The Vikström Papers

—

Leviathan

Published by Long Midnight Publishing, 2025

copyright © 2025 Douglas Lindsay

All rights reserved. No part of this publication may be reproduced or transmitted in any form or by any means without permission of the author.

Douglas Lindsay has asserted his right under the Copyright, Designs and Patents Act 1988 to be identified as the author of this work.

All the characters in this book are fictitious and any resemblance to actual persons, living or dead, is purely coincidental.

ISBN: 979-8311369664

By Douglas Lindsay

The Vikström Papers:

Restoration Man
Jacob's Point
Shadow Tide
Leviathan

The DI Buchan Series:

Buchan
Painted In Blood
The Lonely And The Dead
A Long Day's Journey Into Death
We Were Not Innocent
The Last Great Detective
I Wanted To Murder For My Own Satisfaction

The DS Hutton Series

The Barney Thomson Series

DCI Jericho

The DI Westphall Trilogy

Pereira & Bain

Others:

Lost in Juarez
Being For The Benefit Of Mr Kite!
A Room With No Natural Light
Ballad In Blue
These Are The Stories We Tell
Alice On The Shore
The Arlington Revenant (2025)

THE VIKSTRÖM PAPERS

—

LEVIATHAN

DOUGLAS LINDSAY

LMP

For Kathryn

1

'A talking monkey? I'm going to guess the little fella's a capuchin.'

I give the therapist a sideways glance. She's looking at her notepad.

'You get this a lot, huh?'

'It's not unusual.'

'Aren't you supposed to say that when I tell you I think I'm Tom Jones?'

'How d'you mean?'

She's young. Maybe that joke didn't make it to her generation.

'This is different, though,' I say. 'There is an actual capuchin. His name's Joey. He was involved in a case I was working a few months back.'

'And this capuchin called Joey can talk?'

'No, the actual Joey can't talk. He belonged to a woman I busted on the case. He vanished after that. No one knows where he is now.'

'So Joey just talks in your dreams.'

'Yes.'

'Every night?'

'Every night.'

'And your cat, who's called… Hightower, this cat also talks in these dreams, but he can't talk in real life.'

'There we are.'

She scribbles something in her notebook.

Feels like I'm in a movie. I'm from Cambuslang, a dull little town south of Glasgow. There was a time there were three cinemas, and trams up and down the high street, and the place was bustling, but that was way before I was born. The malaise crept in long ago, and now the main street is traffic-dominated, and is a collection of charity shops and betting shops and poundshops and pubs that have been there forever, and cafés that come and go with the seasons. And sure, it's not like therapists don't exist in the UK, and I'm sure there are people right now paying five-hundred-pounds-an-hour to tell a stranger the kind of things that thirty years ago they would have told their friends. Nevertheless, the idea still feels American. Seeing your therapist. Paying for someone to talk to. And there's no way I'd be doing this if I still lived in Cambuslang. But here I am, on the Massachusetts coast, living the American dream.

'What do the three of you talk about?' she asks.

'My love life. They seem pre-occupied with it. We sit at the kitchen table drinking whatever, you know schnapps or cider or white wine, and I'm always trying to talk about the Patriots. I mean, we've got ourselves a quarterback, right? Vrabel's back, things are looking up.'

'My husband follows the Red Sox,' she says. 'He doesn't watch football.'

She doesn't bother saying that obviously she, with agency in her own life, has no interest in sport.

'I try to talk about the Patriots, but all they want to talk about is Natalie. And I'm like, let it go, for God's sake. Nothing happened with Natalie, and I haven't even seen her in four months. Well, you know, there was that once at Target in Danvers. I mean, we ended up standing there chatting in the dairy aisle for forty-five minutes, but that aside…'

'Why did nothing happen with Natalie?'

Now we come to the crux of the matter, and to why I came to Boston to find a therapist. This isn't just about Natalie. It's about Deputy Sheriff Elise Miller.

Elise and I have been a little out of sync recently. It began with her husband, Byron, announcing he was being moved to his firm's Boston office from Manhattan, and therefore wouldn't be spending four nights a week away from home. He was told just before Christmas, and the change is taking place in a couple of weeks.

That easy-come-easy-go relationship Elise and I have had the past few years is about to come to an end. If we're going to continue to see each other, she's going to have to become far more clandestine. Her lies of omission are going to have to become just actual, regular, lies to his face. Much harder to pull off.

The alternative, of course, is that she leaves him and she and I take up permanently together. However, neither of us has suggested that, and the silence of neither of us suggesting it grows deeper and more uncomfortable every time we see each other.

The silence has become a third presence at the table.

And all of that, even that's a lie, because it didn't begin with Byron's unexpected announcement. It began with me unexpectedly falling for Natalie, denying it to myself, Elise realising there was some new spanner in the works at play in my head, and us not talking about that either.

And that's why I'm here, except, I'm not going to mention Elise. It feels wrong. And Elise, regardless of how unlikely she ever is to come across Dr Van Noy here, would be hurt if she knew I'd chosen to talk to a therapist about it, rather than her.

'There's someone else, but I'd rather not discuss it,' I say weakly.

'You're having an affair?'

Dammit, don't we all hate it when someone sees right through us?

Van Noy lays down her pen in a way that makes me turn, and she's sitting back, hands clasped on her stomach. She's pregnant. I'd say she's in her seventh month, but that would be an entirely uneducated guess.

I may feel like I'm in a movie, but it's not so like a movie that I'm lying on a couch. We're sitting on comfortable chairs, a low table with coffee cups and water glasses between us, we're on the forty-third floor, and I've got a sensational view out over the harbour towards Logan, where one's eyes are naturally drawn to the incoming and outgoing air traffic. This is a view that you could just sit and look at all day. Perhaps her clients get lost in it, and then talk freely, as though in a trance.

She lifts her coffee, takes a quick drink, scowls a little because there's no way that coffee's still hot enough, and then sits back.

'I'm doing myself out of business here, but perhaps it's because I've got other things on my mind, and I'm intending to work a very light load in the coming year. Really, Mr Vikström, you do not need a therapist.'

'Drugs?'

'You're lonely. Neither a therapist nor drugs will help that. You need to get out more.'

'Seriously?'

'Yes.'

'I'm not lonely.'

'How many friends have you got in America?'
'Friends?'
'Yes. If you don't count Natalie, if you –'
'She's not a friend.'
'Fine. And if you don't count the someone else you don't want to talk about, because obviously there's something there that transcends friendship, how many friends do you have?'

Usually I'd have a shallow answer about Hightower being my only friend. That seems a little too on the nose.

'I don't have friends. Doesn't mean I'm lonely.'
'Mr Vikström, you're lonely. You're clearly torn between this woman Natalie and this other woman. You need someone to talk to, just as you need someone to have general football chitchat with, and you have no one because you have no friends. And so the cat and the capuchin invade your dreams every night as a mechanism. But everything they say, *everything*, comes from you, so you're basically talking to yourself.'

She pauses, she gives me a significant, *there we are* kind of a look. I have nothing to say.

'Get out more. Talk to people. Make some friends. Find someone who interests you, and hope you interest them, and maybe you can share. It's not difficult, but it starts with you admitting it, and letting people into your life.'

'This is what I'm paying you six hundred dollars an hour for?' I say. Very poor, very defensive.

'No,' she says. 'You've only been here half an hour, and I'm ending the conversation. That'll be three hundred dollars, and really, don't come back. There's nothing I can do for you. It's insane of you to pay someone to be your friend. Just go out there and talk to people in real life.'

I have nothing else. It appears neither does she. After a peculiarly long silence, she opens her hands in a *we're done here* gesture, and indicates the door.

I get up and walk to the door. Turn just before leaving her office, and look out one last time over the view. The airport to the left, the harbour down below, and the ocean stretching away into the far distance. Blue and silver and shimmering in the late winter sunshine. God, that is spectacular.

'Speak to Leanne on your way out,' she says. 'I'll send her the details.'

'Thank you,' I say.

'You're welcome. And speak to Natalie. A wider

friendship group aside, she sounds like she might actually be where your answers lie.'

I hold her look one last time, I nod, I turn away, walk through to the outer office, and then close the door behind me.

Leanne isn't at her desk. Instead, sitting there is Joey the capuchin. Hightower is curled up in one of the chairs in the small waiting area.

Hightower yawns.

'At last,' says Joey, in that broad accent of his. 'You get what you were looking for?'

I wake up. Eyes wide open, staring at the ceiling. Mouth feels dry, which means I was sleeping with it open, and I wonder if I was snoring.

It's cold, but then I went to sleep with the window open. I look to my right, out towards the morning and the grey light of dawn. The ocean is dark and grim, waves breaking on the rocks beneath the front of the house, the small jetty attached to my property largely covered by water. High tide, big waves, the back end of a late February storm.

I pull the duvet a little closer, roll onto my side, and look out across the water.

2

There was a boat that sank a few weeks ago. A small yacht named the *Bel Air*. Just a couple of guys out enjoying an unusually quiet late January sea. No one has any idea what caused it to sink. But it went down, out beyond Grand Bank, which means it went the other side of the shelf. A hundred yards closer to shore, divers would have been able to get down to it, and examine the wreckage for evidence of what went wrong. But the other side of the shelf? That's instant abyss territory. There's the technology to get down to that depth out there in the world, but only when there's money behind it, and the Massachusetts coast guard doesn't have that kind of money.

While the boat is likely lost forever, the first body washed up on the north coast of Cape Ann a few days ago. Sure, it could've washed up anywhere from Canada to the Bahamas, but since then I've taken to going out every morning and having a look along the rocks, a few hundred yards in either direction, just in case the other one shows up. The longer it takes, the more gruesome it's liable to be. The guy who washed up just along the coast from Jacob's Point, had had a couple of chunks taken out of him by some beast or other. Probably a shark, but there are older and fouler things than sharks in the deep places of the ocean.

Actually, bastardised *Lord of the Rings* quotes aside, there's not a lot older than sharks in the ocean. Anyway, if it wasn't for my dreams being haunted on a nightly basis by Abbot and Costello, I'm sure my dreams would be full of half-eaten zombies, their bodies bloated by sea water, crawling up the rocks and banging on my bedroom window. At least the interfering cat and monkey are saving me from that.

Like I said, no credible explanation for the sinking of the boat has yet been put forward. The favourite is the Russians, just because that's where we are again in the world. The Cold War is back, and this time, well it doesn't seem so cold.

Nevertheless, the Russians sinking a perfectly aimless

yacht out in the ocean just for the hell of it, or even by accident, seems pretty remote. So remote, in fact, that they haven't even bothered denying it. And we all know, the Russians deny everything that they do. It's all part of the psyop.

So, no one in authority, and no one with any common sense, thinks it was those guys, and the only problem with countering that narrative, is that the alternatives are just as vague, and just as reliant on guesswork.

I guess I've been waiting for the phone to ring. With the authorities seemingly getting nowhere, it's the kind of situation where someone, somewhere, be it a relative, an insurance company or some other interested party, decides they want a private investigator to get the job done properly, or to unearth the things the coast guard don't want to talk about publicly. However, since my last job at the start of the year – about as low-key a business as ever comes my way, involving a guy in Gleneagles, New Hampshire running a very basic car number plate scam – the phone has been quiet.

Maybe no one's gone down the PI route. Maybe they've gone to some other agency. Or maybe they've come to my agency, and, despite me living on the ocean's doorstep, they elected to go with one of their other people.

That's not the kind of thing that bothers me. Nevertheless, I wouldn't mind the work. Not much doing these days.

I sit at the window and watch the world, and wait for the first sign of a month-old corpse floating in on the tide.

3

Thursday morning, a grey day like any other in February. Sitting at the window, looking out on the ocean. Heading into the city today, to take a look at the Museum of Fine Art. I'm going to educate myself – possibly – and then I'll find somewhere to get lunch. Fish 'n chips, drink some cider, have a wander through the old town while dusk falls. Maybe stop for a coffee somewhere.

Granola and yogurt for breakfast, raspberries and blueberries and a bit of apple. Two cups of coffee, two glasses of water. Today I did not take my morning swim in the ocean. Too cold, too windy, the waves too tempestuous. Stormy weather out there, and we're in for a long haul, these conditions predicted on and off, well into next week.

Haven't seen Hightower this morning. He'll be out there enjoying the elements, catching small beasts. He'll be back sometime, fat-bellied, licking his lips.

A phone starts ringing somewhere in the house, which seems odd, then I remember I left my work phone in the bedroom. It's been so many weeks since they called, I've got out of the habit of carrying it around with me.

'Sal,' I say, answering the phone. 'How are things?'

'You all right, there, coach, you're usually sitting on top of the phone?'

As ever, Sal sounds like she's smiling as she talks.

'Left it in the other room,' I say.

'Sorry, it's been a few weeks, right? You all right to take on a case?'

'Yeah, I'm good. Nothing major on at the moment.'

Nothing major on at the moment…

I don't think there's any lie between Sal and me. She doesn't know so much about my life, after all. I might well have all sorts of things going on. Except, of course, I'm always free to take on a new case whenever the phone rings.

'Cool, cool,' she says.

'This about the *Bel Air*?' I ask.

There's a moment's hesitation, followed by realisation, and I can see her head shaking.

'Right, the boat. Nope, that hasn't come our way, I'm afraid. Hey, that was weird, right?'

'Seems to be.'

'There's always something creepy about random boat sinkings,' she says. 'Like there's some kind of Stephen King level of shit going on.'

'Yeah, that's about the size of it,' I say. 'So, what's the story?'

I settle back into my seat, lift the coffee, take a drink, my heart sinking a little with it. I'd been hoping for the mysterious boat sinking case. Not that I was going to be getting in a boat of any description and heading out onto the ocean to investigate. But I have a fascination with the ocean. It's part allure of the wide expanse, and the distant horizon; part the weather, and the squalls, and the waves, and the colours, and the impenetrable depths; and part terror at all those exact same things.

'There's a movie getting made up your neck of the woods,' she says.

'*Leviathan*,' I say. 'Pretty major operation. They've taken up the old Grissom place on the north of town, but they've also taken every room at the St James Hotel, and at the Market Square on the south side. Everyone was gossiping for a week or two, but it's gone pretty quiet. They seem to be running a tight ship.'

'I wouldn't know about that, but there seems to be at least a little bit of drama. We got a call about one of the crew members going missing. Missing, after a fashion. She left unexpectedly a few days ago. Went to bed in the hotel, cleared out the following morning.'

'No message?'

'Sure, she left messages. I mean, on the face of it, it doesn't seem so weird. And certainly the sheriff's office ain't interested, which is why it's comes to us. I'll send over what we've got, you can take a look, and let me know if you're in.'

'OK, Sal, thanks. I'll get back to you in ten minutes.'

'Thank, coach!'

The phone goes dead.

Well, I guess that's at least a little intriguing. The movies.

I drink coffee and stare out of the window while I wait for

the phone to ping. Rain has started to spatter against the glass. In the far distance, which isn't so far today, a commercial vessel, dwarfed by the vastness of the horizon, inches its way through the gloom.

The phone goes, and I open the message and get to work.

4

It's scenic along here, and the towns are quaint, and some of them are old, or what passes for old in North America, and so the movies come here on a regular basis to shoot on location. Not often they come to Glasgow, MA right enough, as we're a bit of a poor relation to Rockport, Manchester-by-the-Sea and Beverly, but they're here this time. Maybe because the town did some kind of a deal with them, maybe the other towns were busy, or have just had enough movies. Perhaps the producers said, we can't be using Motif Number 1 in Rockport *again*, but that seems unlikely. History does not suggest movie producers are too hung up on originality.

The movie *Leviathan* is being made by Tethys Films, intended for cinematic release, with a deal for streaming on GuLu+. Leviathan, unsurprisingly, is being used as a descriptor of the sea monster that lurks in the depths just off the coast of the fictional town, and as a metaphor for the big business that, in the story, has taken over the town, is controlling the mayor and the local sheriff's department, and is responsible for the awakening of the beast. It is literally the tale of Durin's Bane, the Balrog of Molgorth, freed from its imprisonment far beneath the Dwarven kingdom of Khazad-dûm, but it wasn't like Tolkien was the first to come up with a tale of an ancient monster being disturbed. These are the kinds of stories that have been passed down through the ages, and continue to be told.

It's a large crew, including two people on the storyboard department: the chief storyboarder, a woman named Maria Morgan, and her assistant, or officially the deputy storyboarder, Norah Wolfe.

They're in the third week of an eight-week location shoot. Four nights ago, nothing untoward happening, Norah Wolfe spends the evening having dinner, has a long discussion with Morgan and the movie's art director over storyboarding for the following week, as the storyboarders are running six or seven days ahead of everyone else, after which Wolfe goes out for an hour or two.

The following morning she doesn't turn up for work. They go to her room. She's not there. She's gone. Stuff gone, wardrobe emptied, toothbrush and all toiletries removed, Norah Wolfe has left the building. She leaves a note to Morgan on the bed.

Maria, Sorry, but I have to do this. Not coping well with the shoot. Stress levels through the roof. Have to think about my mental health. Horrible timing, but I know you're on top of things, and I'm sure you'll be fine. Try not to think too ill of me. Norah.

She'd been showing no signs of stress. She'd worked with Maria Morgan twice before on film sets. As with the previous two occasions, she'd been getting on fine. She loved her job, loved being around the set and around actors, but was entirely professional about it. Hadn't drunk much, was not known to ever take drugs.

Morgan called her. She answered, they had a brief chat. A few clichés followed, how she couldn't stand it anymore, and how apologetic she was, and how she was sure the production would be absolutely fine without her. And then she abruptly ended the call, and that was that.

One of the producers then got in touch with her, and the call was more or less repeated.

Norah Wolfe had seemingly left of her own free will, she'd left a note, she'd talked to her boss and sounded unrepentant.

Maria Morgan took the case, such as it was, to the sheriff's office, but given the paucity of evidence that any crime had been committed, they naturally said they were unable to assist. And there the matter lies.

And now someone anonymous from the movie has decided to escalate matters, and has passed the case to Radstone-Kirk, the biggest private detective agency in the six states.

So, that's the gig. Find Norah Wolfe. Twenty-three years-old. Blonde hair with a green tint running through the ends. Pale blue eyes. Graduate of CalArts.

I click off the link, and call Sal.

I literally never call Sal and say I'm not going to take on a case – I doubt any of our people do – but it's all part of the procedure.

'I'm in,' I say, when she answers.

'Terrific. Hey, it might be more interesting than it looks.'

'Or I might find Norah Wolfe propping up a bar in Gloucester,' I say, and Sal laughs.

'You never know, coach, you never know, although you seem to have a way of stumbling into the tricky ones.'

'That's all on you, Sal,' I say, and she laughs again. 'I see the name of the client's missing.'

'For now. There's potential the whole thing gets done anonymously, but in the first instance, she's happy to meet up and chat. You OK to meet later this morning at Al's Diner?'

'Just tell me the time.'

'Eleven a.m. She'll be wearing a red North Face jacket.'

'OK, Sal, thanks. I'll let you know if Thunderbirds are go after the meeting.'

'Thanks, coach, have a good one!'

She hangs up. Outside, a gust of wind, the rain is thrown with greater force against the window. There's a noise behind me, and Hightower pads into the room, leaving a trail of damp pawprints behind him.

'Getting a bit wild out there, eh, furball?' I say, and he settles down on the floor, slumps back a little, then leans over and starts cleaning his backside.

I turn away, and look at window, now smeared with rain and offering little of the outside bar a feeling of grey.

5

I step into the warmth of the Sheriff's office, out of the squally rain. Ricky, as ever, is behind the front desk. Today, Ricky looks sad. Ricky is a heart on his sleeve kind of a guy. I make it my policy to never invest in Ricky's state of mind. He's usually in love, or heartbroken, but maybe he's just sad because the Celtics lost a nailbiter to the Knicks last night.

'Hey, Ricky, Deputy El in?'

'Coach,' says Ricky. 'I'll just check she's free.'

He lifts his phone, while at the same time waving in the direction of the coffee machine.

'You know the routine,' he says, forlornly, and it feels like Eeyore offering Pooh the last of his muffins.

'She's all yours, coach,' says Ricky. 'And take a muffin. Ain't had one myself, but Ed's had three, says other people better start eating them, or he's going to finish off the whole darn lot.'

I take a muffin, and lift the coffee, turn back to Ricky, contemplate a word of concern, settle for nodding a thanks, and then I open the door, and head down the short corridor at the back of the office.

*

'What's up with Ricky?' I ask.

We've both got coffee, and half the muffin each.

Elise dabs her lips with a napkin, then licks them a little.

'I think he's fallen for someone on the indoor softball team, but she, whoever she is, because I don't know everyone on their softball team, she's seeing someone else on the team, so he has to witness them together.'

'Damn. Unrequited love.'

'Exactly. Makes for great art and music, but bitch of a position to be in.'

We drink coffee, we stare at each other, perhaps, in our

own ways, contemplating the shitty position in which we find ourselves. The third person in our relationship, the uncomfortable silence of things unsaid, briefly threatens, and so I say, 'You spoke to the film people?' to keep it at bay.

'Yep, I did, though it was brief. I mean, there just doesn't seem to be a story here. They've really brought you on board?'

'Someone has, but not officially the movie as such.'

'You've spoken to them already?'

'Al's Diner,' I say, check my watch, then continue, 'in forty-five minutes. I'm meeting someone in a red jacket.'

'Interesting. No name?'

'No name. You spoke to Maria Morgan?'

'Yep. It was her assistant who left. But she spoke to her, and it all seemed normal. She gave me Wolfe's number, I called her, she answered, and it all sounded fine. I don't know what else to say.'

'How d'you know it was Norah Wolfe you were speaking to?'

She smiles.

'I asked Morgan a couple of details about the production that only Wolfe would know, and she gave me way more information on the girl than I asked for. I ran it all by Wolfe, and she batted a thousand. The girl is the girl, for reason's unexplained she'd found the situation stressful – and there was no need for her to explain that to me – and she left. It is, mostly, still a free country.'

'Where'd she go?'

'I don't know.'

'You've no idea if she was in Gloucester or Galveston, or anywhere in between?'

'That's just the way it is. She said she didn't want to talk about it.'

'Why?'

She gives me one of those sympathetic smiles of hers.

'I don't know, Sam. I mean, there could be all kinds of reasons. She's not under investigation, no one is in this matter, so really, it wasn't for me to pry. There's no crime here, and so it's one hundred percent not our business. To be honest, I really don't think it's for you either, but if they're willing to pay you, and you're happy to take it on…'

I nod along with her. She's right. Plenty of cases start out this way, and plenty of those go exactly the way you think they will, and you're metaphorically packing your bags by the end of the day.

I pop the rest of the muffin into my mouth, lift the coffee, drain it, nod my way through it, and then get to my feet.

'Fair call,' I say. 'I shouldn't trouble you any longer.'

'I appreciate that, detective. If you unearth anything you think requires the involvement of the sheriff's department, you know where to find us.'

'I'll be on the batphone as soon as it's necessary.'

'I feel you usually leave it until you're dangling from the undercarriage of a seven-four-seven at thirty thousand feet fighting a dragon before calling for help.'

I laugh as I walk to the door, and despite my usual determination to come in here and not invite her round to my place for sex, as more or less happens every time, I can't stop myself. Time is short, of course, the days when I will be so casually able to do this drawing to an end.

'You free tonight?' I say, just before I open the door to whatever outside forces are lurking in the corridor.

She gives me a familiar look, elbows on the desk, hands clasped, chin rested on the back of her fingers.

'Hmm. You cooking?' she asks.

'Am I cooking? Sure, I can cook.'

'Dinner would be nice.'

'Just dinner?'

'I think just dinner. I'll call when I'm done here.'

'Oakie doakie.'

I smile, I open the door, go out into the corridor, then close the door behind me. As ever, nothing was really said there, but I got the sense of it. The sense of an ending.

We've been needing to have the conversation about Byron moving back home full-time. I'd been thinking it would happen at the last possible moment, or more than likely would never happen at all, but that was me living my fantasy, avoiding real life at all costs. I just extended the invitation and Elise was ready for it. She's the grown-up in the room, the one who knows we need to talk it through.

I stand for a moment in the corridor as a hollow feeling starts to grow in my gut, and then I walk quickly away before another door opens, and I find myself in casual conversation with Deputy Ed, or worse, Sheriff Spark herself.

6

I wondered if it would turn out to be the storyboarder herself who'd contacted the detective agency, but I looked up Maria Morgan on IMDb, and the woman standing at the door in the red North Face coat isn't her.

I lift my hand to catch her eye, as she looks around the diner. The place is busier than usual, but it has been since the movie crew arrived. This is a big set-up they brought with them, enough so that even when they're filming, there are plenty of people with time to kill while the cameras are rolling. Nevertheless, most of the people in Al's Diner are locals who are here on the off-chance one of the cast decides to stop by.

The woman in the red coat approaches, coat off, and settles into the seat opposite.

'Radstone-Kirk?' she asks.

Darlene arrives, coffee jug in hand, and pours a cup.

'Sam Vikström,' I say.

'You want to see the menu?' asks Darlene, and the woman in the red coat says, 'You have French toast?' and Darlene says, 'Sure, you want bacon?' and she answers, 'Are you recommending the bacon?' and Darlene says, 'Al cooks the best bacon in the six states,' and the woman in the red coat says, 'I'll take the bacon,' and Darlene smiles and says, 'Can I get you anything now, detective?' and I say, 'I'll have the French toast and bacon too, thanks,' and then Darlene is on her way.

'Everyone knows you're a detective?'

'Darlene knows I'm a detective.'

'She'll know you're working a case, though.'

'I come to Al's all the time.'

'What's your accent?'

'Scottish.'

'You sound like Shrek.'

'I get that a lot, but actually I sound nothing like Shrek.'

'Maybe not.'

'You've got a name?'

'Of course I've got a name, but at this stage I don't want you to know it.'

'That doesn't make sense.'

'Why?'

'Because I'll find it soon enough anyway. The IMDb page for this movie is already packed full of detail. The crew list is long. So if you don't tell me who you are, the first thing I do is waste an hour chasing up every woman listed, until I identify you.'

'The public page on this movie is not very detailed yet,' she says.

'I looked at the business page. There are a lot of people listed on there, and when I have the time, I'll find you. So, please, let's just remove that little bit of intrigue. I will be entirely discreet.'

'How can I know that?'

'There's got to be implicit trust in taking me on in the first place,' I say. 'If you're not going to trust me, then I can't rely on you to be fully honest, and the whole thing starts to break down before we even get started.'

She lifts her coffee, takes a drink, then lays it back down, squinting at the cup as she goes.

'Jesus, you people drink this?'

'You adapt after a few years.'

'How long have you been here?'

'Since the late nineties.'

'Well, I guess you're going to get used to the coffee.' She scowls at the cup again, and then can't help herself, lifts it, takes another drink, shakes her head, then says, 'My name's Patricia Karlsen.'

'The producer.'

'You've done your homework.'

'You must know some of the people in here,' I say.

'Not really. There are some of the crew, but I'm not… look, I'm more on the financial side, rather than the day-to-day running of the movie. More of an exec producer role, but that's become such a washed out, meaningless title… It is what it is. I work with Brian, but he's running the show. I'll be more hands-on when I can.'

'So, tell me about Norah Wolfe.'

She takes another drink. Following the general principles of the third-drink rule, she no longer has to grimace.

'I'm her mother.'

Well, a detective genius I may be, but I didn't see that coming. I look at her across the top of my own cup of coffee, think of the few pictures I've seen of the young woman, and can't entirely put them together. Not that that means anything. Maybe Norah looks like her dad.

'What's the story?'

'Norah didn't want anyone on the set to think she just got the job because her mother was the producer. So she had us pretend we didn't know each other. There's no reason for the producer in charge of finance to talk to the assistant storyboarder, so, you know, don't speak to me for the duration, mom. I mean, it was fine. We get on fine, and I completely understood. This is such a nepo business. She was good at what she did, and she wanted to make a career without her mother giving her a leg up. And having done that, she didn't then want people thinking I had anything to do with it.'

'Did you?'

'Did I have anything to do with her getting the job?'

'Yes.'

'No. She was on board before I was.' She pauses, she lifts the coffee cup, she looks at it, she places it back on the table without taking a drink.

'People didn't know?'

'No one.'

Darlene returns suspiciously quickly, loaded with two plates of French toast and bacon, maple syrup already drizzled over the top, and places them on the table.

'Y'all good there folks, or is there anything else I can get you?'

'Fine, thanks,' we say together, then Darlene winks at me, and heads across the diner to the next table in need.

Karlsen watches her go.

'Did she just *wink* at you?'

'Yep.'

'Does she think we're on a date?'

'Darlene's mind is a mystery to me,' I say.

'I cannot wait to get back to the west coast.'

She takes her first taste of French toast and bacon, a moment, and then the wonder of it spreads across her face.

'Holy shit,' she says.

'Al's French toast and bacon's pretty good,' I say.

She takes another mouthful.

'Wow. What does he put in this?'

'Crack, mostly. Tell me the story. What d'you think's happened to Norah?'

'I don't know, but I don't believe… I just don't believe she was stressed and left the set.'

'Had you talked to her since she got here?'

'Hadn't talked, no. We agreed before we came, no surreptitious meetings. But we exchanged texts every night. She was enjoying herself. This was her dream.'

'You've spoken since she left?'

'Just the first day. She said she'd had enough, and she needed to get out. She really wasn't forthcoming.'

'You think she sounded coerced?'

'Like she was being held at gunpoint?'

'That kind of thing.'

'Hmm…'

A pause for more food.

'I don't know. Look, I'm going to be up front. She was raised by her dad. I didn't see too much of her when she was growing up, and it's really only the last couple years we've started to bond some more. I'm more like a distant aunt, or a family friend, than a mom.'

'OK, so what d'you think's happened?'

'I have no idea.'

'You know where she is?'

'She wouldn't tell me. She said everything was fine, and she just needed to get away from things. She said she was putting her phone on airplane mode, and that was that.'

Well, this sounds promising.

I manage to stop myself giving the camera a side eye. I expect people in the film business are wise to that kind of behaviour.

'You know of anywhere she's likely to have gone? She hasn't just gone home to her dad?'

'Her dad and stepmom died in a murder suicide three years ago.'

'Oh.'

'I always said Todd was an asshole, but I didn't think he'd go that far. Men will be men, unfortunately.'

'There's no way that that tragedy could be connected to Norah disappearing?'

'No. And don't call it a tragedy. It was male violence, that's all. Look, Norah has an apartment in Pasadena. She's not there, I've had it checked.'

'You think she'll have stayed on the east coast?'

'I may be catastrophising here, but I don't think she'll have had any say in it. Something's happened to her, and either she's being held against her will, or she's dead.'

'That seems a leap, given she spoke to you, the storyboarder, and the deputy sheriff after she went missing.'

'She was enjoying herself on set. I've asked around, and no one has the faintest idea why she would just up sticks like that. And now, radio silence. I don't like it.'

'And you'd like me to find her.'

'That's correct. You think you can do that?'

'I can hardly guarantee success,' I say, 'but I usually manage to get to the bottom of things.'

'I asked your agency to put their best man on the job.'

They don't actually work like that, but she can believe what she likes.

I think now we have the measure of where we are, and for a moment we take the time to eat Al's French toast and bacon.

7

Cape Ann doubles for any coastline they like in the movies, be it Alaska in *The Proposal*, (with added CGI mountains), or Long Island in *The Tender Bar*, but usually it is what it is, a movie set in New England, be it *Coda* or *Manchester by the Sea* or *Witches of Eastwick* or *Little Women*.

And so it is with *Leviathan*, the plot of which involves oil exploration gone wrong just off the Massachusetts coast. And you might think, they're not going to drill for oil off the Massachusetts coast, but a) that's hardly likely to stop the movies, b) oil companies would drill in your brain if they thought there was a chance of finding anything, and c) they already tried off this coast, and the only reason there aren't rigs out there in the Atlantic, is because they didn't find any oil.

So, in this movie, they're looking again, or they've got them drilling a little deeper, or in a different location. Doesn't really matter, most folks aren't going to know they drilled out there in the first place. And in the movie the company are lying about what their intentions are, and inevitably the coastline, and the people who live there, will get absolutely fucked. The little guy will get screwed by the leviathan.

They drill for oil, they inadvertently release the kraken. Chaos and mayhem ensue.

'Assuming this movie doesn't fall apart because the assistant storyboarder walked off set,' I say to Hightower, 'I'm definitely giving it a watch.'

Hightower's staring out of the window. The rain's stopped, but the wind is still blowing, and the afternoon is bleak and grey, promising an early evening and a stormy night. I'm at the kitchen table, reading up on the movie, and the people involved. Trying to get my head around as much of the case – if there even is a case – as possible before I throw myself into the action.

'Remember our Lou Carlyle business?' I say, lifting the cup of tea, closing my laptop, and looking at Hightower. The cat stares back at me, though not with any acknowledgement or recognition.

'His father was one hundred percent certain, like in absolutely no doubt, the kid had been kidnapped. Turned out the lad had robbed his parents, and done a runner to Boca Rotan.'

Hightower gives me that sage look that says he understands things. He knows. Humans are assholes.

'But you know, furball, my guts are pretty good, and I just get a feeling. Lou Carlyle, I felt it straight from the off. Waste of time. This one... something's fishy. It doesn't make sense that she spoke to three people, and they all report her sounding OK, and happy with her decision. Doesn't make sense. I mean, it does if she actually quit the movie, but that doesn't sound right.'

We look at each other. Hightower has nothing to say.

'This one's a keeper.'

8

The Market Square is a small hotel on the south side of town, just off the road down to Salem. Ten rooms, all of which have been booked out for seven weeks by the movie production. Bumper couple of months for the hotel, given it would usually be quiet this time of year.

I'm sitting in a small office with a view of the road, waiting for the manager, Becka McDaniel. The office, like the hotel, has that wonderful old British colonial feel to it. There are many artworks of men in uniform, the furniture is heavy, the curtains are thick. It's meant to be historical reinterpretation, a recreation of British style, but in fact just feels like cheesy pastiche, and most Brits wouldn't recognise it, other than from the same old TV shows the Americans watch.

The door opens, a woman in her forties enters, smiling as she comes.

Great teeth.

'Sorry to keep you, Mr Vikström,' she says, then, as she's taking her seat behind the desk, 'No one got you tea?'

'I'm OK, thanks,' I say. 'Just got a few questions, won't take up much of your time.'

'I won't lie,' she says, 'since the film crew arrived, the hotel is full, they're out there working every day, and things have never run more smoothly. I have all the time in the world. We can only hope this movie's a success, and Hollywood comes back for more.'

'That's great,' I say, to fake interest.

'It is. So, how can we help you?'

'You had a guest here by the name of Norah Wolfe?'

'We did. She checked out four days ago. It's literally the only room change we've had since the film arrived, and the rooms are booked out, in the same names, for another four weeks. Four weeks, three days to be precise.'

'Someone else moved into her room?'

'It's been filled.'

'From the film crew?'

'Yes. They'd paid for the room, of course. I believe they moved someone who'd been staying in a trailer out at the Grissom place on North Atlantic.'

'What can you tell me about Norah Wolfe?'

She looks at me a little curiously, then off to the side while she gives this some thought, lips pursed.

'Hmm. I don't think I can tell you anything. I had no interaction with her.'

'How did she leave her room?'

For a moment I wonder if she's going to say, 'By the door,' but turns out she's better than that.

'There were no problems, far as I'm aware. She didn't leave anything behind, there was nothing to indicate it was done in a rush. I can ask Sally if you like. She's housekeeping on that side of the hotel.'

'Sure, that'd be good, thanks.'

She lifts the phone, makes a quick call, a couple of nods, a couple of affirmatives, then hangs up.

'Sally's on her way.'

Silence. Sudden and heavy. Now we're just two people sitting here, with nothing to say to each other, waiting for someone else to show up.

'What brings you to New England?' asks Becka McDaniel.

'Football in the first place. Long time ago.'

'High school, college?'

'The Patriots.'

'Wow. You played?'

'Junior coaching staff.'

'Wow. The glory years. They do already seem a long time ago.'

'Pre-glory years. I was on coach Carrol's staff his last year, but didn't survive that. Now I do this.'

'Damn,' she says. 'You worked for the Pats, that's nice.'

I smile. It's been a long time, but I still like it when people are impressed by that. Most aren't. And having been there pre-Dynasty seems to add weight. Like, I wasn't just there to stand on the shoulders of giants. I was there before there were giants.

'Junior assistant apprentice linebacker coach. Didn't work out.'

'Too bad. You worked with Bruschi, McGinest, those guys?'

Woman knows her stuff.

'I was watching film, and making notes for the assistant coaches, who were making notes for the actual coaches. There were several degrees of separation between me and Willie.'

She's smiling all the same, and no less impressed.

'Very nice. I loved it back then, back before expectations went through the roof.'

'Right?'

The door opens, just as Becka McDaniel and I are getting into the discussion. I find myself glancing at her hand as she looks at Sally. Wedding ring. We'll leave that there then, I've had enough of getting to know married women better than I should.

'Sally, thanks for coming down.'

Sally nods, closes the door behind her, glances a little warily at me, then says, 'Is there a problem?'

Her demeanour says, *what the fuck is it now*? like she's always being summoned to the manager's office.

'There's no problem,' says McDaniel. 'This is Mr Vikström. He's a private investigator, and he's got a couple of questions about the guest who checked out on Monday.'

Sally looks at me, her wariness unassuaged.

'There was a young woman in room…'

'One hundred twenty-three,' says McDaniel.

I pause to consider for a moment that they have a room one hundred and twenty-three in a hotel with ten rooms, then say, 'Norah Wolfe,' and Sally nods. 'Looks like she left the film set unexpectedly. Her mother's trying to get in touch, and can't get hold of her. And… on the face of it, there doesn't seem to be anything suspicious, but her mother's worried enough that she's employed my agency to try to locate her daughter. The last people who'll have seen Norah before she left town would've been here at the hotel, so this is me just starting out. Asking around, not necessarily expecting anything.'

I agreed with Patricia Karlsen that I'd say Norah's mother had employed me to look for her. I obviously don't need to add who Norah's mother actually is.

Sally stares at me long enough that I realise I didn't ask a question. Sally is in her early twenties, and she's not here for any shit from some guy with a foreign accent.

'Did you have any interaction with Norah while she was here?'

'No.' A pause, and then, 'Hardly any. Like, you know, a couple of times I went to clean her room and she hadn't left for work yet, but that was nothing more than, you know, I'll be another five minutes, no problem, like that kind of thing.'

'What about Monday morning?'

A beat. Another.

'Monday morning?' she asks.

'The day she checked out.'

'I didn't see her then.'

'What about her room? Was there anything untoward about it, anything different?'

Another beat.

'Anything different?' she asks.

'Anything unusual? Did it look like someone else had been there? Did it look like she'd left in a hurry? Anything left behind? Anything at all where you thought, oh, that's odd, or you don't see that every day?'

I can see the change in her eyes. There's something to say.

She glances at McDaniel and then back to me. I follow her glance and see that McDaniel has also noticed the shadow of hidden knowledge flash across her face.

'It's OK, Sally,' she says, 'you can talk to Mr Vikström.'

'Well, I don't know,' she says. 'It seems to me to be private information. I shouldn't be sharing it.'

'The woman has disappeared,' says McDaniel. 'It's OK to share.'

'If she's disappeared, why isn't the sheriff here?'

They both look at me now. Seems a reasonable question.

'There's no evidence a crime's been committed as yet,' I say, 'so the sheriff's department won't touch it. If I can sort it without needing them, it's better for everyone. Better for the hotel.'

There's no logic in that. Like, none at all. If there's no crime, there's no need for the sheriff. If I find there's been a crime committed, it's not like Elise will just leave it to me to sort out.

'It's fine, Sally,' says McDaniel. 'Under the circumstances.'

Another look at McDaniel, finally convinced, then she turns back and says, 'She'd had sex. There was evidence, you know, it was apparent from the sheets… She'd had sex.'

'With a man, that kind of apparent?'

'Yes.'

'Did you see the man?'

'I didn't see Miss Wolfe at all on Monday morning.'

'You didn't see them together the night before?'

'I don't work Sundays.'

'Any sign the man had been there other than what he left on the sheets?'

She shakes her head.

'Sorry to be, I don't know, whatever, intimate, but could you tell…' and I finish the question with a slightly vague gesture.

'Could I tell what?' she says. 'What he looked like from his semen?'

Sally finds her sarcasm. Nice.

'Could you tell how recent the deposit was?' I ask bluntly.

'I didn't send it to the lab, and I definitely didn't touch it. But it had dried in, if that helps you.'

'When had you put the sheets on?'

'The previous day.'

'I thought you don't work Sundays?'

'I don't work Sunday nights. I was in in the morning.'

'You put fresh sheets on every day?'

She pauses again, but I think this time it's more of a *what the fuck* kind of a pause at my line of questioning.

'With guests who are staying awhile, we change the sheets every three or four days. I remembered I changed them the previous day because my first thought on Monday, when I got in to work and she'd already left, was damn, didn't need to change those sheets yesterday.'

'Thanks, Sally, that'll be all,' I say.

Sally turns to McDaniel, looking for clearance from the actual authority in the room before she leaves, McDaniel nods, and there goes Sally.

'Well, that's a step in the right direction,' says McDaniel. 'Gives you something to chase, at least. Has there been a mention of a partner of any description?'

'Nope, this is new. Is there a way we can get eyes on this guy? Is there CCTV in the lobby?'

'Is there CCTV in the lobby?' she says, laughing. 'Look at this place. We market ourselves as being from the eighteenth century. We do not have CCTV in the lobby.'

'You have electricity and modern plumbing,' I say, and she

smiles.

'A fair point. But no, no CCTV. We can speak to Malcolm, he'd have been on reception on Sunday afternoon and evening. He might've seen Norah come back.'

'Perfect,' I say. 'Malcolm's on the front desk now?'

I don't remember seeing Malcolm.

A pause, and then, 'No. Malcolm's not in today.'

I look across the desk.

'I'll give him a call,' she says.

'Thanks.'

9

When a young woman goes missing, it's either about money or sex. Every time. Sometimes both, but invariably one or the other. It's practically science.

There's a conclusion to be jumped to here. Norah Wolfe met some guy, they fell in love on a whim, the feeling survived the first night in bed, they left to pursue romance. Why spend your life working on fake drama, when you suddenly find yourself in the middle of your own romantic narrative?

Seems dumb to give your job up for that, consequently impacting your career, but she's young. People do all sorts of dumb shit when they're young.

It might feel too easy, too straightforward, but it ticks the boxes. She leaves in a rush, she knows it's daft so doesn't want to admit it up front, and so lies, even though everyone knows she's lying. She's OK to field calls the next day, but then, having explained herself as best she feels able, she can cut her phone and herself off from the rest of the world, and go and have non-stop, early-twenties sex. Until it gets old, and she realises she's been an idiot.

Even then, though, there's method in her madness. She tells everyone she was stressed. She removes herself from the situation in order to protect her mental health. When the time comes to put herself forward for the next job, she can say she's in a better place, she can hint vaguely that the problem wasn't her, it was those she was working with, and anyone who doesn't know the situation, or doesn't know the individuals involved in this shoot, will, if she plays it well, believe Wolfe, and think Maria Morgan, or the producers, or the head of production design, must be difficult.

That conclusion is an attractive one to jump to. On the other hand, I don't actually want to jump to it. I've got a job here, sports fans, let's hope it gives up a little more than a young couple shacked up in an Airbnb.

I arrive at dusk, ring the doorbell, and stand back. A small house out in the woods, not so far off the highway cutting through Beverly.

The answer is a long time coming, and I've just rung the bell again, when the door behind the fly screen is opened, and a woman in a dressing gown, her hair dishevelled, a mug in one hand, stares at me.

'You're the fella coming to see Malcolm?'

I smile and nod. Seven words, delivered like she was inserting them in my anus attached to a hand grenade.

'He got fed up waiting. He's out back.'

The hotel manager called him less than twenty minutes ago.

'I can go round the side?'

'Sure. Watch the chickens.'

'Watch the chickens,' I say with a nod, and then she closes the door in my face.

I walk around the side of the house. Opening up behind it, and obscured from the road by the bare branches of birch and beech, a small lake, a peculiar flat calm, despite the wind that continues to blow. There's a jetty directly behind the house, with a small rowing boat tied up. There's a man, presumably Malcolm Stewart, sitting in the boat, watching me walk round the house. A lugubrious look about him that says, what now?

I walk to the jetty, paying attention to the chickens. There are a lot of chickens. Quiet chickens, pecking at the ground in silence. In the air the smell of chicken shit.

There's a hint of winter mist on the water, like this place exists in its own strange micro-climate. Early evening chill, as night comes. And although the highway isn't so far behind us, it seems like the sound is swallowed up, and suddenly Malcolm and I are together in an eerie silence.

'Get in,' he says.

I hate boats, but even I can cope with a calm this flat, particularly since we're nowhere near the sea. Nevertheless, it hardly seems necessary.

'I'll only be a couple of minutes.'

'I'm heading over to the far corner. Best place for yellow perch. Chances of catching any, as the little woman will've told you if you'd asked, next to zero, but it gets me out the house and away from Margot, if you know what I'm saying. Get in.'

'I don't want to be stuck in your boat for however long, when I only need you for a minute.'

'I can drop you off at the far side, you can walk round. Ground's not too damp. Ain't been any rain in two weeks. Get in.'

'It's rained every day for two weeks.'

'Not around here.'

People.

'Careful,' he can't stop himself saying, like I'm intending to jump in two-footed.

I gingerly get in the boat, sit down opposite him, my feet in between his, then he detaches the rope, pushes off from the jetty, sorts the oars out, and then makes a few swift pulls, sending us away from the shore.

Another couple, then he rests the oars back into the boat, and we glide for a short while across the still water, before coming to a rest all of forty yards away from the jetty, now much closer to the other side of the pond.

'Deeper than you think,' he says, as he starts to sort out his fishing rod. It's short, and I guess there'll be no casting involved. He'll just be tossing a line and hook over the side.

I look into the water. In the grey of late afternoon, beneath a blanket of cloud, the water is cold and impenetrably dark.

'Used to be this whole thing would be frozen over. This year, though, barely any ice around the edges in early January, and been completely clear since. That's just the way it is.'

'Just yellow perch?' I ask, playing along.

'Fella died here,' he says. 'Long time ago. Seventy-four, seventy-five, round 'bout then. Went for a swim, warm day in April. Didn't figure the pond hadn't heated up yet. Got breathless, got into trouble, didn't make it back to shore. Never did find his body.'

I give him a sceptical glance, then look back at the water.

'They must've found his body.'

'Like I say, deeper than you think.'

'You swim in there?'

'I fish. I don't swim.'

'Just yellow perch?'

'Me and Margot we always say, if we're eating the perch, and the perch are down there, nibbling on what's left of old Jeremiah, does that make us second-hand cannibals?'

He laughs humourlessly.

If I bought this house, and presuming the lake comes with it, I'm dredging the damn lake. Don't care how deep it is.

There's something about this guy, though. He's got a look about him. I'm thinking that perhaps the lake might be three-feet deep, and there was no old Jeremiah.

'Tell me about Norah Wolfe,' I say.

'The girl who checked out?'

'Yes.'

He nods, as he busies himself with the fishing rod. A very basic reel. He takes a live minnow from a Tupperware box, attaches it to the hook, checks the small weight is securely attached, and puts the rod out over the side of the boat, and with a flick of the wrist, and a subtle movement with his fingers to release the line, casts the bait out over the water, about five yards from the boat.

He lets the reel run for a few seconds, stops it, pulls on the line a couple of times, and then settles forward, elbows on his knees, looking at the water.

'Just come out here to get away from Margot. She appreciates it as much as I do. The husband goes fishing, son, that's the secret to a long and happy marriage.' A pause, and then the acerbically delivered, 'Long, at any rate.'

Silence returns, this one seemingly more absolute than before. I look around, the small lake at nightfall, bare trees and mist. The lone, single-storey house the only sign of human habitation in the area. This place is pretty damn creepy. We've all seen too many movies in this kind of setting, and none of them are good. They don't make romcoms and slapstick comedy in creepy-ass lakes at dusk.

'Tell me about Norah Wolfe,' I say again.

He's studying his line, as though expecting twitching to start imminently.

'Seen her around,' he says. 'They're an OK lot, you know. No high jinks, seem professional. You never know what you're going to get when you get a crew like this in for a couple of months. I mean, if it's ugly from the get-go, then you're in trouble. You're in for two months of drama. I don't like drama. But this bunch… seems like they work long days out there, some of 'em work in the evenings, they get back, they eat, they have a couple of drinks, they go to bed. It's the young 'uns you have to worry about, course, but you never can tell. She was the youngest, and I thought, damn, there's trouble. But she was quiet. Don't know what she did on set, presume she was in the film. When she left like that, I thought they'd decided to kill off her character. I mean, that's the kind of thing that happens. The writer or the director suddenly thinks, damn, it's going to be epic if we kill this fella.'

When it comes to it this guy is talking a lot more than the critics thought he would.

'Did you see her on Sunday evening?' I manage to squeeze in while he takes a breath.

He doesn't immediately answer, looking at his line again, his eyes locked in, searching for the slightest tremble. I look around the lake. The trees and the darkness seem to have closed in a little more.

'Sunday evening?' I say.

'Sure, she was there on Sunday evening. Didn't go to the bar. Came in through reception, had some fella in tow. Hand-in-hand. She was smiling, looking like, I don't know what. The cat got the cream.'

'How about the guy?'

'How d'you mean?'

'Was he looking like the cat who got the cream, or was he more like, he knew he was the cream?'

He laughs, harshly and briefly, and then the light relief quickly leaves his face.

'Guy knew the score, sure. He knew what was happening.'

'Can you describe him?'

He looks at me now with a little more intensity, like he's actually seeing me for the first time. A quick glance at the line to make sure there's not some giant catfish on the other end, then he comes back, scratching his chin.

'A bit older than the girl. Caucasian. Let's say about forty. Full beard, long hair. Wearing a pair of eye glasses, pale blue rims. Something about him, you know. Looked like a player.'

'Had you seen him around?'

'Never seen him before in my life.'

'What d'you think he was a player in?'

'The movies. He looked the type.'

'You didn't recognise the guy as an actor, like you'd seen him on shows and stuff?'

'I don't watch shows.'

'Movies?'

'I don't watch movies.'

'You don't have a TV?'

'I watch the Sox. Otherwise, TV's in mothballs five months of the year. Six when we don't make the play-offs.'

'You don't watch the play-offs when the Sox aren't in them?'

'Nope.'

'What was he wearing?'

'The guy with the beard and the blue-rimmed glasses?'

'Yep.'

'Don't remember. Nondescript I guess. I hadn't seen him around the hotel, and he looked quite pleased with himself, so you know, he stood out some. But the clothes? They didn't register.'

'So, they walked through reception?'

'They did.'

'Where'd they go?'

'To the room. You know there are, let me see, five doors off of reception. There's the restaurant, there's the bar and lounge, there's the corridor to the offices, and there's the corridor to the ground floor rooms, with the stairs to the upper floors. That's where they went.'

'Did you see him leave?'

'Nope.'

'How much longer did you work?'

'I finish at eleven pm on a Sunday, so maybe an hour after they came through. Didn't see him leave in that time. And by the time I was back to work, it was Monday afternoon and she'd have been long gone by then.'

'So, that was the one time you saw him?'

'That's correct.'

'And you never saw the girl again after her brief moment of being the cat who got the cream?'

'That's correct.'

'Did you ever see her with any other man?'

He regards me with interest, then nods as he thinks about it.

'Well, that's a good question,' he says, as though surprised I've asked him something pertinent. 'But you know, I don't think I did. Calm. No drama, like I said. And now this. What's the story?'

'I don't know.'

'You think she upped and ran with the guy, throwing away

her career for love?'

'I have to consider it a possibility. Could you do a photofit of the guy?'

'Nope. Kind of a Jesus looking fella, that's all I've got. I had to do one of those photofit things once for the sheriff's office. Didn't look anything like the guy. Just not my thing.'

He gives me a look that says *that's it, pal, there's nothing else in the tank.*

We've drifted pretty close to the far bank now, and I gesture towards it.

'You mind dropping me off here?'

'Sure, I can drop you off. When you get back round, tell Margot I forgot to do the chickens. She's going to have to do the chickens.'

'I'm not telling Margot she has to do the chickens,' I say.

'Any of those chickens die, it's on you,' he says.

'No, it's not.'

He rests the rod against the side of the boat, jamming the end of it with his foot, then lifts the oars and eases us into the side, turning the boat so that I'm more or less by the bank.

'Don't step in the water,' he says. 'The pond floor slips away like it's made of butter. And it's deep. You don't want to fall in there. Worse than old Jeremiah in this pond, my friend.'

10

Me and Elise and dinner. Fennel and bacon braised in chicken stock and vermouth. A glass of wine each.

Outside the wind has picked up, the rain has started again, and the waves are high. One of those times when you can't tell if the rain against the window in the night is actually ocean spray.

Next door, Hightower sits in his spot, looking out at the night, seemingly unsettled by the storm.

'So, you think Norah Wolfe just met a man, fell in love, and off she went?'

'I don't know. Seems a little unbelievable. I asked her boss about it, and it didn't mean anything to her. Norah didn't really hang out with the crew. Kept herself to herself. Says they had a down day last Friday, and Norah spent the day in Salem with another young woman from the set, watching the small boats, visiting the museums.'

'Cheap entertainment.'

'It's a vibe.'

'It's a vibe?'

'Yeah. That's what the youth say.'

'I've heard them. You're too old to say it, though, so you might want to take that into consideration.'

We smile, we drink wine, we eat dinner.

'Never tasted anything like this before,' she says. 'Pretty interesting.'

'I'll take interesting.'

'So, you think this guy was just someone she met while hanging out in a museum?'

'That's the best bet, which is going to make it pretty difficult to track him down.'

'It will. What's the plan?'

'Last place I know she went was Salem, so tomorrow I'm going to go to Salem, armed with a photograph of her, and see where it gets me.'

'That'll be pretty high octane,' says Elise. 'A couple of

hours in the Salem museums, showing people a photograph, and most of those people looking at it blankly, saying, nope, can't help you.'

'Even Tom Cruise is going to need a stunt double when they film that scene for the movie,' I say, and she smiles, and just like that it seems the banality of small talk has come to an end, and I look at my food, and suddenly, taking the audience by surprise, she says, 'We should talk.'

I look up from my dinner, and there's Elise, in all her practicality, looking at me from across the table, something unfamiliar in her eyes. Something sad, as though she's already accepted the forlorn inevitability of this conversation.

I take a drink of wine, lay the glass back down. Stare at the table for a moment, manage to look her in the eye again. I want to retreat to one of my familiar throwaway, glib remarks, but I owe her more than that, and anyway, nothing comes to mind.

It's coming up on five years we've been a thing now, and it's been a lot of fun, and also pretty damned painful. Byron's been working away from home four or five nights a week all that time, her kids have been away the last couple of years, and we've never had the conversation about why she doesn't just leave him. I guess I've never asked because I never really wanted to know. And now Byron's about to be home every night, and push is coming to shove.

She reaches forward, placing her left hand in the middle of the table, and I reach out and take her fingers into mine. Have a strong, uneasy feeling. A familiar hollowness in the stomach.

We rub our fingers gently together.

'Feels like we've lost each other recently,' she says.

'I'm right here,' I say, needlessly, and she says, 'You know what I mean,' with a sad, little crushing smile.

I let out a bit of a sigh, then force myself to say, 'Is this the awkward, how come we never talk about you leaving Byron conversation?'

'Yes, Sam, it is.'

She swallows, loudly. There are tears in her eyes from nowhere, and I wonder how many times she's had this conversation in her head, and if there was ever anything I was able to say that made it all right. Because any time I've had the conversation in my head, there was nothing either of us could say.

'I just thought…,' I say, to get to it, and then words dry up, and then I find, 'I thought you didn't want to leave Byron. That's just what it is, you know. It's part of... it's part of who we are.'

'You never asked me to,' she says. 'And, before you say it, I never offered. And sometimes...'

She looks away, resting her chin in the palm of her hand now. 'Sometimes, I wonder if I would've made that offer if you'd been someone different. I don't know who that would've been, but why is it I won't leave Byron?'

'You love him. He's a good man,' I say, hopelessly.

'Come on, Sam, you don't need to go into bat for Byron.'

I sit back, cheeks puffed out, not really sure what to say.

'I don't want to split up,' I say.

Our hands are still entwined, and finally she pulls her fingers clear and sits back. A tear breaks free and rolls down her cheek. She swallows.

'I don't either,' she says. 'But this has been relatively easy for me since we started. Byron was two hundred and thirty miles away. He never came home unexpectedly. I never had to, you know, I never had to go home having been here, having been with you, and lie to him. I'm not sure I can pull that off.' Another swallow. 'I'm not sure I want to...'

'There'll be... we can still have coffee, meet and chat, and you know... there can be guerrilla sex.'

She half laughs, half cries at that, the same sad smile, the shake of the head.

'Don't make me laugh,' she says.

She sniffs, she reaches into her pocket and pulls out a tissue, says, 'I came prepared,' then she blows her nose, nods to herself, takes a drink of wine, and seems to have been able to banish the tears.

She sighs, she reaches over, squeezes my hand again, then withdraws.

'We need to talk about the girl,' she says, abruptly.

The words *what girl?* immediately come into my head, but I manage to keep them at bay. Elise needs to have the conversation, and even if I'm not emotionally equipped for this level of intensity, the least I can do is not be disingenuous.

'I haven't seen the girl.'

'I know.'

'How'd you know?'

'Because I'd know if you'd seen her. For example, you say

you haven't, but I'm going to guess you saw her in some capacity about a month ago.'

Damn, there we are. All my defences being stripped bare.

'You'd make a good cop,' I say.

'Funny.'

'It wasn't planned. Bumped into her at Target.'

'Doesn't matter. It really doesn't. You could've seen her passing by sitting on a bus, or the two of you could've spent the weekend in Lake Placid, without leaving your bedroom. You're thinking about her. There's just been something there, something that started before Byron dropped his bombshell. You're thinking about her, I can tell, and it's... you know, you need to call her and get her out of your system. Or, you know, the other thing, if that's what happens.'

'She's not in my system.'

'She's in your system, Sam.'

'She knows about me and you.'

'What?'

I swallow, lift the wine glass to temporarily hide behind.

'You told her?' she says, looking hurt in a way I've never seen before.

'No. She was here one night you phoned during the *Mary Celeste* case. She saw your name come up on the phone, so I couldn't deny you were calling me on a Sunday evening. I think I talked my way out of that OK, then she was sitting out there in her car, about to turn up unannounced at my door the following night, when you walked out. You and I, we didn't smooch on the doorstep or anything, but really...'

The hurt has gone, and now she looks worried.

'You should've said.'

'I didn't want to.'

'She's a journalist.'

'I trust her.'

She holds my look, manages to not make any comments about me saying I trust a journalist, then she lifts her fork, moves some food around her plate, then lets the fork drop, sighs heavily and rests her forehead on her hand.

'So, now if you go to her and say, hey let's go out, she's going to say, you're in love with the deputy sheriff, there's no point.'

That is literally pretty much what happened already, though I don't know that I was asking her out romantically. It didn't matter either way.

For once, I manage to keep schtum. Outside, the storm gathers strength, keeping pace with every awkward turn of the conversation.

'Maybe you're just going to have to tell her that you and the deputy sheriff aren't a thing anymore.'

Elise saying it out loud comes like a gut punch, even though that's what we've been talking about, that's where this conversation is inexorably heading.

'Are we not a thing anymore?' I ask.

We hold the look across the table. I'm sure there was music playing when we sat down, but it's stopped, as though Siri has decided there's nothing suitable. The situation demands nothing but the sound of the tumult outside.

'I don't... I don't think we are,' she says. 'For us to be a thing, it'd need me to leave Byron, and...'

The sentence drifts away. She lets out a long sigh. Tears will not come again, not right now.

This is the moment. This is the point where I reach across the table, take her hand in mine, and say, 'Leave him. Call him tonight. Come and stay here with me.'

I have nothing. Silence wraps its cold fingers around my throat.

I'd need to speak to Dr Van Noy, the imaginary therapist, to know if this is fear of commitment, or fear of having stepchildren, or if it's not fear at all, it's just not something I want. And if it's not, how much is that related to Natalie?

'You should speak to the girl,' she says, as though every thought of mine is typing out on a tickertape across my forehead.

'I'm not...'

Suddenly an explosion of noise. Something crashes against the window. A cracking of glass, a shattering. We both leap out of our seats. Then a blur of movement, as Hightower races through the room, hackles raised, disappearing to the other end of the house.

We run into the sitting room, and there on the floor, thrown by the storm, a tangled mass of sea flesh, a great lump of a pale, gelatinous body, tentacles and arms spread around in a tangle. A giant squid, writhing in horror at finding itself in my living room. The window is shattered, the glass spread in ten thousand pieces, and the storm rages into the room, wind and rain and all the force of the wrath of Poseidon.

11

The window repair could wait until morning, but I did everything else that needed to be done, Elise staying at least to help me get the squid back into the sea.

I won't say it went well. We managed to wrap him in a blanket, accompanied no doubt by broken glass, though we did our best. Carted him back out into the tempest, walked about two feet onto the jetty, and tipped the big fella back into the water. I really doubt he'll survive, but he's got a better chance out there, than in my sitting room. Maybe I'll find him washed up on the rocks again in the morning.

I'm saying *him*. Who knows? Hard to tell Mr and Mrs Squid apart when you're a rank amateur.

Not long afterwards, Elise got a call, the storm causing havoc downtown, and she had to leave me to it. And that, without further discussion, was how it was left. Our relationship in ruins.

At that point, the moment of her leaving, I had plenty to distract myself, as the storm was still coming full force into the sitting room. I got the two halves of the old table tennis table from the garage, and nailed them over the window. Bottom one first, then leaning the top one on that while I fixed it, it went more smoothly and was much more quickly done than I imagined it would be. Up until this point in my life, I've not been known for repair skills.

Thereafter, as the wind whistled through a tiny gap between the two halves of the table tennis table, I cleared up the glass, vacuumed, dried everything off as best I could. There was a lamp lost in the tumult, but I've been looking at that lamp for several years, thinking it was time I got rid of it, so we'll call that a win.

And now it's just after three a.m. and I'm lying in bed, listening to the storm outside, and the whistling of the wind from the place where the living room window used to be. Hightower appeared a while ago, to warily watch me in the clear-up process, and now he's sleeping, curled up on the bed. He doesn't usually lie on the bed when I'm in it. Still spooked, though at least he's calmed down.

For me, though, sleep is not imminent. Brain a jumble of confliction and questions. Would a giant squid, which is a pretty big fucking squid by the way, would a giant squid really get thrown through a window by the storm? But if it wasn't the storm, what else could it have been? Godzilla? An even bigger giant squid?

Must've been the storm. That one you don't need to overthink. Life is far-fetched enough as it is, without introducing the possibility of an actual leviathan into the storyline.

The giant squid, tumultuous though its entry to the evening's proceedings was, is not of course the main reason my head is buzzing.

My relationship with Elise just ended. So it seems. Maybe we'll go off, and nothing will happen between Natalie and me, or something will happen and it won't come to much, or life will just go on as it does, and Elise and I will find each other again, and she'll find a way to accommodate our relationship within the new boundaries, and normal service will be resumed.

But this doesn't feel like that. This feels more climactic. We can all live with denial, the difficult questions locked in a cupboard. Once they're out there, however, then everything changes. And this is where we are.

And sure, I didn't say that I was thinking about Natalie all the time, and that she was haunting my dreams, but I didn't need to. Now the end of the affair sits heavily in my stomach, uncomfortable and ominous. Elise has been one of my constants, the past few years.

And perhaps, of course, Natalie has found someone else in the intervening months. I turn up with romantic intent, ring the bell, and the door is answered by some asshole called Chad, a towel tied around his waist, and abs like corrugated concrete.

God, I fucking hate Chad, and he might not even exist.

I reach out, fumble with my ear buds, then stick them in, and start the music playing. George Harrison, *Behind That Locked Door*.

Eventually, sleep will come.

12

Just after nine a.m. Waiting for the window people. I called them last night, they said there was already a queue, but they'd get here early this morning. Could've slept all day, having finally fallen asleep after four, but here I am, sitting at the kitchen table. Bacon on sourdough, two cups of coffee, orange juice and a glass of water. Computer open, going through the social media feeds of Norah Wolfe.

She's of her time, with a variety of accounts, but the most frequently used is Instagram, and for the most part, it's selling her storyboarding services through her artwork.

She's good. I mean, I don't know what makes a good storyboarder over a bad one, but she can draw a human hand and a decapitated head and a plane crashing into a mountain, which seems a decent measure of someone's artistic ability.

Phone goes, but not the window repair company.

'Hey.'

'Just checking in,' says Elise. 'You OK?'

'You mean the window, or the thing?'

'I mean the thing, Sam. Sorry, I felt like I just kind of dashed off.'

'Duty calls,' I say. 'And, I'm not sure. Sad. How about you?'

'Not sure.' A pause, and then, 'Sad.'

Silence threatens, which is never good for a phone call, then we retreat to the practical.

'I haven't been into town,' I say. 'How's it looking out there?'

'Ugly. Lot of damage, though I guess we've seen worse. Should have most infrastructure back up and running, order restored, by midday. You got the window people coming?'

'I'm on the list, just have to wait for them.'

Silence again.

Yep, that's how it's going to be. We need space after last night, or it needs one of us to be able to say some amazing breakthrough thing, but I have no idea what that would be. I'm not sure Sorkin would even be able to write either of us a line at the moment.

'I should get going,' she says. 'Just wanted to make sure you're OK.'

'Have a good day,' I say, brain whirring, desperately reaching for something better, as the silence extends and we both wish we could think of a way to end the conversation that might lighten the awful weight of this.

The phone goes dead, call ended.

I stare at it, as it returns to the home screen. Just hanging up made sense. Even *goodbye* would've seemed inadequate. Why say anything?

*

'It's a shitshow out there,' says the woman who's come to repair my window. I thought there might be two of them, given these are large panes of glass we're dealing with, but the first thing she said was that the company had had to split up all their teams. Calls from all over the cape, and beyond. 'And people,' she continues, 'people can be assholes when they're stressed. You know, you're thinking, maybe I should aim off, but isn't that the measure of someone? Deal with your stress, while still respecting others. How hard can that be? But nope, there's a lot of aggression, and there's a lot of passive aggressive bullshit. One woman, she said to me – do you have coffee by the way?'

We stare at each other for a moment.

'This woman,' I say, 'she asked if you had coffee, or was that you changing the subject and asking me if I have coffee because you want a coffee?'

She laughs, nodding to herself.

'I talk a lot, you'll get used to it by the time I leave. I was asking if you have coffee.'

'I'd been going to offer the first time you stopped talking,' I say, and she laughs again.

'Coffee would be great,' she says. 'Super-hot, lots of hot milk too, if that's not difficult. I like coffee hot, Marky says my mouth must be asbestos, but that's just the way it's always been with me. And I was saying, this woman, she was so mad I was like twenty minutes later than I'd said I'd be. I mean, twenty minutes late, are you kidding me? On a day like this? And she's trying not to get angry, but I can see she's angry, and I said, just let it out, darlin', I don't care, and she said I am this close to dropping the F-bomb. This close. And I thought, we're through, darlin'. I did the job, got out of there, and never said another word to her.'

'You don't like the expression F-bomb?' I say.

'It's the dumbest thing to come out of America in the last fifty years, and that's a damned high bar, by the way.'

'Yeah, I agree, it's dumb,' I say. 'If you're going to use bomb for the word fuck, where do you go for cunt? The C-apocalypse?'

She laughs again, more loudly this time, then says, 'I like event horizon,' and laughs some more. 'Look, this ain't getting the baby bathed. Tell you what, you get the coffee, I'll get started on the window, might need you to give me a hand, and before you know it, this place is going to be good and toasty again.'

*

'A giant squid?'

She's on her way out. Repair done, everything cleared up, table tennis table back in the garage, the sitting room looking just like it always does.

'A giant squid flew through the window,' I say. 'Tossed by the storm.'

'That seems a little far-fetched.'

'Saw it with my own two eyes.'

'Like Phil Collins in *In The Air Tonight*?'

'Exactly like Phil.'

'You might have had too many beers, my friend.'

'You've seen no other instances of creatures thrown up by the sea?' I ask, and she shakes her head, still with that look about her that says she's not buying the story.

'Hey, I'll let you know if I find someone with a shark in their kitchen,' she says, as she gets to the door.

And the instance of the window repair woman is done.

*

The phone rings five minutes later. Patricia Karlsen, the film producer. I don't have anything for her yet, other than the likelihood her daughter got a boyfriend, and ran away to have sex, and I'd been hoping I'd get another day or two before having to speak to her.

'Mr Vikström,' she says. 'Can you talk?'

'Sure. I'm afraid I haven't made a lot of progress.'

'That's OK, I wasn't expecting you to have unearthed Norah already. There's been a development, which I can only hope is unrelated, but I'd be grateful if you could come out to the film set.'

'Sure. Where are you filming today?'

'We're on Rake's Island.'

'Really?'

'Why wouldn't we be?'

Because I don't want to go out to the island, mainly.

'Isn't the weather killing you?'

'It's problematic, but cinematically, it's perfect. Saving us a lot of money in expensive studio time recreating these kinds of conditions.'

'What's the development?' I ask, prevaricating before I agree to anything. I really don't want to get in a boat to go to that island, even though it's only a couple of miles off the coast. Two miles in a small boat in rough seas is two miles too many.

'One of our junior wardrobe people has died. Drowned. No one saw her last night, she didn't turn up for work this morning. We were calling around, looking for her, then one of the camera guys found her body on the rocks.'

'You sure she'd drowned?'

'I'm not a pathologist. That's how it looks. There was no gunshot wound, no bruising around the neck. The only sign of anything was a bad cut on her head, but we're thinking maybe she slipped, banged her head on the rocks, and fell into the water.'

'When was the last time anyone saw her?'

'Yesterday afternoon. We evacuated the island earlier than planned because of the weather. Ultimately, she wasn't on either of the boats, but she kind of got missed in the bedlam. It was a bit Saigon '75, to be honest.'

'No one had any contact last night?'

'Not that we've heard. Looks like she got left behind, and then… there are places to take shelter out here, but maybe she was looking around, trying to find some way off the island.'

'Wouldn't she just have phoned someone?'

'You'd think. So, look… it feels like an accident, but at the same time, it doesn't entirely tie up. That's why I'd like you to take this on, in addition to finding out about Norah.'

'You should call the police.'

'That's in hand, but I'd like you to look into it too.'

'K. Any relationship between Norah and the dead girl?'

'How'd you mean?'

'Maybe they were friends on set, maybe they shared something.'

'I hadn't thought of that.' A pause, and then she says, 'Damn.' Then, 'You can come out here? We've got a boat leaving in about twenty minutes.'

I would rather shoot myself in the face than get on that boat. I would rather take a bath in tarantulas. I would rather crawl over broken glass just to eat the long-dead carcass of a putrefied cockroach. I would rather walk naked down Commonwealth Avenue with ten thousand nameless faces shouting *Shame!* as I go. I would rather watch *Wicked.*

'Yeah,' I choke out. 'I'll be there.'

'Thank you.' A pause, and then, 'The boat leaves from Manchester harbour.'

'Manchester?'

'Sure.'

'Isn't there somewhere closer? That must be over three miles from there.'

'It's a fast boat, it's fine.'

*

Two minutes later I'm at the front door, coat, beanie, phone, car keys. Don't bother with the Walther PPK. Hightower is standing in the kitchen doorway. His face says, 'You're going out? Seriously? What if another squid flies through the window?'

'I can't explain it, furball, but seriously, I don't think that squid flies through the window if I'm not in the house.'

He looks dubious, which is fair enough, because that doesn't make any sense. Nevertheless, sometimes you get a feeling, and that squid, in the height of a storm or not, felt like a message. From the sea gods. And I'm about to make myself extremely vulnerable to the sea gods.

'You'll handle it,' I say, and then I'm turning away, out of the house, and already my stomach is churning.

13

The small harbour in Manchester-by-the-Sea is busier than you'd expect on a cold Friday in late February, but I suspect it's mostly the well-to-do checking up on their yachts. The boat operated by the movie company is obvious, nevertheless. A large motorboat, alarmingly high-sided, given that we're going out onto seas that are still vigorous, if not as tumultuous as last night; white with a blue roof, and with several people either already on board, or milling around on the quayside.

I spot Elise from some way off, in amongst the throng, then I realise that the pathologist, Dr Troy, is also there, and there are a couple of those random CSI guys who pitch up every time something untoward's taken place.

Hmm, this is beginning to look a lot like the authorities taking this more seriously than the producer implied.

I don't know why the sight of all these people in life vests makes it worse, but it does. Obviously they're making people put on life vests, yet there's something about it that says, wear this, you're going to need it.

'Hey,' I say to Elise, who turns away from speaking to one of the crew. She looks a little surprised, then nods.

'They've asked you out here too, have they?'

'They have,' I say, then I clutch at a straw by saying, 'but you know, if this is your show, and you don't want civilians tagging along, I can bale out.'

She glances at the boat, she nods sympathetically. I can see her physically having to stop herself reaching forward and squeezing my hand. Or maybe I'm imagining that, because that's what she'd be doing in happier times.

'You OK?' she asks.

'Nope.'

'If you don't want to get on the boat, don't get on the boat. But it's not our show. Usually we'd get the coast guard, or the Manchester office, but... well, that was one helluva storm, and there's a queue for those boats. We need to get over there, and gather whatever evidence we can. The movie folks said they had this thing rented, and to be honest, I'd rather be on this than what the Manchester boys have.' A pause, and then a small shrug, and then, 'So, here we are. If you feel compelled, buckle up.'

She looks around, she finds who she's looking for, she says, 'Cynthia there will give you your life vest. Leaving in… two minutes…'

Her voice drifts away. She glances past my shoulder, she looks a little disappointed, she turns away, starts talking to one of the crew again.

I turn. Natalie Slater is walking quickly towards us, the slightly discomfited look on her face indicating she's already seen the deputy sheriff and I talking to each other. Or maybe I'm just projecting. Perhaps she's given neither me nor Elise a second's thought these last few months.

'Hey,' she says.

'You heard about the dead girl,' I say.

'Sure. You know who it is I talk to, to get on the boat? Is it… it's the deputy?'

'It's the movie company's boat. You could try Cynthia who's giving out the life vests. It's a bit chaotic, so you might be better lying about who you are. I doubt they're going to want a journalist at this stage.'

'Can I say I'm your partner?'

In the chaos, the chances of the producer finding out I aided and abetted a journalist getting close to the film set and scene of the accident, or scene of the crime, are slim.

'Sure,' I say with some reluctance, even though I've no intention of saying anything else.

As it is, Cynthia is not running a tight ship. She needs to get the boat moving, she sees two people looking to get on board, and she gives us both life vests without bothering to check.

*

Natalie and I sit next to each other on the way over. She tries to make conversation at first, but doesn't get far.

'Sorry. I'm terrified,' I say.
'You're terrified?'
'Can't talk.'

'It's just a boat. It's literally built for this,' she says.

'I'm going to sit with my head between my knees, rocking back and forth, humming a mantra.'

A small wave hits the bow of the boat, and I stiffen, touch her leg in a moment of terror, then remove my hand, eyes already closed, make a small gesture of apology for touching her like that, then lean forward, arms wrapped around my head, head against my legs, curled up in as much of a tight, foetal ball as I can manage.

*

It doesn't help.

14

Still going through the recovery process. Fear takes a lot out of you.

'You OK?' Natalie asked, as we were getting off the boat. I couldn't speak. I imagine I was pale. I nodded. She squeezed my arm, she said, 'I'll let you recover,' and I managed to say, 'At least we don't have to do that again,' and she flashed that great smile of hers.

Now I'm sitting in silence, at the top of a slight rise, looking down over a stretch of rocks to where the body of Roxanne Baudot still lies, tossed up by the waves, like a giant squid. Unless, of course, she never drowned at all, she was murdered and her body was dumped there.

To my left, on the eastern side of the island, a small settlement of ten holiday homes, only two of which are currently occupied. The film set is round the headland, but this is a small island, and the sounds from there, the shouts and the occasional clank from a piece of machinery, can be heard, and every now and again someone comes in to view.

The show, as the show usually does, is going on. The only person from the set currently in attendance at the scene of the potential crime, is the principal producer, Brian Faraday. I'm not sure where Natalie's gone. She was here for a while, checked out the scene, managed to get a couple of surreptitious photographs on her phone, talked to a couple of people, though I don't think she would've learned much, and now I expect she's round with the film crew, attempting to be equally clandestine.

Down in amongst the melee, I notice Elise detach herself, she looks around the area, and then she walks up the short hill to where I'm sitting. My equilibrium is almost restored. About time I got up and went to ask questions. No point in enduring that bloody awful journey, if I'm not going to attempt to make something out of it.

'How you doing, chipper?' she says, and I can't help smiling.

'Just about back in the land of the living. I'm hoping there's a five-star hotel, and I can hunker down for a couple of months.'

She smiles, she nods, she turns, making a gesture towards the ocean.

'I don't think it's going to be so different on the way back.' A pause, and then, 'Maybe worse. Although, having said that, it wasn't actually all that bad coming over here in the first place. I think maybe...' and she kind of shrugs apologetically, tapping the side of her head as she does so.

'I know. It's just... you know I never tried to deal with it, because I always thought, I'll be fine. I won't need to get on a boat again.'

'You can dream,' she says, then she looks around the island. 'What happened to your friend?'

'I don't know. I presume she's over there, attempting to draw people into verbal indiscretion.'

'She was nice,' she says.

'How'd you mean?'

'She was squeezing your arm. Concerned about you.'

'I didn't even notice.'

'Then she caught me looking at her, and she looked apologetic, like you know, I'm not trying to steal him off you or anything, and I said, really, you're being nice to him, it's fine, he needs it.'

'And the two of you had this conversation with your minds?'

'We're women. We have powers. Anyway, I like her. Despite everything. You should speak to her.'

I don't say anything, and she quickly fills the silence with, 'Daniel thinks the victim was murdered. The blow to the head didn't come from slipping and falling.'

'How can he tell?'

'He's a professional. Not one hundred percent out of the question she hit her head on the rocks, but his opinion is this is foul play. She did drown though. Ultimately that was the cause of death. It's possible whoever struck her did not intend murder, but that's where we've ended up.'

'Damn. You going to close down the production?'

'Not yet. I'll speak to the producer, see how we can accommodate each other. No point in messing with their thing if we can work around it. How're you getting on with the missing girl?'

'Haven't addressed it at all since we spoke last night, but this,' and I gesture in the direction of the corpse, 'this makes it look like there might be something else going on.'

She's nodding.

'You know if there was a connection between the two? Roxanne and Norah?' asks Elise.

'I asked Rebecca Karlsen already, and she didn't know. It hadn't occurred to her.'

'She said she'd ask around?'

'Yep.'

'K. You speak to anyone else I might want to talk to?'

'There's the fellow on reception at the Market Square who reported seeing Norah with a man on Sunday. You probably want to talk to him. Better if you catch him at work, I think.'

'I'll keep it in mind. OK, thanks.'

She looks over her shoulder, then turns back. Something about her that says she wants to say something else, an *about last night* kind of a comment, but it's too soon, and she thinks better of it.

'See you on the ride back,' she says.

15

Standing on the edge of the film set, looking east, out over the ocean. Worryingly, it does not look too bright away over there, like there's another storm brewing far out to sea.

'If we're lucky, it'll hit the coast further south.'

Have been granted fifteen minutes with the movie's principal producer, Brian Faraday. He's English, though his accent seems to have been formed from spending a life working in film. Sounds like the kind of generic English accent you get in movies, that people don't have in real life. The equivalent of Hugh Laurie or Benedict Cumberbatch's Anywhereville USA, American accent.

I was sitting in a café in Rockport one time, about five minutes to six. Place was closing up, I was the last guy left in there. In walks Jeremy Irons, and the local mayor, or the local something or other. Not sure why Irons was in town. Rockport being Rockport, maybe he was scouting a movie location, if that's the kind of thing he'd do. 'Just looking to have a quick coffee,' says the other guy, the mayor or whoever. And the café owner says, 'We're closing, sorry.' No negotiation, just off you fuck, we're shut.

And I sat there, looking at my empty cup, thinking, *what are you doing?* I mean, I don't like the rich and famous getting favours, just because they're rich and famous, but seriously, this wasn't much of a favour. This was a cup of coffee. You've got a literal *Die Hard* villain in your establishment. Make the guy a coffee, give him a muffin for God's sake. Get his photograph, stick it on the wall.

Hey, we had Simon Gruber in here the other day.
The fuck's Simon Gruber?
Hans Gruber's brother.
Really!? That fucking guy!? I'm coming round there so I can say I drank a cup of Joe in the same place as Hans fucking Gruber's brother, man.

That's how it would've played out. But she either didn't

know who he was, or wasn't interested anyway. She chased him, and they went elsewhere.

That café's closed down now. Cause and effect, sports fans, cause and effect.

Where did all that come from?

Right, this producer with the generic English movie accent reminds me of Jeremy Irons.

To our right, they're filming a scene where the leviathan of the movie's title is emerging from the sea, and chasing a couple of people up the rocks. None of these people are scheduled to survive. Sadly, the leviathan is going to be done by CGI, so rather than being chased up the rocks by a guy in a giant lizard costume, they're being chased by a bloke carrying a very long pole, with a purple ball on top, so that they've got something to focus on, when they look up in terror at the monster's teeth.

'You spend a lot of time around here?' I ask.

'First time I've ever been to this coast,' he says. 'Nevertheless, weather tends not to move in a straight line over the sea. A universal constant.'

The only constant around here is that the weather will do whatever it damn well pleases. Sometimes it'll come to nothing, and sometimes it'll put a giant squid through your window, and when a storm is still in its genesis, it's impossible to tell which way it'll go.

'What kind of monster are we looking at?' I say, indicating the guy with the purple ball on the long stick. 'Godzilla?'

'It will be smaller, sleeker, faster moving than Godzilla. Closer to the *Alien* xenomorph. You can see by the height of the ball representing the head.'

'The aliens in *Alien* are called xenomorphs?'

'That's correct.'

'Who knew?'

'A lot of people,' he says. 'This seems rather frivolous. I understood you wanted to talk about Roxanne.'

'Roxanne's dead, possibly murdered, a few days after another of your crew, Norah Wolfe, goes missing. You think there might be a connection?'

'No. And I already said that to the sheriff.'

'It's the deputy sheriff, and I'm not working with her. She won't share anything with me. I'm working for Norah Wolfe's mother, and Mrs Karlsen okayed me coming over to the island,' and I pause for the tut and the head shake at the mention of

Karlsen's name, and that seems to me to be the kind of thing I should bank for later, 'so let's say we just zip through this without the additional commentary.'

'Very well.'

'Given the two people involved so far, could you predict who might be next, if someone was to be next?'

'No. They worked in different units, there was no reason for them to spend any time together. Not work-related reasons, at any rate.'

'D'you know if they spent time together unrelated to work?'

'I didn't, but Alice says they went out together on Friday. There was a day off, they went to Salem. Chasing the ghosts of long-dead witches, I presume.'

'Roxanne was with Norah in Salem?'

He gives me the look.

'That's what I just said.'

'Who's Alice?'

'My assistant.'

'It's OK for me to speak to Alice?'

'If she's free.'

'You didn't know anything about that?'

'About what?'

'About Norah and Roxanne going into Salem for the day.'

'Why would I?'

'You won't know if anything happened while they were in Salem?'

'Obviously not.'

He gives me an annoyed glance, then turns back to the purple ball boy, chasing the screamers up the rocks. They are on at least their fifteenth shot of this. No wonder movies end up so expensive. I doubt your average viewer is going to be able to do the Pepsi challenge between any of those shots.

'Any issues with either Roxanne or Norah so far?'

I get another half-glance, though his eyes don't make their way entirely to my face.

'Any issues...' Deep breath. 'Not that I'd heard. While the work on any movie is necessarily collaborative, our production, like most others, is a pyramid. I'm at the top. Both these girls were near the bottom. Neither of them had come into my orbit. You'll need to speak to Arthur about Roxanne, and to Maria about –'

'I spoke to Maria,' I say, and he nods and waves away that part of the discussion.

'Arthur's not on the island. Back at base, putting together plans for the mall fight.'

'You have the leviathan go into a mall?'

A moment, and then he turns and gives me a look.

'No,' he says, slowly, 'like it's your damn business. There's a literal fight,' and he raises his fists, 'between a couple of the human protagonists. You know, stresses build, they could erupt anywhere, just so happens to be at the mall.'

'That's probably better than the monster leaving the sea and heading for Taco Bell for a burrito.'

I get a grim stare, then out of nowhere he laughs.

'That was funny,' he says. 'Are we done?'

'Sure,' I say, and he nods, says, 'You should speak to Alice,' and then he moves quickly away, and before he's within fifty yards of the set, he's shouting at someone to get their attention.

*

'Something happened, but I wasn't sure what it was. It didn't seem important. I mean, when Norah went off, and everyone was like, what the hell just happened to her, I don't think anyone was asking if it might've had something to do with Salem on Friday.'

'So, how'd you know something happened?'

'Roxanne was a bit funny on set on Saturday. Not her usual self, you know.'

'She was in wardrobe?'

'Sure, and her work was fine throughout. But I had to speak to her about something, and I could just tell, you know? Something was off. Like, just a half-second out of kilter.'

'Did you ask what it was?'

'I did. She said it was nothing. But then, when I asked about Salem, the same kind of a shadow crossed her face, and she had the same reluctancy to talk. I guess I'm putting two and two together, and who knows what it makes?'

'What are your guts telling you?'

'Oh, my guts are telling me something went down between them, I just don't know what.'

'How long did this reserve of Roxanne's last?'

'Well, it's over now.'

'Any chance that it started before Friday?'

'Well, I just noticed it on Saturday, but I can be unobservant about people, 'specially when I'm wrapped up in a shoot.'

'You think whatever was bugging Roxanne, might've also been the reason Norah left the set?'

'Maybe. Maybe not.'

'What d'you think happened between them?'

'Honestly, I don't know. If they told anyone, it wasn't me. I think you'll find you're in, *what happens in Salem, stays in Salem* territory.'

'You think it might have been romantic?'

'Jeez, I have no idea. I don't know about them.'

'But then, ultimately sounds like Norah went off with a man.'

'I guess. That doesn't mean anything, does it? Hey, maybe they fought over the guy.'

'In Salem?'

'Go figure.'

And that's about that for Alice, the assistant to Brian Faraday, except just as we're going our separate ways she says, 'You know, there's something, just something about this shoot. It's felt a little, I don't know, off. Just off. Like there's something lurking over there, in the shadows.'

'That's a bit vague.'

'That's all I've got.'

'Something sinister?'

'I don't know. Sinister? Maybe.'

*

'You making any progress?' asks Rebecca Karlsen.

She looks drawn. Worried. Scared even. This is a pretty big movie to be running, which is bad enough. Then your daughter disappears, and it wasn't without a word, but it was still strange. And then one of the crew gets murdered.

This has potential to turn into the kind of disaster movie production that people make ninety-minute Netflix documentaries about. Or, at the very least, it makes Internet lists of Top 50 Movie Shoots That Were Completely Catastrophic. Images of a guy chasing people up a rocky shoreline carrying a purple ball on a stick ain't going to help, but that's the magic of the movies I guess. They all look like that before the computer people get their hands on them.

'Norah tell you anything about going to Salem on Friday?'

'Last Friday?'

'Yes.'

'Sure, she said she went with... damn, she went with Roxanne. Gosh, I'd completely forgotten about that. Did something happen?'

'No one seems to know. Did she say anything to you?'

'She mentioned on Thursday evening she was going, but didn't mention it again. I never heard from her on Friday evening, and then the next interaction we had... I don't know why I'm having to think about it, I've read our messages to each other about ten times since she left. We exchanged a line or two on Saturday, but there was nothing... it was just about that day. I'd forgotten about Salem, and she never mentioned it. You really think something happened in Salem?'

'Did she say why they were going there? What they were going to see?'

'I didn't ask. I just assumed they were going to Salem for the same reasons anyone goes to Salem.'

'OK. I'll maybe go down there, go to the main tourists spots, see if anyone remembers them.'

'You need photographs?'

'We're good. I've already got them off the Internet. That aside, I don't feel I'm getting anywhere. How about you? You know if anyone has any idea why someone would want to kill Roxanne?'

She shakes her head, the pained expression returns.

'It's... I'm at a loss. We all are.'

'Has she got a close friend on set?'

'I really don't know, but no one's claiming her as a close friend. Everyone's just... confused.'

We turn at the approach of Deputy Sheriff Miller, who looks much as she does at work every day. She's not stressed by the trials of a movie production, nor by the undulations of a boat on a short stretch of ocean.

'Mrs Karlsen,' she says, 'we're going to head back now. Thanks for all your help.'

'If there's anything else I can do.'

'Of course. We'll be in touch. Roxanne's parents are being

notified, but, as you know, they're in France, so this will be a distant interaction, unless they decide to come here to bring their daughter's body home. I'll let you know if that's going to happen.'

That thought also seems to shake Karlsen a little further, and then she nods, and says, 'I'll keep you up-to-date with anything…' and the words run out, and she finishes the sentence with a gesture.

'Detective,' says Elise, turning to me, 'the boat's heading back if you want to tag along. I guess it'll be back and forth the rest of the afternoon, so it's your call.'

She turns and looks out across the wide expanse of ocean, stretching towards an encroaching, troubled horizon.

'However, this is going to get worse before it gets better, so it's up to you. Tomorrow morning's going to be a flat calm, so maybe you want to stay the night.'

'Tomorrow morning's a flat calm?'

'Yes.'

I look at her, I look at Karlsen.

'Does anyone stay on the island overnight?'

'We might tonight, still under discussion. And there are a couple of people in the houses over there, but they're pretty pissed we're even here in the first place, and taking no interest in us. But you know, if you want to stay here overnight, it's your call.'

I look at her, I look at Elise. I can see the brief flash of sympathy in her eyes, but we're not alone here, and she can't be showing any sign of affection.

'Sounds like you come now, or leave it until morning,' she says. 'But now means right now. Thank you, Mrs Karlsen.'

The women nod at each other, Elise gives me a last look, and then turns away.

Dammit.

'I should go. I'll get down to Salem. Should get there before the museums and the tourists shops close.'

'Thanks for everything, detective.'

I turn away, walking quickly up over the slight rise after Elise.

16

The trip back across to the mainland makes the first journey seem like sitting in the rowing boat on Malcolm the receptionist's millpond out back.

It is terrifyingly tempestuous. Two people are sick. I'm not sick because I'm consumed by fear. Like the brain can't cope with both things at once, so it thankfully shuts one of them down. No sea sickness, just gut-wrenching terror.

I mean, we never lose sight of land. There's no reason to have this level of fear. Sea sickness is entirely understandable. There's just nothing to be done about that. But fear? That's all in my dumb head.

Once again, I'm wiped out by the time I get back to the mainland. Practically crawl off the boat, legs weak, at the other end. Natalie must have remained on the island, so she wasn't there to see this pathetic display of pusillanimity. As soon as I'm on land, I think of her, and that she'll be taking a later boat back, and wonder what fresh hell she'll go through. Maybe they'll stop sailing, and they will all just spend the night out there. It's a movie set, it's not like it's not kitted out to have people survive overnight.

'You OK, soldier?' asks Elise, standing side on to me, trying not to look too invested.

I'm bent double, hands on my knees, trying to adjust to no longer needing all that adrenaline that's been coursing through my body.

'It's over, so yes. You OK? Sorry, I barely even looked at you to see if you were all right.'

I look up, and she smiles, then I finally I manage to stand up straight.

'Won't say I enjoyed it, but you know, it happened. We're here now.'

I let out a long breath, shake my head.

'God, I'm pathetic,' I say.

I see her glance around, making sure there's no one within

earshot.

'You know, seeing you like that, it makes me think of the fact that I know, *I know* you're even more terrified of heights than you are of being out on the ocean, then I think of what you did on that lighthouse last year. In weather worse than this, and heights that were equivalently much worse than what you just went through.'

I have nothing to say. We stare at each other.

'That's all,' she says.

She takes a small step away, retreating from the conversation.

'You should still speak to the girl.'

She turns away, and walks quickly along the small harbour wall. I watch her go, and then look back at the boat. It's bobbling around, tied up to the harbour, but I can see they're already getting ready to head back out to the island.

The cadaver is in the back of an ambulance, the crime-fighting crew have disembarked with all their stuff, and they're just getting loaded up, ready to leave.

I walk back towards the boat. The captain, cigarette in hand, watches me approach.

'You all right there?' he asks.

I stop, then stamp a couple of times on the quayside concrete floor.

'Seems solid enough,' I say, and he laughs.

'Not in your element out there, huh?'

'Oh that? I was fine. Just thinking about the Pats blowing the number one draft pick. That was so dumb.'

He laughs again, then turns and looks out over the ocean. The arrival of rain little more than quarter of an hour away.

'How many more trips are you going to make out there?' I ask.

'Yeah, it's getting ugly,' he says. 'I'm going to say two, tops, but they're going to have to be snappy. Has to be two, if we're getting everyone off that's out there, but they need to be back-to-back. Don't want to be on the water a couple of hours from now.' He takes a draw on the smoke, then makes a gesture out towards the island, which, from here in this sheltered inlet, we can't actually see. 'I've already radioed the folks out there. Either they start packing up now, and we,' and he makes an about-turn gesture, 'soon as we get out there, or they commit to leaving folks on the island, and we make one more trip, in slower time.'

'Well, good luck. It was a pleasure 'n all, but hopefully we'll never see each other again,' and he laughs, nods, takes a last draw, flicks the butt onto the ground and then steps on it.

I turn away, take a last look over my shoulder at the subdued sea in the Manchester inlet, and then I walk to the car, and settle into the driver's seat, feeling safe and comfortable, and just a little bit of an attention-seeking fraud.

17

There are a lot of witch museums in Salem, their names quickly blending into one. And I don't know, of course, if that was why the two women came to Salem. It is the thing that distinguishes it along this coast, the thing that gives the place international recognition, but maybe they came here because they'd already done Rockport, Gloucester, Manchester, and Beverly, and they were working their way down the coast.

I get my first hit on the photographs of the women at the third try. The Salem Witch Museum. Doesn't mean they hadn't visited the first two places I'd tried, but it could be different people who were on. And it's not like I can ask to check anyone's security footage from Friday.

'Sure, they were here. They're what now?'

'This one's missing,' I say, indicating Wolfe. I've already decided not to mention that Baudot is dead. People get twitchy around murder. Young women going missing though, there's a bit more intrigue there.

'That's too bad. She was here on Friday. You say she went missing after that?'

'She was back in Glasgow at the weekend, checked out of her hotel on Monday morning. To be honest, this isn't that exciting. She called some people later that day. It was just a little off that she walked out on the movie they're making up there, and her mum's worried about her, that's all.'

'This is why the P.I.'s asking the questions, and not the local cops,' says the old guy, nodding.

'Yep.'

'I don't think I'm going to be able to help you here,' he says. 'What can I say? There was no drama. These two girls, the guy they were with. They came through here, bought their tickets, went into the museum. Not sure I saw 'em leave, but I might just've been distracted. We had a few folks in on Friday. A bus tour. From China. Seeing those folks more 'n more. Good for business, I guess, but some folks don't like it.'

'There was a guy with them?'

'Sure. Nothing remarkable about any of these people, but I got memory, see? I'm not saying I'm smart, I just got that eidetic memory, you know.'

'So, you remember the guy?'

'Sure.'

'You remember what he looked like?'

'Sure I do. Tall. Six-five, maybe six-six. Thick hair, but not long. Dark. Dark eyebrows. Dark complexion too, I guess. White, but with something in him. Maybe Italian. I don't know. I don't know Italians, it's just how it feels. *Capisce*?' he says, and he laughs.

'Thick, dark hair, tall, dark complexion, possibly Italian.'

'That's your guy.'

'Did he seem to be with one of the women?'

'Like a couple?'

'Sure.'

'I was wondering that myself. They came in, they wandered around looking at books. The ladies wandered over here, they bought three tickets, the fella comes up as they're paying. I was wondering who he was with, but it was hard to tell. Kind of decided the girls were a couple, the guy was, I don't know, just some guy they were with.'

'Which of the women paid for the tickets?'

He indicates Roxanne.

'She bought all three. Hey, it's seventeen-fifty each, what does that tell you? I don't know.'

'Maybe they were taking it in turns at each museum.'

'Maybe. Maybe not.'

'Anything distinctive about what the tall guy was wearing?'

'Jeans, padded check jacket. Hey, it's winter in New England, everyone wears the same damn thing around here.'

'So, you decided the women were a couple?'

'Maybe I did, sure.'

'Was there any affection between them?'

'Nah, it was just… they were comfortable together. Heck, they were probably just friends, right? Women get comfortable together in a way men don't.' A moment, and then he chuckles. 'Just an old man's fantasy,' he says, and he chuckles again.

'OK, thanks, boss,' I say. Fish a business card out of my pocket, and place it on the counter. I like this guy, decide I might as well come clean. 'This one was found dead this morning. Murdered. She only died last night, so it's not related to these two being here on Friday, so you might not have the police around, but this tall Italian guy, he's going to be of interest.'

He doesn't seem at all bothered about having the police round.

'I should give 'em a call,' he says. 'I'll wait 'til I see it on the news, see what they're saying. Don't want to land that fella in any trouble, but then, maybe he deserves to be in trouble. You see a fella with two women, then a week later one of 'em's missing and one of 'em's dead…'

He ain't wrong.

'Thanks. You think of anything else, or you see this girl again, you'll give me a call?'

'Sure,' he says. 'I can do that.'

And I'm off.

18

When in Salem.

Standing outside the antique shop of Gerry Nine Fingers. I've been to the museum where his wife, Dr Montrose works. Managed to speak to someone on the desk there – they recognised the women, and had a similar description of the guy – without making contact with Dr Montrose, which is a bonus. Talking to her always feels a little like going into combat, unarmed.

Talking to Gerry, on the other hand, is like watching an episode of *Curb Your Enthusiasm*. Not that I actually like *Curb Your Enthusiasm*, but the real life version is pretty funny.

I find him in his usual position, leaning over an old maritime antique, a small tool in hand, magnifying glasses on. The bell tinkles above the door, I close the door behind me. Outside the storm is beginning to build, the rain is falling, and it looks like we're in for a repeat of last night.

I think of the giant squid.

'A portentous gust of wind,' says Gerry, looking up. 'Long time, no see. Oh, wait, no it's not. It's only been about four months. You here to buy something maybe? Or are you just wanting to pump me for information? I'm like a reference library to you. I'm like Wikipedia. I might as well start calling myself Gerry-dot-com. Every six months I should ask you for donations.'

He says all this looking through his magnifying glasses, then he finally takes them off and lays them on the counter. He leans forward, fingers spread out, displaying the missing index finger on his left hand.

I approach, smiling. Can't help it. The man's irascibility is good fun, that's just how it is.

'Was passing by, thought I'd stop for a chat.'

'I'll bet. You know your trouble?'

'Enlighten me.'

'You're lonely. You got no friends. You been living here

for twenty-five years and I'm the only guy you ever met you can talk to. Lucky for me, huh?'

Yeah, all right, Gerry Nine Fingers, I get enough of that from my dream therapist.

'You recognise either of these women?' I say, placing the photographs on the counter.

He's probably right, of course. I mainly come in here for a chat. No reason why Roxanne and Norah would've come to Gerry's antique shop over any other. There's a museum a block away they might have visited – though the person I just spoke to didn't recognise them – but there are still about twenty antique shops between here and there.

Gerry regards me warily, and then looks at the two photographs. He toys with me, like he's actually thinking about it, then looks up and shakes his head.

'You know they've been along here at some point?'

'They were in Salem last Friday, doing the tourist tour. I know at least they visited the Witch Museum, the Salem House, and the Cape Ann. They may have been to other places, I'm just going door-to-door, see if there's anything doing.'

'You seriously been into every antique store?'

'I haven't been into any antique stores. You're right, I've got no friends, and I just came in here for a chat.'

'Well, isn't that pleasant? I can't help you with either of these two. What else d'you want to talk about?'

'They were seen with a guy, tall, six-six maybe, kind of Italian-looking, dark hair, eyebrows.'

'A six-foot-six Italian guy with eyebrows? Are you kidding me?'

'Nope. That's the question.'

'No, I don't know any six-foot-six Italian guys. Jesus.'

OK, so this might've been a mistake. The appeal of Gerry's amusing irascibility has quickly worn off. I turn away, and look around his cabinets of seafaring wonders. I do like most of this stuff, so there's that, and I walk away from the counter, and look in a cabinet that seems to have a few new items from the last time I was here.

'What's that you're working on?' I ask, while studying a pocket compass, which has been cleaned and restored, the label next to it stating it dates from 1751.

'An astrolabe,' he says. 'It's from the nineteenth century, so it's never been used in anger, it was always just there for presentation or ornamental purposes. Clean it up, fix the gearing, some schmuck'll pay something for it.'

'I like this compass,' I say.

'You like the compass?'

'Sure. I like the design of the rose, the shape of the needle.'

I don't turn to face him as we talk. He senses my genuine interest, and he walks around the counter to take a closer look.

'Yeah, right, that one. Yeah, I like that too. Got it in an auction down on Long Island. Two hundred bucks.'

It's got a price ticket on it of twelve hundred. The fact that he just told me how much he paid for it is a clear indicator he presumes I've no intention of buying. But I really like this.

'That your usual kind of mark-up?'

'Market value,' he says. 'I'm not interested in ripping people off. The thing was a piece of shit when I bought it. Thing of beauty now, look at it. You'd pay fifteen hundred for that in Boston, closer to three grand you walked into the wrong store in Manhattan.'

He looks at me, he has a moment of recognition, he nods.

'It's Swedish,' he says. He snaps his fingers. 'Despite that accent of yours, there's got to be some Swedish in you with that name.'

'Grandfather.'

'Nice. Still alive?'

'Died in nineteen-seventy-three. Dad's dead as well, so really, the Swedish connection's long gone.'

'There's still you,' he says, then he barks out a laugh and turns away, starting to walk back to the counter.

'I'll take it,' I say.

He turns, he looks curiously at me.

'You'll take it?'

'Yep.'

'I don't do, you know... My margins are slim, I can't be doing concessionary rates or nothin'.'

'Of course,' I say, slightly offended he'd assume that was what I was thinking.

'Oh. Well, that's great. I'll just get the, eh... yeah, I'll get the box.'

*

'Who are they anyway, the two girls?' he says, when the deal on the compass is done.

'You know there's a movie filming up in Glasgow?'

'I heard about that. Heard they're out on Rake's Island, disturbing the birds.'

'They're there now.'

'Jesus. And those girls are working on that movie?'

'They were. One of them left on Monday. She's vanished. Her mum's employed me to find her. The other one turned up dead today. Sheriff's office think she was murdered.'

Unusually for Gerry, there are no glib comments tossed my way at that. The unexpected compass sale has obviously put him in an unusually good humour, the tale of a young woman getting murdered a dent in that, even for someone as comically curmudgeonly as Gerry.

'Damn,' he says. 'This guy, the Italian guy, he's a person of interest?'

'Not for the feds. Not yet, anyway. I just came here asking around, looking to see if anyone saw the girls. Turns out they did, turns out this guy was seen with them. No one got a name, though.'

'The guy never used his credit card?'

'No one's said so far.'

'Maybe he bought them coffee or lunch.'

'I've been stopping in cafés and the like. Nothing as yet.'

'You should try the Stand Alone.'

'You think?'

'That place is weird. It's like it exists on some other dimension.'

'How'd you mean?'

'You know, some people can't see it. Like the door, you know it's a red fuckin' door man, how hard is that to see, but some people, I don't know, they just walk right by. Never know it's there. But there's a type of person, you know. Sometimes they can see the light, and sometimes,' and he taps the counter with his left ring finger, 'sometimes they can see the darkness.'

We stare at each other across the counter. I check the time. Almost five-thirty, the day outside getting dark, the storm whipping up this side street from the harbour.

'I'll check it out.'

'You've been there before?'

'Sure.'

'You can see the door?'

'Sure.'

'You know that some people can't see the door?'

'I never thought about it.'

He looks along the counter, the astrolabe he's working on is still there, and he pulls it closer to himself, and lifts the magnifying glasses.

'Maybe you don't need to think about it,' he says. 'Go to the Stand Alone. Speak to the Jigsaw Man. One of those girls is dead, fair chance they'd be able to see the door just before. The universe would've known they were going to die.'

He slips the magnifying glasses on, lifts a hand in farewell, and bends over the astrolabe, elbows on the counter. A moment, then he seems to change his mind, and lifts the glasses on to the top of his head.

'Tell you what,' he says. 'Give me copies of those pictures. I'll ask around for you. I know people who know things. I know people you can only dream about.'

He laughs. I say, 'Open your phone, I'll air drop them,' and he says, 'Sure thing, chief. Gerry'll have this shit sorted in no time.'

19

Playing the piano, while for the second evening in a row, a storm batters the front of the house. *Stars Fell On Alabama.* Nice chord structure: the insertion of the Gm between the C and the A7 in the opening line, the progression through the G7+ between the D9 and the C. I love all those old chords, the kind of thing that was lost with the arrival of the three-minute, three- or four-chord pop song.

Not that I'm much of a follower of the modern artist. For all I know Sabrina Carpenter could have a G7+, a C#dim and an F7sus4 in every bar.

Hightower hasn't left my side since I got in. The wee man's still freaked by the incident of the giant squid. Wait, he's been freaked a lot longer than that. It was like he's known for a couple of days that the squid was coming. He's been agitated. But then, the weather's been bad for a while now, and it's obviously getting to him. Hiding under the bed a lot.

Let's hope that what he senses out there is just bad weather, and not something more sinister.

The Stand Alone was closed up for the day. It's late February, there wasn't much doing anywhere I went in town. No surprise really. So, tomorrow morning, back down to Salem. This tall Italian guy is pretty much all I've got going for me at the moment. And I'll need to speak to Elise, see if there's anything happening from their end. They'll be able to speak to the crew of the movie in a way that I can't, regardless of Karlsen's part in my investigation.

There's a knock at the door. I stop playing, I glance at furball, who lifts his head out of his paws, ears erect, instantly wary.

'It's OK,' I say. 'Giant squids don't knock.'

This wisdom doesn't seem to help.

Down the hallway, see the figure standing outside through the window. Take a moment, didn't expect this, then open the door.

'Hey,' says Natalie.

'You look freezing. Come in. Why aren't you wearing a coat?'

'I drove.'

'And you've been standing out there?'

'I could hear you playing the piano.'

'With this wind?'

'It's sheltered at the front. Under the awning, you can barely hear it. You can hear the piano though, because you have windows open all round your house, like some kind of a freak.'

'You've stood out there listening before.'

'I have. I like it, it's nice.'

A slightly awkward silence, before I think to say, 'Any time you like, you can come and sit here, and I'll play for you. You don't have to stand in the cold.'

'I might take you up on that.'

'How long were you out there?'

'An amount of time.'

I smile, and finally move, and we walk through to the kitchen, the storm rattling the windows.

'Hot drink or alcohol?' I say.

'I didn't… I don't mean to invite myself over or anything. I just, you know, you looked like you had a hard time today, that's all. Just checking up on you.'

'Oh, I'm fine. Sorry, bit of a drama queen.'

'We've all got our terrors.'

'I prefer it when mine aren't on such public display. Anyway, back on dry land – or, you know, soaking, rainswept land – I'm fine. How about you? It must've been a hellscape coming back later in the day.'

She laughs.

'Oh, boy. The movie people, most of them stayed over there. I mean, it was wild, but they were like, this is great. You know, the director and the cinematographer were like excited kids. It was pretty infectious. Absolutely nuts, but nice to see people enjoying their work, I guess. So, there weren't so many of us on the last boat. Most of them were sick. But I grew up going out on dad's yawl. I'm used to it. I love it, in fact. Guess I'm just lucky.'

'Why didn't you stay out on the island?'

'I was wandering around most of the day, chatting to people as casually as I could, then I got busted.' She drags a thumb across her neck. 'There's a producer, an English guy, Brian Faraday, he took the time to find out I was a journalist, then he lost his shit. They'd all been assuming I was with the sheriff's office.' She shrugs.

'You've written it up already?'

'The news has been filed. Job done for the day.'

'Glass of wine?'

'That'd be nice, thank you. White wine if you've got it. Any of the other colours, if you don't.'

*

I share my day. I'm not possessive about my cases. I'm always happy to share with anyone who might help, or might be able to use what I've learned. If the case gets solved, that's all that matters. She shares some of her day. Maybe all of it. I can't say that she'll be as generous as I am. Don't know her well enough.

Doesn't sound like she learned too much. I feel the answer to the mystery of Roxanne's death is more likely to lie with Norah Wolfe and the unknown Italian, than it is with the crew of the film. Not many of them seem to have had anything to do with her, and it sounds like the production is going OK for the moment. On schedule, on budget. That, at this stage one imagines, is the Holy Grail of film production.

The day's events have been discussed and deconstructed, and with it comes an inevitable silence. Or, at least, a silence soundtracked by Junior Mance on the piano. Hightower is in the kitchen with us, sitting by the window, keeping his distance nevertheless, an eye on the storm as much as he can have given the reflection.

'You want another glass?' I ask.

'I shouldn't,' she says. 'Car's out front, and I need to get going sharp in the morning, so I really need to drive home tonight. But thank you.'

And with that, silence comes again. The refusal of the drink top-up is the kind of thing that leads to the departure, but she likely doesn't want to leave, any more than I want her to leave.

Inevitably we start talking at the same time, then we both stop, and we both insist on the other talking, and obviously I insist a little more strongly as she acquiesces, then she says, 'How's the deputy?' then she winces, like she wishes she hadn't said it in the first place.

I take a drink of wine, nod in answer. We come to it at last. Actually, she's only been here about twenty minutes.

'Think we might've split up,' I say.

'Oh.' Then, 'You *think* you might have split up?'

I nod.

Down the rest of the wine, set the glass back on the table.

'I don't know. Don't know what to say. It's been a bit off recently. There's a thing that's going to happen… you don't really need to know about that. But really, I guess it's been off since…'

Here we go. I'm not at my best in these situations, which is one reason I've largely avoided them all my life. Elise and I were always at our best when we ignored the pain and the nuance and the contradictions. I find talking rarely makes things better.

'Since…?'

'I met you.'

'Oh. Bar that time in Target, we haven't seen each other in four months.'

I look gormlessly across the table. It would be nice to be someone who could take control of this kind of conversation, bending it to one's will, or at least being able to have some agency in which way it'll go. When I stumble blindly into this kind of thing, I'm more like James Bond, that time he was a cunt, dancing in a hurricane.

I lift the glass, drain the dregs, lay it down, and then go to the fridge. I stand with my back to her, trying to make the decision, or rather, building up to doing the bold thing I already decided to do when I was in Gerry Nine Fingers' antique shop a few hours ago, then I lift out the bottle of wine, place it on the table, and say, 'I'll just be a moment.'

She looks a little non-plussed, then I turn away, through to the bedroom, lift the small box with the Swedish compass that I placed in the bedside drawer, then return to the kitchen.

She's sitting in the same position when I get back. Glasses empty, wine bottle untouched.

'I saw this in a shop in Salem today,' I say.

I place it on the table in front of her.

'You bought me a present?'

'I bought you a present.'

'Why? Sorry, that sounds ungrateful.' A beat. 'Yes, ungrateful. Question withdrawn. Thank you, that's really kind.'

I don't know what it is, but having made the decision and handed it over, and seeing her as hapless as I am in this situation, I find myself relaxing a little. I sit down, pour another small glass of wine, but leave her glass for the moment.

With the air of someone opening a bomb, she lifts the small, unwrapped box, and removes the lid. There it lies, the renovated eighteenth-century Swedish compass.

She doesn't look at me. She studies it for a few moments, then lifts it out of the box, and looks more closely at the design of the rose. She swallows. She holds the compass in the palm of her hand, her elbow on the table. Hasn't taken her eyes off it since she opened the box.

Feel goosebumps on my arms, on the hairs on my neck.

She swallows again, and finally lifts her eyes.

'I love it.' A beat. 'Eighteenth century?'

'You can tell that without looking at the provenance?'

'Like I said, I went out on boats with dad all my life. He taught me the old ways.'

'You never mentioned that,' I say.

'The first time we really talked during the *Mary Celeste* case, I got drunk, and I couldn't remember if I'd told you or not. I guess I thought I had. Now, I guess I didn't. How did you know I'd like it?'

'Hope rather than expectation,' I say. 'I like it. No reason you should, I sup –'

'I love it,' she says, cutting me off. Then, inevitably, 'I also know how much this is likely to have cost.' Tick-tock. 'You shouldn't have done that.'

'I know.'

She holds my gaze for a moment, then looks back at the compass. Her eyes still on it, she reaches out, lifts the wine bottle, pours herself a small glass, downs it in one, then walks around the side of the table, pauses for no more than a second, places her fingers softly on my face, then leans in and kisses me on the lips, her lips moist and tasting of wine.

20

'Everybody needs to calm the fuck down. Calm, the fuck, down, people.'

There's been a lot of jibber-jabber. Me as much as these two clowns, so I can't really complain too much.

Me and Hightower and Joey the capuchin, sitting around the kitchen table, working our way through a bottle of Wild Willi Gold. I should never have allowed myself to be dragged into this conversation, but here we are. For a while I was sure I was talking to my therapist, and she was telling me that my compass move was a triumph, and I should maybe try giving more people antique Swedish compasses, then all of a sudden I was back here, at my kitchen table, and these two muppets are telling me I gave the compass to the wrong woman.

I think it was Joey who said the line about everyone needing to calm down, though I'm sure I'd already thought about saying that. Words and intentions seem to be interchangeable.

'I can't give it to Elise,' I say. 'I can't give anything to Elise. Elise doesn't want anything from me, other than what I can already give her. And now, now I'm not sure I can give her anything at all.'

'Some of us like Elise,' says Hightower. 'But no, we don't get a say in it, do we? What about me? What about Joey, huh? We're the kids who get screwed over in the divorce. Well, don't come blaming me if *I* turn out to be a serial killer.'

'Right?' says Joey, before downing a shot, and slamming the glass on the table.

'You're already a serial killer,' I say. 'You're a predator. You're a born-ready, killing machine.'

'Whatever. Just maybe think about the kids before you go breaking up with your married friend, that's all.'

'I have no choice! I'm in love with Natalie. That's just how it is. You can only fight this kind of thing so long.'

'Oh, listen to yourself,' says Joey. 'You ain't in a romantic drama, pal. This is crime drama. At best, maybe, and this is a long stretch, *maybe* you're in a slightly surreal psychological thriller, but there's not a lot of nuance here. Don't go bringing talk of romantic drama to the table.'

'My table, I'll bring whatever I want.'

'Your table? Is it *your* table?'

I look at the table. Maybe he has a point. My table isn't charcoal grey. And my table isn't this large, and doesn't have eight seats around it.

Tap-tap-tap.

A noise from the window. Dark outside, nothing to be seen except the reflection of the kitchen. I can see myself in the reflection, but neither Hightower nor Joey. I look for them, wondering if they're vampires, but they're no longer here.

Tap-tap-tap.

I get up and walk to the window. Suddenly the kitchen lights start to dim, and I can see outside a little better.

Tap-tap-tap.

A crow on the window ledge, tapping at the lock.

Big-ass crow.

Of course, it's not a crow. A raven. There's a raven at the window, trying to get in.

'What d'you want?'

It looks at me. Suddenly there's silence when there hadn't been silence before. Usually there's the sound of the sea, there's the wind, there's rain against the window, there's the hum of the fridge, there's music playing, there's *something*.

Silence.

The raven cocks its head to the side. Its beak opens, like it's cawing, but there's no sound.

Something approaching. Something big. A second, an instant, then a crash of glass, and a formless black shape smashes through the window.

My heart explodes, and I sit bolt upright in bed, my body out of nowhere a hundred percent adrenaline.

'Oh my God,' says Natalie, sitting up beside me. 'You OK?'

I lean forward, panting heavily, trying to get my breathing under control, the dream already diminishing, smothered by reality, the way dreams are, pushed back into the dark recesses of consciousness from where it somehow managed to escape.

She touches my arm. I flinch slightly, she pulls away, and I say, 'Sorry, sorry, I…'

Deep breath. Turn to the window. Outside, the early morning is calm. The grey light of dawn making its first appearance upon the far horizon. The sea as flat as promised.

I glance at Natalie, who's settled back a little since I flinched at her touch.

'There are demons,' I say, and she looks no less worried, then I think I should clarify, and it comes out as, 'I have demons,' and she says, 'You do, don't you?'

Finally I lie, head back on the pillow, eyes open, staring at the ceiling. A moment, I feel her fingers edging towards me beneath the covers, and I take her hand into mine.

*

'I don't know how this is going to sound,' she says, as she drinks a quick cup of coffee before heading out into the day.

'Uh-oh.'

'It's not what you think.'

'How d'you know?'

'Because I realise what I just said might've been the precursor to me distancing myself, or saying, that was nice 'n all, but maybe we should just be careful here…'

'OK, fair enough.'

'It's not that.'

'Good. What is it?'

'I don't know if I should say it now, it's going to sound, I don't know… actually, I just don't know how it'll sound.'

'Let me judge.'

'You might judge me harshly.'

'You've seen me weak-kneed and terrified on a boat, and you've seen me shoot awake, haunted by God knows what monsters in my head, and you're still here. I'm not judging you.'

'I just wanted you to know that I came here last night...' Deep breath. 'I just thought, I don't know what's going on with you and the deputy, but I want to see you, and it's time to at least *try*. So. That's all. I just didn't want you to think I slept with you because of the compass.' She looks a little abashed, then adds, 'I was going to sleep with you anyway.'

'Why didn't you take a second glass of wine, then?'

'I was trying not to be too obvious.'

'You jumped me after I gave you a present. That was pretty

obvious.'

I say that straight-faced, then we both start laughing.

The laughter goes, we smile at each other across the table. In the background, BBC Radio 3 breakfast show on delay, which Natalie put on while making coffee. Currently playing Miles Davies, which I hadn't expected. But then, what do I know of BBC Radio 3?

She lifts her coffee, and downs it.

'I should go. Speak to you later?'

I nod.

'K. I'm... you know, whatever, I'm free tonight if you are, but you know...,' she says.

'Me too. I'll call you.'

She smiles, she taps her bag as a final thank you for the compass, and then turns and walks quickly from the house.

The door closes, and then I stare at it, looking at the space where she's just been. I take a drink of coffee, and lean forward and rest my chin in the palm of my hand.

'That came out of nowhere,' I say to the room.

I glance at Hightower. He gives me one of his bored looks, and yawns.

21

I guess I've never really thought about it before, but there is something odd about the Stand Alone café. Hard to say what it is, which is why I've never taken the time to think about it. Even though it's in the middle of a row of shops, opposite the harbour in Salem, it seems to live up to its name. Like it's detached, alone in its own separate world.

But there's more than that. You feel invisible when you're in there, like the people walking past have no idea it exists, and that doesn't make any sense.

This is why it's good not to overthink things.

Same goes for relationships.

The Jigsaw Man is in the corner, and we nod at each other as I enter. I take a seat, have a look at the menu. French toast with maple syrup, bacon and berries leaps off the page. Still got the taste for it from two days ago.

'Hey,' says the waitress, and she's pouring coffee the second she arrives at the table, then she says, 'Juice or water?' and I say, 'Orange juice, please. No, make that apple,' and she says, 'One apple juice it is. And are you wanting anything to eat today?' and I say, 'Can I get the French toast, bacon, berries, the whole kit and caboodle,' and she smiles and says, 'Excellent choice. Anything else?' and I say, 'Nope, I think that covers it,' and she smiles and says, 'Cream's on the table, and I'll be right back with that juice,' and off she goes.

I sit and look out of the window while I wait. Trying not to think too much about last night. Trying not to disappear into a mire of infatuation. Also trying not to think about Elise, and how hurt she'd be if she knew. And maybe she does know. She's smart. And for all her talk, all her *get in touch with the girl*, she's not fooling anyone.

Unless, of course, she's happy for us to split up, relieved at no longer having to feel guilt, and setting me up with someone else is all part of the process.

Overthinking, coach. Put your brain in neutral.

The apple juice arrives, I glance at the waitress's name badge, and say, 'Can I ask you a quick question, Julie?' and Julie takes a look around the café – there are only three other tables occupied – then says, 'Fire away!'

I place the pictures of Roxanne and Norah on the table.

'These women were in Salem together last Friday. So, eight days ago. I'm just going around, trying to find the various places they went. I wondered if they'd come here?'

She looks troubled, and then she indicates Roxanne.

'I saw her on the news. She's dead, right?'

'That's right.'

'You a cop?'

'P.I. The other girl's also missing, though she might just have taken herself off. Her mother's hired me to find her, and I was on that case before Roxanne was killed. I've no idea if there's a connection between the two events, but I do know they came to Salem together one day last week.'

'Hmm, last Friday? I wasn't on that day. You want me to ask the Jigsaw Man?'

As ever, I love that even the staff call the Jigsaw Man the Jigsaw Man, like that's what it says on his passport.

'If you don't mind.'

'No problem.'

She smiles, she lifts the photographs, she walks over to the Jigsaw Man's table, where he's sitting in his corner, doing a jigsaw of an image I can't see from over here. I watch them talking, Julie gesturing in my direction, then the Jigsaw Man breaks character by indicating for me to go over and speak to him.

I get up, I contemplate lifting my coffee and apple juice, then he makes another gesture that I should do exactly that, then I'm over beside him, sitting down opposite, and looking at the jigsaw he's about halfway through. A Bruegel winter scene. Nice picture. The box on the seat next to him states the title as *Winter Landscape With a Bird Trap*.

'Similar to the one you did before,' I say, and he smiles at the recognition.

'*Hunters In The Snow*,' he says. 'Same fella.'

He lifts his coffee and takes a drink. 'You don't mind joining me for breakfast, I'm just about to eat.'

'Are you sure, I don't want to trouble you.'

'No trouble.'

He taps the table. The pictures of the two women are still there together, side-by-side.

'They were here. The pair of them, with one other. Tall, dark, something of the Italian about him.'

'I've heard tell of him being six-six.'

'That would be about right. You don't have a photograph?'

'No. I didn't know of his existence until I came to Salem and started asking around to see if anyone had seen the women. Quite a few people had, and most of them mentioned the guy.'

'That makes sense.'

'Why?'

'This is who they are. Without the third party involved in their day in Salem, they would have been something else entirely. I don't think, for example, they'd have been able to find their way in here.'

'Why is that?'

'Some things just are, Mr Vikström.'

This is the kind of answer one expects from the Jigsaw Man.

'So, tell me about the guy,' I ask.

Food arrives, two plates of French toast and bacon and berries. She places them on the table – the Jigsaw Man first of all placing a mat on top of the jigsaw – then she says, 'Maple syrup coming right up.'

'Interesting man. Dark. And I don't mean his complexion, I don't mean his hair, his eyebrows. There was a shadow over him. He was haunted. You know, I had a thought…'

He lets the sentence trail off, thinks about it, and then decides to start eating. I watch him for a moment, then let him dictate the pace, and join him in food.

The waitress returns with the maple syrup, and the Jigsaw Man and I pause to pour the syrup across the French toast.

For a while we eat in silence. Not much conversation around the place. Behind me, the door opens and someone enters the café. I don't turn to look. There's a radio playing bluegrass. I don't recognise it, but it's a nice sound.

In the silence, the flavour of the food explodes in my mouth. Nothing else to think about. My eyes rest on the tangled branches of upside down snowy trees at the top of the jigsaw.

'I wondered if maybe he was a spirit,' says the Jigsaw Man out of nowhere. 'That the women didn't know he was there. That he was following one of them around.' He studies the two photographs, and then indicates the one of Norah Wolfe with his knife. 'This one. He was following her around. It wouldn't have been the first time we've had a spirit in here, though it's rare.'

'Yet, that wasn't it. He spoke to Kelly, he placed an order. At some point he became part of the conversation with the women. They reacted to him, not just the other way around.'

'It wasn't a *Sixth Sense* scenario.'

That seems flippant, and for a moment I regret opening my mouth, but the Jigsaw Man smiles.

'Yes,' he says. 'That was exactly what I'd been thinking to begin with, and then, it appeared it was not the case. At one point he even laughed. I didn't think he had laughter in him.'

He looks at me earnestly across the table, another moment, and then he resumes eating. I look up at the ceilings, turn, and look along to the door and above the coffee counter.

'No CCTV I'm afraid,' he says.

'Would you be able to draw him?'

The Jigsaw Man lifts his eyebrow, without looking at me. Back to concentrating on breakfast.

'What makes you think I can draw?'

'Maybe I don't think you can draw, I just asked if you could. But yes, now that you mention it, I do think you can draw.'

He smiles and then continues eating. Another two mouthfuls, his plate not quite finished, then he pushes it to the side, and I see him look over towards Julie.

'I'm sorry, but I'm sure you'd like me to press ahead. If you don't mind moving back to your original table to finish eating, I shall draw you a likeness of this third person.'

'Of course,' I say, finding myself relieved that I'm to be released from the Jigsaw Man's presence. There's a benevolence about him, and certainly no threat, and yet there's an intensity there that's quite intimidating.

Julie lifts my plate and coffee, and carries them back to my table by the window, and I take my old seat, glass of apple juice in hand. I glance back at the Jigsaw Man, who's in discussion with Julie, then turn away and determine not to look at him again.

*

Breakfast done, on my second cup of coffee, no more than

twenty minutes later, when the Jigsaw Man approaches my table, a couple of pieces of paper in hand.

He lays the first one down. A4, the bulk of it a head shot drawing of the man that's been described to me by three different people around the town. Dark hair, heavy-set eyebrows, black eyes. There's no malevolence there, but the Jigsaw Man has perfectly captured his haunted air.

To the side, in much smaller scale, a full-length drawing, side on, showing a slightly bent posture, a hangdog look about him, as though he carries the weight of the world.

'Thank you,' I say. I want to say that's spot-on, or you've really caught him, but since I don't actually know what he looks like, all I can say is that this is a bloody good drawing. I stay quiet.

He lays the second piece of paper on the table. On this, he's drawn a head shot of Natalie. He's caught her perfectly, her eyes smiling, her lips slightly parted, looking straight at the viewer.

'I…,' I begin, and then say the only thing that really comes into my head. 'What the fuck?'

He smiles at that, more broadly than he'd smiled before.

'You'll want to gauge how well I've caught the third man. The third person, sorry. Naturally, the phrase the third man rolls more easily off the tongue. I drew a picture of someone you already know, so that you'll be able to calibrate how well I might have represented this man.'

'This is like a photograph,' I say, indicating the drawing of Natalie. 'Except… I don't know, there's more than that. It's like, it's like you've drawn out her inner…' I let the sentence go for a moment, because I don't want to say beauty, and then I say, 'Beauty,' anyway, and then, 'But seriously, how d'you even know her?'

'Miss Slater comes in here when she's in Salem. She's a regular. I read her work. She writes well.'

'OK, well, OK, that make sense. But how did you know that I'd know her?'

The Jigsaw Man smiles. A moment, and I realise he's not going to answer, then he places his hand on my shoulder, squeezes gently, and turns away.

I watch him go, and then look back at the drawing of Natalie.

God, she's gorgeous.

Heavy sigh, and then I turn back to the drawing of the guy.

If he's caught this guy as well as he has Natalie, then holy shit, he's right.
Haunted.

*

A few minutes later I go to the counter to pay the bill.
'No check,' says Julie, and she nods towards the Jigsaw Man.
'Really?'
'You were his guest this morning.'
'Thank you.'
'You're welcome.'
I look over towards him, contemplate walking over there, then Julie says, 'It's OK,' and I look at her, and I understand, and turn away to the door.

22

Before leaving Salem, I stopped off at the other places where people had said they'd seen the two women, with the man. Out of three establishments, there were two of the people I'd spoken to yesterday, and both of them reacted like there'd been a minor explosion in their brain, 'Holy shit, that's your man right there,' said the guy at the Witch Museum. 'The hell drew that? That's some Da Vinci level shit.'

*

And now I'm stopping off to see Rebecca Karlsen before going to see Elise. I called Elise, made sure she'd be around. Tried to sound normal. Tried to sound like I hadn't slept with someone else last night. Of course, I'm known for my acting the way Gary in *Team America* was known for his acting, so the second I spoke she probably thought, *ah, crap, he didn't just talk to the girl...*

I find Karlsen at their unit base at the old Grissom place, a colonial-era property to the north of Glasgow. She's in an office in a large trailer, close to the security barrier they've set up around the pop-up facility.

A grey day again, wind beginning to pick up, though it's yet to disturb the still waters of the ocean.

The guy on the gate called her to make sure she was happy to see me, and I knock and enter, closing the door to the trailer behind me.

This is a nice trailer, by the way. Karlsen behind the desk at one end. Another, currently unoccupied desk by the door, sofas and a small kitchen area at the other end.

'Mr Vikström,' she says. 'Come in. Grab a coffee, take a seat.'

'Really, I won't be staying, I –'

'It's been a helluva couple of days, Mr Vikström. I've just cleared my schedule for twenty minutes. Get some coffee, sit down. I don't care what we talk about.'

I smile, nodding at the instruction.

'OK, but I'll skip the coffee. Think I've had four already this morning.'

'You're way behind some of us, but I won't force you.'

I sit down, the A4 of the haunted man loosely folded over in my hand.

'What can I do for you?' she says.

That's an interesting first question in itself. Not, is there any news of Norah?

I place the picture on her desk, and she leans forward to take a closer look. I watch her as she examines it, and see the slight shudder, which she shakes off, and then she looks up.

'And this is?'

'You don't know this man?'

'I don't.'

'He was in Salem on Friday with Norah and Roxanne.'

She looks back at him, then makes a small gesture to the drawing.

'Where'd you get this?'

'A guy in a café down there. Said they came in for lunch.'

'A guy in a café? He must've studied them pretty close. Unless this looks nothing like him, but this, whether it looks like the guy or not, is a beautiful piece of art. Who drew it? John Singer Sargent?'

'He has particular talents,' I say. 'You don't recognise this guy?'

She's shakes her head.

'Nope. Kind of glad I don't, to be honest. There's something…,' and she shudders again.

'The guy who did this, that's what he said. He had an aura about him, like he was haunted.'

'And he was hanging out with Norah and Roxanne?'

'Looks like he spent the day with them. Went to a couple of museums, had lunch, had hot chocolate somewhere else.'

'This guy doesn't drink hot chocolate. He drinks neat Scotch, with a vodka chaser.'

'Maybe it was just the women who had chocolate. I didn't get that level of detail.'

'The guy who drew this, I bet he had that level of detail. He tell you what this guy had for lunch?'

'I didn't ask, but he did at least have lunch.'

She studies it for a while longer, then shakes her head.

'Nope, I'd remember him. Can I keep this, ask around?'

'I need to keep it. About to take it to the sheriff. But you can copy it, or take a photo or whatever.'

'I'll just take a picture,' she says, and she lifts her phone and stands over the picture to get a good angle.

I leave her to it. She takes a few shots, then sits back down, quickly scrolling through the photos to make sure she caught it right, then she nods to herself and sets the phone back on the desk.

'So, this is where we are,' I say. 'I'm finding myself focussing on this day in Salem, because these two women are connected in some way, and this guy is inserted in the drama and it feels like it should be significant. But maybe it's a red herring, and it leads us down a dead end path.'

'That's your job, Mr Vikström. If that's how it's to turn out, let's hope you get there quickly. I'll pass it round, and let you know if anything shows up. The sheriff, I presume, will have access to a lot of national databases. You'll hopefully have some luck there. And what about the receptionist at the hotel who saw Norah return with a man on Sunday evening. Have you shown this to him?'

'I haven't, and I will, but this doesn't meet his description of the man Norah was with.'

'Damn. Well, OK, we are where we are.'

'You're not going out to the island today?'

She laughs ruefully, shaking her head.

'That's for stronger heads and hearts than mine. I got the boat after you yesterday, and that was utterly hellish. I think I threw up everything I've eaten since Thanksgiving. Good God. But Laurence loves it out there. Says he's getting terrific material, and the dailies look wonderful. There's a feeling... I don't know, I get a feeling like this shoot is haunted in some way, and Roxanne's death truly is the stuff of nightmares, but so far, the death aside, and I admit that's a damned big aside, it's going well, you know. On schedule, on budget, dailies looking terrific.'

She taps the desk three times.

'The town's hoping they can grab a bit of the business that usually goes the way of Rockport and Manchester,' I say.

'Hmm, not sure that's going to happen. Rockport's got its thing, and some of the streets in Manchester are so perfect it's like they were designed by Hollywood. But don't worry, I'll give Glasgow a good write-up on my Movie Producers WhatsApp group.'

'That's not a real WhatsApp group, is it?'

'No, it's not,' she says, smiling.

'Right, I should get on. You ask around, I'll go and speak to the deputy. The sheriff's department owes me nothing of course, so they could take this picture, run with it, identify the guy then not tell me. No reason they should.'

'Why don't you run with it for a while first then. Isn't that what Bogart would've done?'

'Maybe. But what needs to happen here is that we find your daughter, and catch whoever killed Roxanne. The quicker that happens the better. It's not about me getting the glory, and it's not like I'm trying to spin the work out as long as possible. If the sheriff finds your daughter, that's great.'

'Thank you,' she says. 'You're a good man.'

'Practical, at any rate,' I say, getting to my feet.

I make an *I'll call* gesture, then leave the trailer, hit by an unexpectedly cold wind as soon as I step outside.

23

Elise is on the phone when I walk into her office, and she indicates for me to take a seat, nods a few times to the person on the other end of the line, then wraps up the call, and stares at her computer screen, with the face of someone trying to process information, and being a little too stressed to think clearly.

'We all good?' she says, finally, looking round.

'I'm good. You look a little frazzled.'

'The mayor's losing her shit. Doesn't want the movie production to run into a brick wall.'

'Hasn't so far. They seem quite happy with how it's going. To be honest, seems like they're being very pragmatic. At least it was a junior member of staff who was murdered and not the star or the cinematographer, that kind of thing.'

'Maybe they could speak to the mayor,' she says caustically, and then, 'What can I do for you?'

We stare briefly across the desk – I had wondered if I'd come here, intent on not mentioning anything personal, and then just blurt out, 'I slept with Natalie last night!' – such is my level of guilt, but her stress precludes that. She's not here for that this morning.

'It's about Roxanne and Norah spending Friday in Salem.'

'We weren't really focussing on that. It's six days before Roxanne was murdered.'

'That's fair. I'm coming at it from that angle because of Norah, and that's my remit here.'

'Cut to it, Sam,' she says.

Damn, she really is brusque. Maybe she does know, have you thought about that, coach?

I place the Jigsaw Man's drawing on the desk, and she asks the question with a small movement of her chin.

'The two women weren't alone. They did a couple of tourist spots, ate lunch, went to another café, all with this guy. I don't know who he is. I got this from one of the café owners.'

'He drew this from memory?'

'Yes.'

She really studies it now, in the slight twitch in her eyes signs of her seeing how disturbed the guy looks. She reaches forward, pulls the drawing a little closer, and then runs her fingers over it.

'You think it's accurate?'

'Yes. I've seen other drawings he's done, and he can nail people.'

'Who are we talking about?'

'The Jigsaw Man at the Stand Alone.'

She sighs, nodding.

'Guess that makes sense,' she says. 'Is it OK if I keep this?'

'Wouldn't mind if you made a photocopy for me. Also wouldn't mind if you'd tell me if you find anything when you've run it through all your facial recognition apps.'

She stares across the desk, and nods.

'Sure, will do. Thanks for bringing it in.'

We stare at each other across the desk. This is the moment of weakness. This is the silence that creates a window for personal matters to be discussed.

I'm thinking stay strong, coach, knowing full well I'm as weak as a spoonful of coffee in a gallon of boiling water, when she once again inadvertently saves the day. Or quite possibly advertently saves the day, for all I know.

'Sorry, Sam, I've been really short. Head's spinning. Supposed to be away this weekend, Byron and I actually had plans for once, and then the mayor gets on the phone to the sheriff and the sheriff gets on the phone to Ed and me, and so here I am.'

'That's OK. I should leave you to it.'

She takes a deep breath, thinks about whether there's anything else to say, then gets to her feet, lifting the picture.

'I'll make some copies. You might as well keep the original, doesn't make any difference to me.'

'How's the investigation into Roxanne's murder coming along?' I ask, walking behind her, as she goes through to the admin room.

'Early days,' she says. 'The film crew packed up in a hurry on Thursday afternoon, scrabbling around, with the captain more or less standing there tapping his watch, threatening Clooney's fate in *Perfect Storm*. In a jumble of arms and legs and inexpertly packed equipment, they got off the island.'

She pauses to check the copies, compares the top one to the original, nods to herself, then offers me the original back.

'You want this?'

'I'll trade it for three copies.'

'Deal,' she says. 'No one on either sailing can recall Roxanne being on the boat, but then, she was a pretty low-key member of wardrobe, and not many of them can remember her actually being on the island in the first place. But we do at least have a visual on that from a couple of people who worked with her, so it looks like she got left behind.'

'Isn't it most likely she got tossed onto the rocks by the storm, banged her head?'

'That's certainly what we'd all like to have happened. Sadly, as well as the head knock which Troy had already picked up as being most likely delivered by human hand, she also has bruising on her arms, consistent with being manhandled. We're pretty certain she was murdered.'

She taps her fingers, I presume debating whether she's going to provide me with the rest of the information at her disposal.

'There's a little more, but this isn't just *you didn't hear it from me*. You didn't hear it, period.'

'Roger that.'

'Separate to her murder, she'd previously likely been raped. Anally and vaginally. The bruising on her arms that we already talked about, that was fresh. There was bruising and signs of her having been used for extremely rough sex. Impossible to say whether that would've been consensual, but usually... usually it's not consensual.'

'How many days previously?'

'Between two and seven.'

'Does that mean Troy couldn't tell, or it had happened several times over that period?'

'The latter.'

I nod, don't bother passing comment. Damn, why are there always assholes abusing women?

'You think someone stayed on the island with her?' I ask.

'Our working hypothesis is that she was murdered before the boat left. The island's big enough for that to have happened, away from the shoot and the houses. None of those who recall her being on the island in the first place, have any recollection of her being there in the hour or two before departure.'

'What about the houses? A couple of them are occupied, right?'

'No one saw anything, and those people are not currently under suspicion.'

'So, you think her killer is someone from the crew?'

'Or someone from the boat's crew. Or someone who snuck on the boat. That's the thing with two sets of people. Movie crew, boat crew. OK, one was much bigger in number than the other, but if there's someone there you don't recognise, you're likely just to assume they're part of the other crew.'

'Karlsen, the producer, she doesn't recognise this guy, but she said she'll show it around.'

'OK. Rather you'd left that to us, but I'll get down there and do that too.'

She gives me a look, then immediately retracts.

'Sorry, she's your client, and it's for you to answer to her, and you've brought me the thing. Could be that our guy here,' and she looks at the picture, 'he's got nothing to do with it.'

'As you pointed out, it was nearly a week before Roxanne's murder, so maybe you're right.'

She walks away, out of the door, across the corridor, back into her office.

'Sorry, Sam, I just need to get on with this,' she says, as I follow her back into her room.

'Of course, I'll leave you to it.'

We smile, a perfunctory look, I hesitate for a minute, but all I'm doing is lingering in the danger zone, and then I turn away.

I stop in the doorway, then turn back. Elise has already lifted the phone, now she places it back and asks the question with her eyebrows.

'The squid through the window at my place,' I say, and she looks a little more curious than before, and says, 'Yeah?'

'It happened, right?'

'It happened?'

'My dreams are so weird at the moment. Sometimes it feels like they're blending with reality. It's… it's a bit of a mind fuck, to be honest, and the squid thing seems so unreal.'

'I was there, helping you get the damned thing back into the ocean,' she says.

I nod, I stand for another moment, then finally say,

'Thanks,' and she smiles, a little more affection in it than she's shown since I got here, and says, 'Unless this is also a dream, in which case, maybe we're both being mind-fucked.'

We smile, she makes a gesture shooing me out of the room, she lifts the phone, and I turn away and walk back down the corridor.

24

Back to the Market Square hotel to speak to Malcolm Stewart on reception, hoping he's there, because if he's not, then I'm going to have to go back out to his strange house, with his strange wife, the strange chickens and the strange mill pond out back.

I'm probably being unfair on the chickens.

The place is quiet as I park outside, but then, presumably the vast majority of the guests are out on Rake's Island, or at the movie's unit base, doing whatever it is those people are doing.

Into reception, and Malcolm is there, sitting behind the counter, doing that thing where he looks like he's working studiously, when in fact, he may well just be playing Angry Birds, or some more modern game that I've never heard of because I don't follow the games that people play online.

He watches me approach, he glances back at his computer, he presses something – which I'm going to say is him exiting the game – and then I'm at the counter, and he's sitting innocently beside a wallpaper screen of a New England lighthouse in a storm, a great wave crashing upon it. Might even be the lighthouse out at Jacob's Point.

'Malcolm,' I say.

'You know, my family left Scotland in seventeen-forty-eight,' he says, by way of hello.

One is never sure what to say when presented with that kind of information.

'That explains the name,' I manage.

'I'm actually Malcolm Stewart the fourth, but that sounds a little… pompous, sometimes.'

Sometimes.

'What can I do for you?' he asks, mercifully. These conversations generally have no place to go other than me having to say that no, I don't know Allan Stewart who lives somewhere in Perth.

At least he seems a little more agreeable, now that he's at work. Perhaps he resented being interrupted on his mill pond.

I place the copy of the Jigsaw Man's drawing on the counter.

'Wonder if you've ever seen this man,' I say. 'And I know he doesn't meet the description of the man who entered the hotel with Norah Wolfe on Sunday evening, but is there any possibility it could be the same man, and he disguised himself in some way?'

He studies the drawing, an eyebrow raised sceptically as he does so.

'This is…,' then his words dry up for a moment, and he shivers. 'This is interesting. Did you draw this?'

'It doesn't have a peg nose, so no,' I say.

'No, I can see that. I don't mean to be rude, but there's a depth here that I don't think you'd be capable of, even if you could draw.'

I almost laugh. He might not have meant it, but that was pretty fucking rude, by the way. Manage to keep it to myself, stop the smile coming to my lips, and wait for him to pronounce. What I was hoping for, the immediate reaction of, 'Oh that's Mad Eric, here's his phone number,' obviously isn't happening.

'No, I don't know him. I don't think I want to, either. If this is a good likeness, then he's haunted. And this, this body in profile, it implies height.'

'Somewhere in the region of six-six.'

'Then definitely not the man who came here with Ms Wolfe on Sunday evening. He was not much taller than her. A wig, perhaps, to aid in his disguise, but he wasn't losing nearly a foot in height.'

'OK, thanks. Is there anyone else on duty at the moment?'

I get another eyebrow. He pushes the picture a little closer to me on the countertop, then leans further into the discussion.

'There are others here. Is this man known to have been at the hotel?'

'No, but that doesn't mean he wasn't.'

'Is he a person of interest?'

'Officially, in the investigation into Thursday's murder, not yet. Not as far as I'm aware. However, he's of interest to me, and I'd just like to ask. No harm in it.'

Another dismissive look, then he lifts the phone, presses a single button, waits, and then says, 'The private detective would like to speak with you, Mrs McDaniel. Just a quick question.' A nod, an affirmative, then he hangs up. 'Mrs McDaniel is coming.'

'Thanks.'

And almost instantly, there's the sound of a door opening, and then footfall in the corridor, and then McDaniel the manager walks into reception.

'Mr Vikström,' she says, a lot more brightly than Malcolm the receptionist, 'how can we be of help?'

*

I'm taking the two-minute drive through town to the St James hotel, the other establishment the film crew have booked out for the duration.

Feel, out of nowhere, like we're in the dog days of the investigation. No car chases, no explosions, no shoot-outs. Nothing dramatic. Pillar to post, asking everyone the same question.

Have you seen this man?

None of the staff currently working at the Market Square had done. Of note, however, was that Roxanne Baudot had been staying at the St James, rather than the Market Square.

The phone rings as I'm getting out of the car. Elise. And I know it doesn't make any sense, but I feel an urgency in the ring.

'Hey,' I say.

'Bingo. Got a hit on your guy straight off the bat.'

'Really?'

'Yep. Person of interest in Washington state, in connection with a triple murder. Three girls, young women anyway, found dead in a cabin in the woods.'

'When was this?'

'About a year and a half ago. The girls had just set off on a hiking expedition.'

'What age are we talking?'

'Two of them had just finished college, they had the summer to go and do whatever. The third was a high school friend of theirs, who was trying to make it in the movies. They went hiking in the north-west. They were last seen with Thomas Riddick at a roadhouse diner on a Thursday evening in July. They went off into the woods, told people they were camping there. Never heard from again. You know, phone reception is what it is around there, and it took a while for folks to realise they were missing.

'They were found, ritualistically murdered, in a cabin 'bout three miles from where they'd eaten their last meal. And it had been their last meal. Remnants of the burgers they ate were still in their stomachs.'

'The one trying to make it in the movies? Any chance there's a connection there?'

'The last thing she worked on was a schlock horror called *Midnight Princess*. Seems she was pretty low down the cast list.'

My turn to say, 'Bingo.'

'Bingo?'

'That was made by the same company, the same producers, same director, as *Leviathan*. Not sure how much of a crossover there'll be in terms of the crew, but there's potential to be a lot. But, significantly, Norah Wolfe worked on that, though not Roxanne.'

'You know that off the top of your head?'

'I've already cross-checked the movies they worked on. This crew, this production team, they're obviously keeping as many of the same people together as possible. There's some coming and going, but there's a core unit of talent.'

'Damn. OK, I'll get looking.'

'And this guy Riddick? We know what happened to him?'

'Vanished. He was seen to leave the diner at the same time as the girls, and for all anyone knows, he could've turned on his heels and gone in the other direction.'

'They didn't get any DNA from the cabin?'

'They got nothing from the cabin.'

'How did they know his name was Thomas Riddick?'

'He was staying at a motel next to the diner. He'd already checked out. Told the guy on reception he had a cabin in the woods.'

'If the cabin was only three miles away, why did he stay at the motel in the first place?'

'He'd arrived by bus late the previous night. Guess he didn't want to walk off into the woods that late.'

'And we know his name's really Thomas Riddick?'

'Nope, but that's who he is on the wanted list.'

'Crap,' I say, another obvious thought finally coming to me. 'The feds.'

'Oh, yes, the feds.'

'You've notified them?'

'I've notified the sheriff. I expect we'll hear soon enough. And, I'm afraid I'm going to need everything you've got on this. Doesn't mean you won't have the FBI at your door anyway, but if you could give me details of the places where the three of them were seen.'

'Yep, I'll write it up.'

'And I'm going to need the name of the guy who made the drawing.' A hesitation, then, 'Don't think the Jigsaw Man's going to really cut it with the feds.'

Damn. It was him who offered to do the drawing for me, but suddenly it feels like I might have landed him in it. The Jigsaw Man does not seem like the kind of guy who wants to have to deal with the FBI.

'I'll see what I can do,' I say, and Elise laughs.

'Good luck with that approach,' she says. 'Look, I'd better go. Just be careful out there, now we know there's a triple murderer in the game.'

'Hey, you too.'

'Will do.'

We hang up. I take a moment, staring straight ahead at a near-deserted car park, the bare branches of birch behind, the hotel to my left.

'Come on,' I mutter, then I'm walking towards the hotel onto the next stage of the dog day afternoon.

25

A more modern affair, the St James, with none of the Market Square's kitsch. I've been in here a few times, as it's the kind of place people are more likely to come when just passing through, or when meeting illicitly or stopping off in town for some nefarious purpose.

Natalie is sitting in the waiting area of reception, laptop on her knees, typing, her fingers a blur, beneath a long, narrow painting of the coast just south of here. In fact, that includes the bit of coast where I live, but the painting either dates from before the houses being built, or the artist decided to exclude them for artistic purposes.

I don't remember seeing that when I came here before.

'Oh, hey, how long have you been standing there?'

I look down at Natalie, looking at me with a curious smile.

'Just got here.'

I glance around the place, which feels even more deserted than the Market Square.

'No one on reception?'

'He's just taking ten minutes. I'm waiting for the manager. You've got an arrangement?'

'Nope, just doorstepping on the off-chance. Looking for someone.'

'You got a lead?'

I stare at her. Damn. This is the issue with having a thing with the deputy sheriff and having a thing with a journalist. There's no way Elise told me about Thomas Riddick so that I could pass on the information to Natalie.

'You do have a lead,' she says. 'I can see it on your face. But you don't want to tell me. Which means you possibly got the lead from Deputy Miller. Hmm.' She looks away, she runs this scenario through the matrix.

'Nope, that's fair,' she says. 'You don't want to get on the wrong side of the deputy sheriff. Assuming you haven't told her anything about last night, and you're already on the wrong side of the deputy sheriff.'

'I didn't tell her about last night.'

'OK. That's good. I mean, that's for you, your business. Anyway, I really need to get this written.'

'You unearthed anything new?' I ask, and without stopping typing, she says, 'Oh, we're sharing, are we?' and I say, 'Touché,' and then there's movement behind reception, and a man who looks not dissimilar to Malcolm Stewart IV at the Market Square emerges from a door behind, and even from here I can smell that he's been smoking, and he looks at me, chin lifted, asking the question.

I glance at Natalie, who looks innocently at me, and says, 'You have someone to talk to. Fill your boots, detective, I promise not to listen,' then returns to her keyboard.

I look at her for a moment or two, but she's playing her part, then I walk over to the reception desk, ID out of my pocket, and place it on the countertop. He looks it over, then lifts his head.

'How can we help?'

'I'm working for the crew of *Leviathan*, and –'

'Mrs Karlsen mentioned you. She asked that we be accommodating. I thought you might be here sooner, if I'm honest.'

'Roxanne Baudot was staying here?' I ask.

'Yes, she was. I cannot let you see her room, however. The sheriff's department has locked it down.'

'That's OK. Was there anything remarkable about Ms Baudot while she was here? Did she stand out in any way from the rest of the crew?'

He seems to accept that that's a reasonable question, looking across the reception area into nothingness while he considers it.

'I don't believe so. To be frank, none of them are standing out. There's Mr Faraday, the producer. He's in charge, and he likes people to know it. That's why all the big shots, the stars and the important crew, that's why they're all here. We don't mind our position in town as the lesser of the two hotels, the cheaper end of the market. Usually the people at the top of an organisation would stop over at the Market Square, and we'd get the junior staff. But Mr Faraday preferred us, and therefore all the senior creatives had to stay here, while the junior staff stayed at the Market, or in their other accommodation at the old

Grissom place. I believe Mr Curtain, the director, was not too happy, but he lost that battle.'

'So, how come Roxanne Baudot was staying here? She was junior staff in wardrobe.'

He leans a little into the counter, a knowing smile slowly coming to his face.

'Good question, Mr Vikström.'

'That's why I asked.'

'I think you can use your imagination.'

I hate it when people speak on the edge of understanding. Because you probably know what they're getting at, but then, he's American and I'm from Cambuslang, and there's always the chance something gets lost in translation.

'She was sleeping with one of the more important crew or cast,' I say.

'You didn't hear it from me.'

'D'you know for a fact that was happening, or is that supposition?' I ask, ignoring the bullshit *you didn't hear it from me* line.

A moment, then he repeats, 'You didn't hear it from me.'

God, I hate people.

I have a folded-up copy of the drawing of Thomas Riddick in my pocket, and I take it out, and lay it out in front of him.

'You recognise this guy?' I ask.

He looks at the drawing, his eyes narrowing, he starts to shake his head, then a shudder runs through him. He shakes it off, then says, 'No, no I don't. Who is that anyway? Is this who murdered that girl?'

'A person of interest,' I say.

'To the police, or you?'

I turn. Natalie's standing beside me, a step or two back, looking at the drawing of Riddick.

'To me. He's the one seen with Wolfe and Baudot in Salem last Friday.'

'Your tall Italian looking guy,' says Natalie, nodding. 'Don't suppose you could give me a copy of that?'

'I think it'll be public pretty soon. Like, this afternoon levels of soon. How about, if that hasn't happened by the end of the day, I'll give it to you. But it can't go in a story, if you've just got it from me.'

'OK,' she says. 'Not sure you're throwing me much of a bone there, but then I don't suppose you need to throw me anything at all,' and we kind of smile knowingly at each other.

'Are you two a team?' asks the guy. 'Like some sort of TV crime-fighting duo? The gumshoe and the gonzo hack.'

'Gonzo hack?' says Natalie, laughing. 'I'll take it.'

'And no, we're not,' I say. 'So, you don't know this guy?'

'Never seen him.'

'Tell me who you think Roxanne Baudot was sleeping with on the crew.'

He looks at me a little curiously, and then laughs.

'You've got a nerve.'

'Yeah, I know. Look chum, we're none of us idiots here. Receptionists know things. And guys like you on reception,' and I tap the side of my head. 'Some receptionists can see and not understand, and some will see nothing, even when they're looking straight at it. But you? You see all human life pass through here, and you know what's happening. You understand what's going on. You're smart.' I tap the side of my head again. 'I think you know exactly why Roxanne Baudot was staying at the St James.'

He smiles ruefully, shaking his head, then he looks at Natalie.

'Does he talk like that to everyone he wants to get an answer out of?'

'Only the really smart ones,' she says, and he laughs.

'I said you were a team.'

'Give me a name, and I'm out the door,' I say.

He's thinking about it, but I'm not sure he's going to crack.

'There's something about Roxanne,' says Natalie, her tone suddenly a little more introspective. 'You can tell from the photographs. There was an energy, a freedom. You know, I don't know how certain they are that she was murdered. The way they're talking, they sound pretty sure. But I can see her deciding she was going to spend the night alone on that island. Right?' she adds, looking at me, but fortunately she's not looking for me to act in response. 'She would just have been like, this is *dangerous*. She was like totally the kind of person who would arrive fresh and new on a film set, and think, God, I am going to embrace this. I'm going to enjoy every damn minute, and if I can have any of these people on this crew, I'm going for it.'

She looks at the guy, she looks at me, she looks back at the guy.

'Right?'

She's got me convinced about Roxanne, and I know she's making it up.

'Maybe you're the one with the smarts,' he says. 'That's exactly who she was. Could tell the second she came through.'

He looks at us both, casts his glance around the reception area, and waves a bohemian hand.

'I know you were buttering me up, but you nailed it. You see everything. All human life. Ha. I like that. All human life. You certainly do. And she was out for whoever she could get, and the higher up the food chain, the better.'

'Brian Faraday?'

'Why not?'

'Laurence Curtain?'

'Girls like that, they start at the top and only work their way down if they're not getting anywhere. We've all seen the shows, right? You watch shows?'

'Do I watch shows?' I ask.

'Sure. D'you watch shows? P.I. shows, detective shows?'

'Never. I watch the Pats and the Red Sox.'

'You should watch the shows, might help you understand people. Might help you understand crime. A young woman gets murdered? There's sex involved. There is *always* sex involved.' You don't need to watch shows to know that, big guy. 'Now sometimes, the young woman might not be interested in the sex, and that gets ugly. And sometimes she's all about the sex, and that's ugly in a whole other way.' He pauses, he looks between the two of us, he says, 'You should watch shows.'

'You care to be specific with names?' asks Natalie.

'I don't think I'm going to go there, honey.'

'OK, that's fair,' I say, 'but Roxanne is dead. Roxanne has likely been murdered. You can keep your counsel as much as you like, but there's a possibility that one of those people she was sleeping with didn't like her sleeping with everyone else. Or didn't like *something* about her.'

'Listen,' he says, straightening up. He's gone. Snap of the fingers, and he's decided he's said enough. 'You can make all the arguments you like, but I'm not going to be the one who points the finger at some guy who's just been having a bit of fun, and then the sheriff or the feds or the C-I-of-A runs a check on the fellow and finds out he's got a drugs conviction from five years ago in California, and suddenly they're treating him like he's Ted Bundy, or that Zodiac Killer. You want to pin something on some poor schmuck, you go right ahead, but you ain't getting it from me.'

We stare at him, he stares at us. I try to think of a way to retrieve the situation, but to be honest, if Natalie wasn't here, I would've given up already. I've got nothing, and I'm just standing here to give her the chance to recover.

'We done?' says the guy eventually.

'I can still talk to the manager?' asks Natalie. 'You're not actually kicking me out?'

He laughs again.

'If Mr Wallis says he'll talk to you, then he'll talk to you. You take your seat, and I'm sure he'll be right out.'

'Thanks for your help,' I say, smiling, and he gives me a wry smile in return, then Natalie and I retreat to the comfy seats, where I first found her, beneath the painting of the Cape Ann coast.

We sit down, a low coffee table between us. She glances in the receptionist's direction, to find that he's no longer there, and then says, 'He's not wrong. Sex. It's a killer.'

'Yeah,' I say. 'Sex or money, that's what it always comes down to.'

Damn, I can't be sitting here staring at her all afternoon, however much I might want to. Things to do, a case to solve. I get to my feet, nodding as I go.

'I'll leave you to it,' I say.

'Sure you can't leave me that portrait you've got there?' she asks, eyebrows lifted.

'You have a contact at the FBI?'

Her shoulders straighten a little.

'Why'd you ask that?'

'You're a journalist, you write crime stories. I presume you have contacts. You have one at the FBI?'

'I might have.'

'You don't have to be so vague, I'm not going to ask for her name.'

'What are you going to ask? And nice, you're right, it's a woman. Look at you.'

I take a breath, let it out long and slow, look around the reception area, just as the receptionist fellow looked around the room, then say, 'You might want to say you've heard they've got something going on in Glasgow, Mass. That's all.'

'And do they have something going on in Glasgow? This is a federal investigation?'

I answer with raised shoulders.

'Which means your guy there…,' she says, indicating the pocket into which I placed the picture, 'that means you know who this is. That means you've shown it to the deputy, and if the feds are involved, it means your man there is wanted for a crime out of state.'

I give her an open-handed gesture in response.

'I need to go. Good luck talking to the manager. Let me know if you get anything interesting out of him.'

'Might,' she says with a smile.

'Give your FBI contact a call, see what she has to say,' I say, and with that I hold up my hand, smile, and turn away.

'See you, gumshoe,' she says to my back.

26

Back home, at the kitchen table. Toast, a bit of cheese, some salad. Also drinking kombucha, like some sort of millennial psychopath.

I'm going to look up the story of the Washington state, cabin in the woods murder. See what beans the Internet has to spill. See if the locals had anything to say about it. People usually have something to say on the Internet.

Then there's looking for connections between *Leviathan* and *Midnight Princess*. Exactly how many of the crew worked on both, and who were they? That, unfortunately, is going to add a tonne of names to the suspect list.

First though, I'm going to take a breath. And sure, this hasn't been a hundred miles an hour, fist fights and car chases, gun battles and climbing El Capitan while fighting a gorilla. Nevertheless, I've been focussed on this damn thing since I got up this morning, and I'm just going to take fifteen minutes.

Lunch, and the view from my kitchen window, out over the cold ocean, the gunmetal grey beginning to be peppered with silent, staccato white, as the wind finally translates into waves, and the next storm builds.

Hightower appeared as soon as I returned, and has positioned himself in the seat opposite. Sitting upright, watching me eat, like he's expecting me to say something. So far I'm enjoying the silence, the magnificence of the endless sea, and the slow passage of a commercial tanker across the hazy, distant horizon.

Trying not to think about Natalie. My relationship life has been so safe the last few years. Sex without attachment, a girlfriend without commitment. More than just a little bit melancholy at times, but ultimately nothing to interrupt the smooth passage of my life here on the coast.

And now I've completely messed up and fallen for someone without a husband, while still, of course, being in love with Elise.

'Don't look at me like that,' I say to Hightower.

'You're taking fifteen minutes,' says the cat. 'Don't ruin it by focussing on your love angst.'

'Good point.'

Finish off the toast, sit back, look out over the ocean again. Glance at my watch, look over my shoulder at the time on the cooker, and then turn back to Hightower with a shake of the head.

'Dammit, I can't even concentrate on not concentrating. We need to talk about the case.'

'At last,' says High. 'I've been sitting here like a moron.'

'So, let's just break down what we have, because things usually end up a lot simpler than you think they're going to be, right?'

'Yep,' says High. 'Complex plotting is invariably a thing of fiction.'

'So, we focus on what we've got in front of us. Two young women meet on a film set. They don't appear to have worked on anything together before, so this was them meeting for the first time. Storyboarder and wardrobe. They don't work together at any point in the last few weeks, but that doesn't matter. Drinks in the bar, sandwich during lunch break, whatever. They meet, they hit it off.'

'Maybe they shared a man. Or men,' suggests High.

'Maybe they did. Or at least, bonded over the one guy who messed them about. It's only been three weeks, so let's not go thinking there's been *that* much sex happening. The sex might be important, but let's try not to focus on it.'

'Roger that.'

'The first day off from filming, they decide to go to Salem. Well known tourist spot around here, nothing unusual in it. While there, they don't seem to have strayed from the norm. They went to the usual kind of places. Witches, maritime folklore, cafés. A grand day out. The only odd thing was that they weren't alone. They were joined for the day by Thomas Riddick. But not everyone who remembers them, also remembers the guy, which makes it sound like they maybe came across him at some point early on.'

'So he picked them up.'

'Or they picked him up. Maybe, just to make it about sex again even though I said we shouldn't, maybe they'd had everyone on the crew they were interested in, or who was available. Here was fresh meat.'

'Except we know the guy's a suspected triple murderer,' says High. 'And he's suspected of killing someone who worked previously on a Brian Faraday film.'

I finish off the kombucha, then lean on the table, looking out over the sea.

'So, two days later, Norah has a guy back at her room – first time that's happened, by some accounts, though she could have gone elsewhere, of course. Then she leaves the set of the movie the following morning. And three days after that, Roxanne is murdered.'

'I know there's a lot of murder in this dumb country,' says High, 'but look, we have a presumed murderer in the cast of characters, and then someone gets murdered.'

'Pretty big coincidence,' I say, and High nods with his chin. 'Perhaps Norah going off is nothing to do with Roxanne. Other than their day in Salem, there's little to connect them. This might just be me getting hung up on that. Maybe Norah's just done what we thought she might have, and left for love.'

Hightower does not look impressed.

'You might not like the idea, furball,' I say, 'but it's the kind of dumb thing young people'll do. And, to be honest, not so young. We're all forever dumb when it comes to relationships.'

'Ain't that the truth.'

'The real connection we might need to establish here is between Roxanne, and Nella Lombardi, the victim in the cabin in the woods who'd been working on the Brian Faraday movie.'

'Ultimately for you, though,' says High, 'this is of no significance. As soon as you reasonably separate the murder from the disappearance, the murder becomes of no concern. Your remit is to find out what happened to Norah Wolfe. And fact is, Norah Wolfe could be in Florida, she could be north of the border, she could be having tea with the king of England for all you know.'

'Listen, furball, he's the king of the United Kingdom, don't be conflating –'

'Whatever. Look, pal, it's time you got down to work.'

'What does that mean? I've been working.'

'You've been getting out and about, because that's what you like doing. It makes you feel like you're doing something, whether you achieve anything or not. But what you need to be doing is working the phones. You've got contacts. The agency has contacts. Ports, airports, train stations, bus stations, car rental companies. Come on, man, you know this stuff. If Norah Wolfe is currently having tea with the king of England, then she'll likely have passed through Logan, and you're going to be able to find that out. So, sure, if you want to do the cool stuff, trying to solve the murder, and trying to find the haunted shadow of a creepy killer, on you go, but you have no idea if it's relevant. So why don't you do what you know is relevant?'

Hightower stretches his neck, looks out of the window for a moment, and then gets down from the seat and walks languidly through to the sitting room.

He has a point.

I also need to stop talking to myself.

Maybe my non-existent therapist also has a point.

*

I multi-task. Or, in fact, dual task.

Make a lists of all the numbers I need to call, all the contacts I have, all the people that will either be able to check travel hubs, or will know someone who can do it on my behalf, including Sal at Radstone-Kirk.

At the same time, I've got the story of the Washington state, cabin in the woods triple murder on my laptop, and I read everything I can find about it, including all the crackpot theories on Reddit and Facebook. And, it turns out, there are a lot of crackpot theories.

Nevertheless, a couple of hours in, the phone calls don't seem to be getting anywhere. And as for the crazy Internet theories, there's one I actually quite like the sound of. Yet it is what it is. A crazy Internet theory. And right in the middle of trying to dig deeper, there comes a knock at the door.

I'm into the hallway, assuming this will either be Elise or Natalie, and not taking the time to think about the complications of either, and then I see the dark suit through the frosted glass, and I pause, and then I think, shit, FBI, and I think of the Jigsaw Man and how I meant to tell him they might be coming, and it'll have been me who sent them his way, and I open the door, and there's a man in black, straight out of a movie – although at least he's not wearing sunglasses on this grey day in February – and he holds forward his ID and says, 'Agent Barnes, Federal Bureau of Investigation. I hear you've been interfering in a federal homicide case. I'm going to need everything you've got so far.'

I stand in silence for a moment, heart sinking, then say, 'I suppose you're going to want a cup of black coffee,' and Agent Barnes says, 'I don't drink coffee after six a.m. You going to let me in, or do things have to get nasty?'

27

We're at the kitchen table, where the vast majority of my life is conducted. I've made myself a cup of tea. Agent Barnes did not want tea.

Agent Barnes is either permanently ill-humoured, or he's perfected his interviewing style over the years. This is who he is. A guy in a bad mood. Impatient, in command, and needing other people to get on his level.

He's studying the Jigsaw Man's drawing of Thomas Riddick, checking it against images on his phone. At least, I assume that's what he's doing, as he's holding his phone at an angle that prevents me seeing it, and I'm making no effort to look.

Sure, there's a certain comedy to a permanently angry authority figure, but in real life, he might well just be the guy who arrests you out of badness, or puts his fist through your face with the impunity of federal law.

He lays down his phone, and takes a ballpoint pen from the inside pocket of his jacket. He then does not also produce a corresponding notebook in which to write, but he does hold the pen, intermittently clicking the end.

'This is not my investigation,' he says bluntly.

'OK...'

'You're going to ask me why I'm here.'

'I'm going to ask if you're really with the FBI.'

'I showed you my ID, of course I'm with the FBI. You can call the Boston office if you like. I won't give you the number in case you think I'm setting you up. We're in the phone book.'

'So, why isn't it your case?'

'There's an agent coming in. She's been hunting this guy for eighteen months. It's her case. I'm just gathering the basic intel, then sending her everything we have, then I stand down.'

'When's she due to arrive?'

'I can't tell you that.'

'Because you don't know, or is it a secret?'

I can't help smiling at the question, which gives him the excuse to ignore it.

'You'd better hope this guy gets found before she arrives. Agent Cameron doesn't like private dicks sticking their nose into Bureau affairs.'

'Thanks for the heads up.'

'It wasn't a heads up. You're going to have to tell me where you got this image.'

Nice interviewing technique. Warm.

'I went round museums and stores and cafés in Salem, most people who'd seen Roxanne and Norah had also seen this guy. One of them drew that for me. I returned to the other places, and they all said, yep, that's the guy. Like, bang on, that's the guy.'

'You said that to me already.'

'Yeah, but in different words.'

Nope, nothing. Not a flicker.

'Who did the drawing?'

'A guy in the café where they had lunch.'

'There's a reason you don't want to tell me his name?'

There are two reasons I don't want to tell this guy his name. The first is that I wanted to warn the Jigsaw Man in advance. And while you might think I could lift the phone and call the café the minute Agent Barnes leaves, I don't have the number. I checked, and the Stand Alone is not listed anywhere. Not in the phone book, not on the Internet.

I don't think the Jigsaw Man will actually mind. I mean he's smart, he must have known there was a possibility law enforcement might turn up at his door if his artwork played a part in the case. A heads up would be polite, that's all.

And then there's the possibility of Agent Barnes going to Salem and not finding the Stand Alone café, even when I tell him exactly where it is. That doesn't make sense, but I get the feeling some people can't see it's there. That's certainly what the Jigsaw Man said, and there's just something about the place when you're there. A feeling like you've stepped through the wardrobe into Narnia.

But then, there was the time I had lunch with the Canadian scientific vessel crew member in there. He was just a guy. If he could see it, why wouldn't anyone else? For that matter, I too, am just a guy. Nothing special about me, sports fans.

'You look like you're talking to yourself,' he says. 'In your head.'

I stare blankly across the table, then lift my tea. Didn't feel I could eat anything while he was there, but a cup of tea without either cake, a biscuit or a piece of toast is incomplete.

From nowhere I think of Bruce Forsyth.

'You're still talking to yourself. Tell me the guy's name.'

'I don't know his name.'

'Tell me the name of the café.'

I take another drink of tea.

If I tell him the name of the café, and he goes there, and can't find it, then he's back here, thinking I've lied. Wondering how it was I came by the picture of Riddick. Then I face the option of either coming under suspicion, and having to answer all sorts of questions, or taking him to the Stand Alone, and walking in, leading the feds straight to the Jigsaw Man.

Bad optics. I really don't want to be that guy.

'You know at the Bureau we have people working on brain implants, that'll be able to record thought. Think about that. A year from now, maybe two, we'll be sitting here, and I will be able to literally read your mind.' He stares harshly across the table. That's got to be bullshit. 'Sadly, for now, all that chatter that's going on in there,' and he leans across the table and jabs me in the forehead, 'is lost on me. So will you pretty please with all the bells of Switzerland on it, tell me where you got the drawing of Thomas Riddick?'

All the bells of Switzerland? Man, that's a lot of bells.

'The Stand Alone. It's called the Stand Alone café. The owner did this. I don't know his name.'

Agent Barnes rubs his chin, leaning on his elbow, looking down at the drawing.

'That's the first thing to make sense since I got here,' he says.

'Is it?'

'The Jigsaw Man, of course. Helluvan artist.'

'You know the Jigsaw Man?' I ask, unable to keep the surprise from my voice.

'Everyone at the Bureau knows the Jigsaw Man. I'm going to keep this,' he says, tapping the picture. 'What else have you got?'

'I don't think I've got anything else.'

'Really? How long have you been on this case?'

I don't answer. No one's saying I'm a *good* private

detective.

'You've been on this case since Thursday morning,' says Barnes. 'And your work is known at the Bureau. You have good results. You know how many P.I.'s there are in America?'

'About ninety thousand?'

'Including those operating in an unlicensed, unauthorised capacity, there are one hundred, twenty-three thousand, two hundred, seventeen. That was as of last Monday, the last time the figure was updated. Our records show that you're in the top five percent in terms of positive results.'

'You literally just made that up.'

'Don't get too excited, most of those hundred, twenty-three thousand are morons who conduct their business sitting on their ass in their mother's basement. Tell me what else you've got, I don't believe this is it.'

I take a drink of tea. I take a glance out to sea. Evening beginning to encroach from the east, the horizon slightly clearer, though now empty of traffic. Everything about the view a shade of grey.

I turn back to Agent Barnes, take another drink, and then tell him everything that's happened so far, right down to the squid flying through the window.

*

'I made a mistake there, didn't I?' I say, when I've wrapped it up, and he's stopped asking me questions.

It didn't take so long to relate the events of the last two days. Despite him blowing sunshine up my arse about my detective abilities, I really haven't got very far. And you may wonder why I'm talking to the feds in any case, but the same applies here as it does to talking to Elise. I don't care who finds Norah Wolfe, and the feds are far more likely to be able to do it than I am.

I neglected to mention the thing I just found on the Internet before he arrived, but then, that's just a thing I found on the Internet, not an actual clue.

'Go on,' he says, his tone suggesting he's heard everything he wants to hear, and he's going to be bored from now on.

'We didn't talk about a quid pro quo.'

He gives me a grim look, he clicks the pen one last time, then he slips it into his pocket. Takes a last look at the drawing, which has stayed on the table in between us the entire time, and then lifts it as he gets to his feet.

'Interesting,' he says.

'You've got nothing you can share?' I ask.

'Why would I do that?'

'So I don't get in your way. Agent Cameron's way, sorry.'

'You're not going to get in Agent Cameron's way,' he says. 'In fact, you are going to stay so far out of Agent Cameron's way, you're going to be on a different planet.'

'As we've discussed, I'm not investigating the murder. I'm not interested in Thomas Riddick. All I want to do is find Norah Wolfe. I find her, and I'm done.'

'That doesn't interest me.'

'I know. But here's what I think...'

'I don't care *what you think*.'

'I think the Bureau could find out where she is, like just in passing, and you wouldn't tell anyone, because there's been no crime committed. You wouldn't care.'

'That's a very good point.'

'So if, by chance, the Bureau already knows where she is, or finds out where she is, I'd be grateful if you could tell me.'

'You want us to do your job for you?'

'Like I said, it's something you might find in passing. I just happened to find this guy for you. If you happened to find Norah, you could let me know. That's all.'

He stares grimly across the table.

'You think finding out where Thomas Riddick was eight days ago is really of much use to the Bureau?'

'At least you know roughly where he is.'

'Sure, because you can't get far in eight days.'

He turns, a few quick strides along the hallway, and he's gone.

*

I send a text to Natalie.

Sorry, the FBI lead might not come to much.

She replies straight away.

Already discovered. You owe me. x

I type **Let's talk about that** in reply, then delete it and don't send. Instead I reply with the laughter emoji, and try to put her out of my mind.

28

A man and three women walk into the woods, and are not heard from again. Several days later the bodies of the women are discovered, brutally murdered. The man vanishes.

There are inherently a lot of unanswered question in that simple outline of known facts, but the question at the heart of it – why he would kill the women – barely needs an answer. Men don't need a reason. Every day, around this dying earth, lots of men will be killing lots of women just because they can. The number one reason for murder on the planet? Men are assholes towards women.

Riddick's disappearance and the non-solving of the crime, however, leaves a vacuum, and there's nothing the Internet likes more than a vacuum. Known facts will not prevent the kooks and lunatics of the world postulating absurdly on literally any given story, so they're certainly not going to be put off by a blank canvas. And each theory is, of course, spoken of with such certainty that any reader would be a fool to disregard it.

So we have such great theories as:

Thomas Riddick was the ex-husband of one of the women, or, at least, the ex-partner. He suspected his ex was now a lesbian. He pretended to bump into them by chance, played the part of being delighted for his ex, then followed them, and killed them. No proof is given of why anyone should believe Riddick and one of the women might have been together, or had even known each other previously.

The women were killed by feral woods people, who likely also killed the man, removing his body for harvesting purposes. This is a very popular theory, the ritualistic nature of the murders adding credence to the idea that backwoods pagans might be behind the killing.

Aliens, of course. Killed the unneeded women, then took the guy so they can keep him alive on board their star cruiser, where they'll harvest his semen to use to impregnant the alien species, creating a new hybrid warrior breed. Like the Uruk-hai, but, you know, space! I think this one falls apart with motive. If there are a bunch of alien women looking to get pregnant, just come to earth. There will be scores of men who'll have sex with you, doesn't matter what you look like, or what form of life you are.

As sure as eggs is eggs, when you have an alien conspiracy, you also have a government conspiracy. It's practically science. A couple of people assume it was the FBI, of course, the bogeymen of over seventy percent of American conspiracy theories. But there was also a solid one, which blames the National Ranger Service. This has the four walkers uncovering some wrongdoing by park rangers, and the rangers taking care of business to make sure their secret didn't get out. Obviously, in this theory, Thomas Riddick was also murdered, his body buried deep in the woods, thereby allowing the blame to fall seamlessly at his door.

Boy, isn't the guy who wrote that theory going to be embarrassed when he finds out Riddick's still alive?

No, of course he's not. He's barely going to look up from whatever piece of conspiracy-laden bullshit he's currently writing to notice.

There are those, and there are many more. The grim, the bizarre, and the utterly preposterous, all rolled into one great melange of online absurdity.

And where there are aliens to blame, and the government to blame, you can also bet that someone thinks that hothouse of liberal sodomy and perversion, Hollywood, will be to blame. This theory has its genesis in Nella Lombardi having three movie credits, and her two friends just having finished law school. Smart movie, starting with actual facts to lure in the gullible reader.

The theory is that Lombardi would have been promised great things in return for sex. All kinds of sex. She had given the sex, or submitted to the sex, however you'd like to put it, but then had not seen a lot in return. She was getting antsy, and had started making threats. Give me decent parts in movies, or else I go public. The Sodom and Gomorrah of Hollywood laid bare.

The women meet up to go walking in the woods. The legally-trained friends have already been discussing with Lombardi the approach to take. Blackmail, backed by the law. Something like that. The writer of this theory doesn't know whether the other two women were taken out because of what they knew, or because it was expedient to do so. Either way, Thomas Riddick was paid for his trouble, and promised invisibility thereafter. Job done, women murdered, he vanished into the ether, never to be heard from again.

That's the theory. I like it, bar one aspect that I would have framed differently. The Sodom and Gomorrah of Hollywood is hardly news anymore. No one would be shocked. No one would care. This isn't nineteen-twenty, and we're not in Kansas anymore. Everyone knows the movies is a drug and sex hellscape. And you know what, even if it's not, everyone *thinks* it is anyway, so where's the shock value?

There's no way those girls would've been murdered to cover up the sins of an industry. But the sins of one person? That's far more likely.

And when you look through the three movies in which Nella Lombardi had begun to construct her career, one name stands out.

Brian Faraday, movie producer.

29

I'm with Natalie at the St. James Hotel, having first established that the crew hadn't decided to spend another night on Rake's Island.

I'm interested in Brian Faraday, but I don't want to speak to him again. Not yet. Perhaps I might not be able to speak to him anyway. He may well just tell me what I can do with myself, I've had my ten minutes, and that's all I'm getting. Either way, I just want to get the vibe, be amongst these people, and see where it gets us.

I spoke to Elise briefly, but it's a weekend, and Byron is at home, and they have plans of some sort, even if they've been heavily curtailed. We talked about the case, we said we'd see each other sometime during the week. I feel I ought to talk to her about Natalie, but over the phone, when she was just about to go home to her husband for the night, wasn't the time.

Natalie arrived at my doorstep just as I was heading out.

'Oh,' she said.

'Hey, you OK?'

'I thought we'd kind of agreed to see each other.'

'We had. I was going to call. I've got something I want to do.'

'Oh, OK. I should…' She looked around, a little lost.

'I'm going to the bar at the St. James,' I said. 'You want to come?'

'You meeting someone?'

'Nope. Just assuming the movie people will frequent it in the evening. Was going to hang around, see what was doing, maybe try to talk to one or two of them.'

'You got anyone in mind?'

'I'll tell you on the way.'

'OK, sounds good. But don't expect too much. I tried this move earlier in the week, before there was actually a murder to report, just to see if I could get any sort of inside scoop on the movie, for a behind the scenes piece. It was pretty dead.'

'We'll give it a go, and if there's nothing doing we can have a drink, then come back here. If you want.'

'We'll see how the drink goes,' she said, with a smile.

And now we're walking through reception, and the same guy's on duty, and he smiles to himself as we pass through, and then we're into the bar, which is pretty busy, and I raise my eyes at her, and she says, 'John Adams,' and I go to the bar and say, 'A John Adams and a glass of dry white wine, please,' and the young woman at the bar says, 'Chardonnay or a Sauvignon,' and I say, 'Chardonnay's great, thanks,' and she turns her back to get the drinks.

Natalie sits down at a table for four near the bar. Solid move. We take up two seats, hope the bar fills out, and two movie crew folk join us at the table, giving us an easy in.

I look around the rest of the bar. Recognise about half of the people here. Not sure how many of them will know I'm a private detective. Not many, I wouldn't have thought, I wasn't especially intrusive out on that island. They're more like to know me as the Guy Who's Scared Of Boats, without necessarily knowing who I am.

As I walk to the table, drinks in hand, this is confirmed when I pass a guy who says, 'You finished chucking up yet?' laughing as he says it, and I just lightly laugh along and don't bother denying the vomit.

I pass the drink to Natalie as I sit down, we clink glasses, we stare briefly at each other across the table, then we both turn and start the business of surreptitiously looking around the room.

'There are twenty-three people present,' I say, voice low. 'There are currently one hundred and seventeen people in Glasgow attached to the movie. That's, what, less than a quarter of the people on the film.'

'Nineteen-point-six-six percent,' she says. 'Rounding up.'

I look at her, wondering if she just made that up. Take out my phone, make the calculation. Nineteen-point-six-five-eight-one-one-nine-seven percent.

'You've got a gift for that?' I say.

'I can do it. Whether it's a gift or not…'

'Very impressive.'

'Thank you. It's been of little use.'

'That's because you're a gonzo journalist and not one of those *Hidden Figures* scientists. Missed your calling.'

'I'll pass that on to dad, he'll be delighted to get the back up.'

She lifts her glass, salutes me, takes a drink.

'Anyway, a lot more people not here than are,' I say. 'Nevertheless, the ones we want to see are at the back there. Who's the girl?'

She looks over her shoulder, turns back after a quick glance.

'The writer. Alison. First movie, though she's done a few TV scripts. This is her break.'

There's a table of four at the back of the room. They're not paying any attention to me, which means I can pay attention to them. The two producers, Brian Faraday and Rebecca Karlsen, plus Laurence Curtain the director, and Alison the writer.

It's apparent Faraday is in charge. Maybe it's because he's the oldest at the table, but I don't think that's just it. He's the reason everyone's here, he owns the movie, he's the boss. He may not be part of creative, but in his mind anyway, everything about the movie will be dictated by him, and everyone else in the room owes him for the opportunity.

'Have you spoken to him?' I ask.

'Faraday?'

'Yep.'

'Tried to. He wasn't interested.'

'What about Laurence Curtain?'

'Similar. Got a brief word in, but didn't get very far. He hates the press, unless it's the New York Times or Vanity Fair. The Cape Ann Herald, not so much.'

'Did he hit on you?'

'Did he hit on me?' she says, laughing. 'No, he didn't hit on me.'

'There are various narratives developing here, and one of them is that Roxanne was at this hotel because she was sleeping with people. Possibly Laurence Curtain. You read about him online, and there are stories. A lot of stories. He likes attractive women.'

'Let's clarify that. He likes attractive *young* women.'

'The guy's about your age.'

'He is. And I'm a good ten years too old for him, maybe more. He looks at me, he sees experience and stretch marks and tits that are already heading south. He ain't interested in me.'

'Your tits are great.'

'Thank you, but whether they are or not, he doesn't know,

does he? Every story you read about him, every single one, the women are twenty-one, twenty-two. He likes tits that are perfect and perky and look like they're barely out of the packet. And you know what? He's never going to change. Forty years from now the guy'll be a washed-up movie director in his seventies, and he'll still be chasing after twenty-year-olds.'

'So, how did it go, exactly?'

'When I tried to interview him?'

'Yep.'

'He was out there, waiting to be picked up and driven down to the harbour.'

'It's a seven-minute walk.'

'It's the American way. Whatever, he's out there, waiting to go, so I grabbed him. I introduced myself, told him who I worked for, asked if he cared to say a few words to add to the piece I'm writing on the movie production coming to Glasgow. He looks at me for, I'm going to say, a solid thirty seconds. I wasn't sure what was happening during those thirty seconds. He might've been trying to intimidate me, he might've been trying to recapture what I'd actually said, as he possibly wasn't paying attention when I spoke to him, I don't know. Either way, his brain finally clicks into gear, his head cocks a little to the side, and he says, 'The Cape Ann Herald?' and I say, 'The Cape Ann Herald,' with a bit of a smile, because, you know, I like the Herald, I'm always happy when they send me a commission, it's a good newspaper, then he says, and I couldn't possibly hope to mimic his level of derision, he says, 'What in the name of all fuck even is that?' And I was still looking at him, wondering whether I should attempt to get past his natural superiority barrier, or whether I ought to just ram my pen as far as I could down his throat, when his driver arrived.' She lifts her glass, she takes a drink. 'But sure, he was this close, *this close*, to hitting on me. If I'd just hung around in his presence for another five minutes.'

A loud laugh comes from that table, and we turn. Faraday. The others are laughing with him, seemingly genuinely amused, rather than just laughing along with the emperor to gain favour. Hard to tell without being in on it, though.

'I looked through Faraday's list of movies and hadn't heard of any of them,' I say.

'You watch horror movies?' she asks.

'Never.'

'He makes horror movies.'

'But I've still heard of horror movies. *The Exorcist* and *Midsommar* and *Hereditary*, I've heard of those, even if I haven't seen them. I don't know this guy's films, though. And there doesn't seem to be much box office.'

'It's not about box office with Tethys Films. He got a couple of small movies made, nothing major, didn't do much business, but he's a producer. He showed his chops. He showed he could put a package together, see the financing across the line, get into festivals, and maybe a limited theatrical release. That's a solid start. Then he had a critical success, which is good in the business, just a different kind of good to making money, and then he did his deal with GuLu+, and he got Curtain on board. Five movies. So he works for them now, he's got their backing, and they like what he's doing. Their first two were straight to streaming, so there's no box office, but this is a step into the big leagues.'

'OK, that makes sense.'

'This is his third of five, so they're right in the middle and riding high. Biggest budget, biggest cast yet.'

'I don't know any of the cast.'

She smiles, and then subtly indicates a guy sitting a couple of tables away.

'You seriously don't know Ryan?'

I not so subtly turn and look at Ryan. It's always someone called Ryan, though this is neither Ryan Reynolds nor Ryan Gosling. I think I would've known by now if either of those fellas were in the movie, not least because Elise wouldn't have shut up about it.

'Nope.'

'You need to start watching movies other than *Lord of the Rings*.'

'I watched *War of the Rohirrim* last week.'

'Funny.'

We look around the room. The burble of relaxed conversation, the ever-flowing movement. People getting up to go to the bar, to the bathroom, outside for a smoke. People coming back into the room. A table of four slowly clearing out, getting ready to call it a night. No one else has arrived after us, so the chances of anyone now sitting at our table seem remote. It's only just after nine, but there's an end of the evening feel to the place.

'Look at Faraday,' says Natalie, and I follow her gaze.

Having led the table in laughter a short while ago, he's quickly lost interest, and is detached, staring across the room. At first it looks like he's staring at nothing, then I notice his eyes are on a young woman, at a table of six, mostly men, of a similar age.

'Who's he looking at?' I ask.

'That's the lighting team, though the chief grip's not there. He's,' and she scans the room, then shakes her head. 'No, he's not here. Just his squad.'

'Faraday's willing her to look at him, and she's steadfastly not.'

'He doesn't have Jedi powers,' she says. 'Too early to say she's avoiding him, but perhaps she is.'

'You know anyone who's definitely slept with him?' I ask.

'Nope. That would all just be assumption.'

'You think Roxanne was one of them?'

'Seems possible.'

'Oh, there we go,' I say, as the girl glances in Faraday's direction, there's the merest of looks passed between them, and then, having done what he needed to do, he allows himself to become interested once more in the conversation at his table.

'Who's going to get up first?' I ask.

'She is.'

'Really?'

'He needs to see her leave. She's likely already got a key to his room. He might be the boss, but he's not really in control. If he leaves first, he's scared he'll go to his room, he'll make himself gorgeous, he'll pop a couple of Cialis, and then he'll lie there waiting for her to arrive. Tick-tock, tick-tock. The seconds pass into minutes. He can't go back down, that would be humiliating. He can't go to her room, because she shares a room, or maybe she's staying at the Market Square. He could send a text, but he's wary of putting anything in writing, because he's done that before and been caught out by it, possibly had it used against him. So he can't text, he can't call, he can't go and find her. He's trapped, clean and scrubbed, in his gilded cage.' She lifts her eyes at me, she smiles. 'So he makes sure she goes up first.'

'And what if she's not there when he gets there?'

'Then he knows straight away she's stood him up. He *knows*. Knowing is crucial. That way he can accept defeat, rather than prepare himself for triumph, and be left hanging.'

The girl gets up from the table, whispering into the ear of one of the others as she goes, then she says, 'Night!' to them all, waves at someone on another table, then slips quietly out of the room.

'And there she goes,' says Natalie. 'Another poor girl sacrificed at the altar of movie promises.'

'Obviously not put off by what happened to one of the last ones,' I say.

'I don't think these girls are seeing cause and effect.'

She lifts her beer, downs the rest of it, and sets the bottle back on the table, running her tongue across her moist lips.

'You want another?' I ask.

'I do not.'

I look at my half-drunk glass of wine.

'No need to knock it back just yet,' she says. 'It'll be something of a non-event, but I want to see Faraday leave. And then you can finish your drink.'

She lifts her eyebrows. She smiles.

*

We leave not long after Faraday has left the bar. On our way, I glance over at the table where he'd been sitting. Karlsen and the writer are leaning in towards each other, looking at something on a phone. The director, Curtain, is looking at Natalie and me as we go. He's not discomfited by being caught watching us. He lifts his drink, then finally turns away.

30

Sunday morning. Back out on the ocean, on a small rowing boat. I wasn't expecting that to happen, but it's fine. Practically a flat calm. The Atlantic is quite agreeable when it's this flat. Not even much of a swell. I can take this. And it's actual science that when you go out on the ocean and it's calm, it's guaranteed to stay that way.

Nevertheless, slightly troubling there's no land in sight. I don't think that was part of the deal when I agreed to come out here.

'Where's the cat?'

I'm not alone in the boat, even though I thought I was a moment ago. Joey's sitting at the back, a small fishing rod in hand, the line drifting on a light breeze, out across the water.

'He hates the sea,' I say. 'He loves looking at it, he likes living next to it, but hates, you know, boats. Hates going on boats.'

Joey turns away from the line, and looks the couple of yards along the boat towards me.

'Sounds like you're talking about yourself there, pal,' he says. 'Hey, where's the coffee?'

'I didn't bring any coffee.'

'You're killing me, here. You bring bisqwits?'

'No, I did not bring bisqwits.'

'The hell are we doing out here then?'

I look at him. I sit up, and look around the ocean. The sky above is flat and grey. Impossible to tell how high the clouds are. Doesn't look like rain, just a ceiling of constant grey, a great blancmange of impenetrable nothingness.

'I have no idea which way is land,' I say, and Joey laughs.

'You're in the ocean, chum, every way is land. Just depends how far you want to travel before you get there.'

'But which way to Cape Ann?'

He looks a little confused at that, and then turns and looks off into the far horizon, turning right the way round in the boat as he does so, and somehow not getting tangled up in the fishing line. Then he looks at the sky, searching for the sun.

'I have no idea,' he says. 'Like, zilch. Impossible to tell what time of day it is. Hey, maybe this guy knows.'

I turn, and coming up behind there's a man in a motor boat, the sound quite distinct in the silence of the calm ocean.

'Where'd he come from?' I say, but Joey doesn't answer.

The putter of the boat changes a little as it slows, and then the motor boat, dwarfing our little rowing boat, comes alongside.

'Hey, how you doing?' says the guy.

'A little confused,' I say.

'That happens a lot. You've come out here to die?'

'What the fuck?'

He laughs lightly, but not *at* me. More at the circumstances in which we find ourselves in the middle of the ocean.

'This is just so common. Really, this ought to be explained better before you come out here.'

'Who by?' A moment, then for some reason I feel the need to say, 'By whom?'

He looks at me a little curiously, his brow wrinkling.

'Well, that's a good question. Hey, maybe that's part of the problem. Maybe I need to speak to my people.'

I have no idea who this guy is, or what he's talking about. Or, in fact, who his people might be. I turn to look at Joey. Joey's gone. In his place, at the other end of the boat, is Elise. She's naked, drinking a glass of wine.

'You know what's going on?' I ask.

Elise looks a little apologetic.

'Sorry, babe,' she says.

'What about?'

'I know I said, go and speak to the girl, sort yourself out. But I was kind of hoping you'd speak to her, then realise you'd be better off with me. Once I'd got my head round it, I'm sure I'd've been good coming round to your place in the afternoon. And what age is she? Thirty-five, thirty-six maybe? Clock's a-ticking, you know what I'm saying.'

'That's not a thing anymore.'

'The biological imperative isn't a thing anymore? Good luck with that.'

I turn and look at the guy. He's still there, on his boat, behind the wheel, keeping it tucked in close to the rowing boat.

'Hey,' he says.

I turn back to Elise.

'So, am I here because I slept with Natalie?'

She takes a drink of wine, looks a little sheepish again.

'Check the big brain on Brett,' she says.

I'm still a little lost, and now we just stare at each other across the short distance of the boat. I wonder if she's wearing sunscreen, because even though the sun's not shining, it's not great being out on the ocean like that.

'You should cover up,' I say.

'Oh, don't worry about me, I'm not staying. Doesn't look like you worry too much about me, anyway, does it?'

She downs her glass of wine, holds it at her lips for a moment, then tosses the glass into the water. I wait for her to follow, but she doesn't move. I turn to look at the guy in the motor boat, but he's gone. The motor boat is gone. I turn back to Elise, now she's also gone.

Just like that, I'm alone.

Dammit, brought out onto the ocean to die.

I look around, thinking for a moment that perhaps this isn't a particularly bad way to go. Then I notice the sea isn't quite so calm anymore. And there are things in the water. Shapes. Large, dark shapes.

'Uh-oh.'

The sky is beginning to darken, the sea is getting a little rougher, the boat starting to pitch in the swell. That's bad, but the really worrying thing is these shapes. What the hell are they?

Squid. Giant squid.

Damn.

I get the sense of something coming, and I swallow and brace myself. The boat pitches forward in a wave, the bow low into the water, and then out of nowhere – or, out of the sea, to be honest – a giant squid, much bigger than the one that came into the living room, soars from the water, seems to hover over the boat for a second, and then as the bow starts to come up, the squid smashes onto the boat, its black eyes looking at me.

For a second I think I'm going to be stuck on a boat with a squid, and then I realise the squid has crushed the boat, and water is rushing in.

I push myself back against the stern. Heart racing, breath coming in panicked gulps.

A long tentacle comes snaking towards me, and then one, then another of the squid's arms wrap around my legs, and I grab on to the side of the boat. It's too late. The squid is too powerful, the integrity of the boat has been compromised.

I'm sucked down. A scream comes to my lips, but no sound emerges, as my lungs fill with water.

I shoot up in bed, gasping for air, my hand grabbing my chest.

The room is cold. The window's open. The sound of the sea, light rain against the glass, the smell of the ocean on the sea wind.

Natalie is next to me, though I don't turn to her yet. I can feel her looking at me, concerned, I'm aware of her stopping herself reaching out, touching my arm, because I flinched last night when she did it.

'Hey,' she says, eventually, her voice soft in the night. 'You OK?'

I stay upright for a moment, and then slump back, head on the pillow. A beat, check the time. Three-seventeen. I reach out, find her in the night, lightly place my hand in hers.

'Monsters,' I say.

She caresses the back of my hand, turning in the bed to look at me. A gentle touch on the side of my head.

'They're gone now.'

Long breath, adrenaline finally dissipating, coming down from the high of imminent death.

I check the time again.

Three-eighteen.

31

'Maybe you need to speak to someone,' she says at breakfast.

'I'm speaking to someone now.'

A bright day outside, at last, but blustery. White clouds racing across a pale blue, early morning sky, waves tossing in an unsettled blue/grey sea.

'You mean, me.'

'Yes.'

'Maybe you need to speak to like a doctor. A psychiatrist or a therapist, or something.'

'I also speak to Hightower.'

I look around for the cat, but he's taken advantage of the bright morning by heading outside to hunt.

She drinks her coffee, settles the mug down on the table, takes a bite of toast, waits for me to look at her.

'Hightower and I don't count,' she says.

'Sure you do.'

I have granola and yogurt and fresh fruit. And coffee.

'This is the trouble with Americans,' I say.

'Oh, this should be good.'

I smile, take a drink, take some food.

'You love to pay for stuff, like it gives it validation. It's not like there aren't actual people on earth who don't need a professional therapist, but the bulk of Americans are just paying for friendship, and because you're paying for it, the advice has more credence. It's like companies who get consultants in to tell them how to run their business, rather than asking their own employees.'

'I thought I was going to be good-humouredly offended, but maybe you've got a point. You must have this in Britain as well, though.'

'Sure, but you're the world leader.'

'It's the American way.'

We eat for a moment, inevitably in the silence drawn to look at the sea.

'So, I'm your therapist?' she says.
'I have lots of friends.'
We look at each other.
'You've never mentioned other friends,' she says.
'Neither have you. We hardly know each other.'
'I have Jilly, and Bethany. I've got the old college gang. I've got three high... wait, four friends from high school. And anyway, it's not the same, because even if you have friends, men never talk about anything other than sport and movies.'

I take a drink of coffee, I lean into the conversation a little to deliver the crushing blow in the argument.

'Sometimes we also talk about TV shows,' I say.
'Funny.'

She finishes off her coffee, pops the last of the toast into her mouth.

'Well, since you're not paying me, I'm afraid I'm going to have to go.'

She gets to her feet. Hesitates before walking off, her bag and coat already dumped by the front door. Then she sits back down again.

'This was nice,' she says.
'It was.'
'I, eh... you know I was stupidly married at eighteen.' I nod. 'Kind of had my guard up since then. But... I don't want this to sound like some dumb song, but I've been thinking about you far too much the last few months, and...' She smiles, she looks away, she laughs at herself. 'God, I don't know what I'm trying to say. This is lovely, that's all. I'll be your therapist. I'll be your whatever you want me to be. Reasonable rates across the board.'

We stare across the table. I don't even bother searching for the right words, because they're not going to be there, and she's not looking for them anyway.

'I'm off,' she says, squeezes my hand, and then she's up, a last smile thrown over her shoulder, and she's gone.

32

'Hey, coach,' says Ricky, as I come into the sheriff's office.

'Ricky.'

The reception area smells of coffee and fresh pastries. No more than forty-five minutes since I finished coffee back at my place, but there's something about that smell.

'Ed or Elise?' asks Ricky.

'Are they both on the movie girl murder?' I ask.

'The movie girl murder,' says Ricky. 'I like that. Sounds like a B-movie from the seventies, except the movie girl was probably a porn star, rather than a wardrobe assistant.'

He smiles, he takes a bite of cinnamon swirl.

'Help yourself, coach. Plenty to go round.'

'Thanks.'

Then he says, 'They're both working the case, but Elise has the lead,' just as I'm about to repeat the question. 'I'll check she's free.'

I head towards the food, lift the coffee jug, pour myself a cup, trying not to listen to the conversation.

'Go right in, coach,' he says. 'She's got a couple of minutes.'

'Thanks, Ricky,' I say, as I grab a pastry.

*

'They're good, huh?'

'You make them?'

'Meg.'

'They're perfect. She should open a store.'

'We keep saying the same thing, and she keeps saying her dream is to work admin for the sheriff's department.'

'Didn't we all have that dream at some point?'

We share the smile, then she nods at the need to get down to business.

'Pretty full on today, sorry. Only got a minute or two.'

'That's OK, I'll eat quickly.'

She says *you're not just here to eat* with a look.

'Checking in,' I say. 'Seeing how you're getting on.'

'With the case, or in life generally?'

'Oh, both.'

'I'll bet. Case is more or less done, far as we're concerned. Couple of days yet before this Agent Cameron arrives, but we've been told to tread water. Once she's here, we'll see. Sometimes the Bureau'll work with local law enforcement –'

'Like in *Twin Peaks*?'

'Sure, Sam, if that's your realistic frame of reference. And sometimes, they won't care for their involvement. We'll find out how this is going to go soon enough.'

'Did you have anything useful to pass on to Agent Barnes?'

'We were limping along a little, not near identifying a suspect. We've pinned down the movement of everyone from the production, once they got back from the island on Thursday. There was a lot of sorting out to do when they returned to the mainland, there were meetings, a skeleton crew spent three hours getting shots of the storm in full throttle.'

'No one unaccounted for? That's a lot of people.'

'We've talked to them all, and yep, the only person not spotted was Roxanne. I mean, OK, we haven't pinned everyone down for the full thirteen hours between leaving the island on Thursday, and returning Friday morning, so someone could've sneaked out after saying they were going to bed at ten. But that would've been a hell of a crossing at that time, and there are no boat sightings. Harbourmaster's got nothing, coast guard's got nothing.'

'Someone must've gone over there at some point,' I say, 'even if they weren't from the crew.'

'I guess they must. Either that, or they were already there, and then they took themselves off by some other means when it was quieter.' A pause, then a small shrug, and then, 'It's a mystery.'

'What d'you think about Brian Faraday?' I ask.

'You've spoken to him?'

'Briefly. He didn't feel any great obligation to talk to me.'

'You must get that a lot,' she says with a smile.

'He seems to like women.'

'Oh, he likes women.'

'Did he say he'd slept with Roxanne?'

'Yes. He also informed me he's slept with three other women currently on set, and that since the beginning of last year, he's had sex with approximately sixty women.'

'Wow.'

'Well, wow's one word.'

'Is his implication that sleeping with her shouldn't make him a suspect in her death, because he hasn't killed any of these other women?'

'That wasn't even an implication. He laid it all out for me.'

'What did you think?'

'As some kind of an alibi, it's lame. I shouldn't share, but I thought he was an asshole. Doesn't make him a killer though. If you manage to get anything out of him, I wouldn't mind hearing about it.'

'I thought it wasn't your case.'

She smiles, and I share the smile, and lift the coffee.

'Got one thing you might be interested in,' says Elise, 'which Agent Barnes didn't care for.'

She looks at her monitor, types quickly, brings up a CCTV image, and then turns the screen round so I can get a good look.

The image is of Norah Wolfe and an unknown – to me at least – man, sitting at a bar, side-by-side, at the counter. The man is on Norah's left, the camera is to her right, and he's turned towards her, smiling, so that the camera, from the wall above the bar at the back, has caught his face perfectly. He's bearded, wearing glasses, and has a beanie pulled down over his forehead.

'This is from Sunday evening at the Seaside Shack.'

'Have you ID'd him?'

'There's nothing.'

'Meets the description of the man seen returning with her to the Market Square.'

'Right.'

'You've been to the bar?'

'Well, that was how I got the image,' she says, trying not to sound like that was pretty obvious. 'It played out over about forty-five minutes. She was at the bar, he sat down next to her, bought her a drink, yadda yadda yadda, they left.'

'Have you checked with the hotel?'

'Not since I got this. I wouldn't have been in a rush to anyway, because Norah isn't our problem. I'd spoken to the bar on the basis that Riddick might've been seen around with Wolfe or Baudot, but this is what we got. I may still be curious how this plays out, but I have my instructions from federal law enforcement, so I'm going to leave it. But, as I say, Barnes doesn't seem to care for it, so at least it gives you an avenue without the risk of pissing them off.'

'Wouldn't want to piss off the feds,' I say drily. 'Can you send it over?' and she nods, presses a couple of keys, says, 'It's done.'

And just like that, work is over, everything that has to be said has been, and now we're just sitting in silence.

I take a drink of coffee.

I want to get up and leave, but the need to talk, or guilt, or something keeps me sitting there.

'What's up?' she asks, reading me like a cheap novel, as usual.

I take another drink. Here I am, the awkward interviewee, hiding behind his coffee.

'You saw the girl,' she says, and I nod.

She stares blankly across the desk. Assessing the situation. For a moment I think she's going to say she doesn't have time to discuss it now, but that particular shadow passes, and she braces herself.

'How'd that go?' she asks, and when I don't immediately answer, she says, 'Oh.'

I swallow. I'm not at my best in these situations, we all know that. I called Sorkin last night to try to get some decent lines, but he never picked up.

'Yep,' is all I manage.

No point in lying.

Feels like a punch to the stomach to admit it, so God knows how awful it feels for Elise to hear it. Sure, all I admitted to was 'oh', but that was a very heavily loaded 'oh'.

She closes her eyes for a moment, she takes a deep breath, her hand drifts to her chest, she opens her eyes. She swallows, the sound loud in the quiet of the small office.

'How was that?' she says, quickly followed by, 'Don't answer that. None of my business. Don't want to know anyway.'

We stare at each other across the desk. I should probably just get up and leave, but of course I don't want to. I don't want to leave her with that. But then, what else is there to say? We had sex *twice*? Nope, not going to help.

'I dreamt about you last night,' I say. She stares blankly

back. 'We were on a boat, and you were naked without sunscreen, drinking wine, and you were annoyed at me, and then you vanished and I was killed by a giant squid.'

That wasn't the wrong thing to say, as such, just a stupid, unnecessary thing to say, and slowly hurt starts to spread across her face, the pain of the end of our relationship in her eyes. She swallows again. The silence is heavy and all-consuming. It overwhelms us.

I'm sitting here waiting for her to tell me to leave, but I don't think she can speak. The fact that I'm holding a cinnamon swirl in a white napkin makes me feel all the more ridiculous, all the more out of my league. I have no place in a conversation of this emotional depth. Why should Elise have to be the one to speak? Why should she have to tell me to get *the fuck* out of her office?

I get to my feet, I lift the coffee off the desk, we look at each other for another moment, then I turn away and walk out, closing the door behind me.

33

There's work to do. You can have all that love angst and hurt and guilt and regret and excitement, the full panoply, you can have all that later, at some unspecified time, when you've got nothing else to do. You do, after all, spend most of your days with nothing else to do.

Malcolm Stewart IV, the receptionist, is in position at the Market Square, behind his desk, having an argument with a guy I recognise from the film unit.

The door ushers in a gust of wind as I enter, and they stop for a moment to look at me, then the guy from the movie turns back to the desk, unconcerned about the addition of *A Detective Entering stage left*, to the scene.

'We're still in America, right?' says the guy. Pollard, that's his name. Something in sound. 'We're still, I don't know, in a first world country, right? We still *function*.'

'You'd like to think,' says Malcolm drily.

I was wrong. Malcolm is not having an argument. Malcolm is being harangued by Pollard, the movie guy.

'Wouldn't we? Well, turns out we're not. We're not in the first world, we're not in a developed country, we're not in America! We're in fucking New Hampshire, backwoods capital of the earth. Jesus.'

'You're in Massachusetts. New Hampshire is twenty-seven and a half miles that way.'

'Oh, terrific. The home of the Masshole, that makes everything just fine. Where are fucking Matt Damon and Ben Affleck? Fucking, the other guy out of the thing?'

I stand to the side, enjoying the show. It will end soon. *Fucking, the other guy out of the thing* is intrinsically funny, and yet we all know he means Mark Wahlberg. Not entirely sure which thing he's talking about, there are so many to choose from.

'I understand Mr Damon is currently filming another instalment in the Jason Bourne saga in Europe, though I don't have any more detail.'

'Jesus Christ.' A pause, he looks at me, he looks back at the guy. 'I've had enough of this crap. Is there *anywhere* in this town I'll be able to get almond milk?'

'Like I say, I've tried. Some has been ordered, and you will have it at breakfast tomorrow morning. Perhaps you could try Manchester or Gloucester.'

'I don't have time to go to fucking Manchester or Gloucester, do I?' he snaps, and with that he turns away, glances rudely at me, stops for a moment, says, 'Nice to see you, seasick boy,' like his annoyance extends to me, and then he harshly pushes the door open, and storms out into the day.

Silence.

I look at the door as it closes over after allowing in another blast of fresh air, and then I approach the desk.

'Morning,' I say.

'Good day,' says Malcolm, with a nod.

'That entire discussion was about the unavailability of almond milk?'

'They never run out in Santa Monica.'

I look back at the door, the window overlooking the car park and the road out of town, but Pollard has already disappeared from sight.

'People are strange,' I say, turning back.

'I won't argue,' he says.

'Is Matt Damon really making another Bourne movie? I love those films.'

'I wouldn't know. I was mocking Mr Pollard in my own way.'

'Ah, too bad.'

'How can I help you today, Mr Vikström?'

I take my phone from my pocket, and bring up the image of the man in the bar with Norah, having isolated him, and lay the phone on the counter.

'You recognise this man?' I ask.

He nods, straight off.

'Yes, of course, and this is why you're here. I'd say this is the man who walked in here a week ago with Ms Wolfe. You've found him, then?'

'I haven't found him,' I say. 'This was taken last Sunday at the Seaside Shack, more than likely not long before they came here.'

He looks at the photograph, he nods to himself.

'This is them meeting in the bar?'

'Far as we know it's the first time. The bartender on duty seemed to think so.'

He taps the counter beside the phone.

'I don't like that smile,' he says. 'You're not trusting someone who smiles like that.'

'Thought the same thing myself.'

He looks at it for a little longer, then pushes the phone back towards me, and straightens up, silently asking if that'll be all.

'This is the only time you've seen this guy?'

'It is.'

'What d'you think?' I ask. 'The hair, the large glasses, the beard, you think it's all fake?'

He glances at the picture again, and then looks to the side, recapturing the brief moment when this guy walked through his hotel reception a week earlier.

'I see where you're going with that. I don't think that beard looks fake, I don't remember thinking it at the time. There's no sculpted facial hair, it all looks natural at the edges. Have you thought about this, though? He removes his glasses, takes off his hat, shaves the beard, gets a haircut, you wouldn't ever recognise him once you see him walking down the street.'

'You're right.'

I look at him, running the matrix, trying to think of anything else.

I can't.

I smile, I slip my phone into my pocket, I tap the counter.

'Thanks, Malcolm.'

'You're welcome.'

And with that, I'm gone.

34

The film crew aren't out on the island today. Apparently they have enough footage of the island in calmer seas, and they're aiming to return tomorrow when the forecast is for a return to stormier conditions.

This morning they're filming in town, on a street, one back, running parallel to Main Street. There are three people standing this side of a barrier, watching the scene being played. I thought there might've been more. But then, the film crew have been here nearly three weeks already, the novelty has worn off, there's no one particularly famous amongst the cast, and it's not like the movies don't come this way on a regular basis.

The other side of the barrier there's one security guy. I recognise him, having seen him out on the island.

This is a much smaller set-up than they had out there. Three cameras, a couple of sound guys, lighting. A small unit set up not far from the barriers, the monitors and equipment turned away from the street, so that no one in the public can see what's going on. Karlsen and Faraday are there, going over papers together. Perhaps it's the script, but really, it could be anything.

Beside one of the cameras, there's a guy with a smoke machine. A small device on the ground, he's wafting the smoke across the street, creating little more than a light, hazy effect, as two people walk out of a building that's mocked up to be the sheriff's office, one of them haranguing the other as they go.

Laurence Curtain is here, sitting in a regular director's chair, leaning on the arm, contemplatively rubbing his chin. Next to him a young woman, his assistant director, leaning into the scene, seemingly paying more attention.

'You are fucking kidding me!' shouts the man, walking behind the sheriff.

The sheriff, typically, is a corpulent man, at least seventy percent stomach fat.

'Listen, son,' he says, stopping to jab his finger into the other man's face, 'I do not kid. For however long you're standing here, for however long you decide you're going to be a pain in my ass, I will not kid. So, you're just going to have to believe me. I am not closing the damned harbour, I am not calling in the coast guard, and I damn well ain't calling in the US Air Force.' Another jab in the face. 'That was the last word. I have had enough of you people and your monster *bull-shit*! There are no monsters. There are no giant sea beasts. There is no leviathan lurking beneath the waves, waiting to pounce on the innocent children of this town. Now, I don't know 'bout you, son, because you seem to have a helluva lot of time on your hands. But I have problems and issues and the good Lord knows what coming outta my ass, so we are done!'

The guy's staring at him, lips set hard, waiting to explode, when the shout of 'cut!' comes from the side.

The tension dies in the scene as the two guys walk towards the assistant director. Sitting next to her, Curtain gets to his feet, makes a small applause gesture to the two guys, says, 'Terrific, Gordon, Eric,' and they nod in return, then he makes a signal towards his assistant, nods and turns away.

He reaches into his pocket for a vape, wanders aimlessly for a moment, realises he's heading towards the barriers where there are actual people standing, then he turns his back on us and walks away to the side.

'How's it going?' I say to the three women on the barrier.

'It ain't like watching the real thing,' says one of them.

'I love this,' says the next. 'The girls are only here to humour me.'

'How many takes have they done of this so far?'

I get three answers simultaneously. ''Bout five.' 'A million.' 'They've been doing this shit since four a.m. fifteen weeks ago. I swear, if I have to watch it one more time...'

The one in the middle playfully smacks her friend on the backside.

'Cut it out, Betsy. One more, then we'll go get us some pie.'

Well, isn't that the motto for all of America? *One more, then we'll go get us some pie.*

'Any controversy?' I ask.

'Hell, no,' says the one in the middle, the most gung-ho about standing here, watching people do their jobs. 'These folks know what they're doing. They got this.'

'How come they did five takes already?'

'This is how it works, honey. They do a bunch of 'em. Scenes like this, you can get the sense of the intensity growing with each one. It'll be off the scale by the time they get to the fifteenth.'

'Don't talk to me,' says the one furthest away.

'And Mr Curtain, what's going on with him? He's letting the AD take care of it?'

The one in the middle shrugs. The one next to me, says, 'Seems that way. He keeps walking off, doing his thing there, talking to other people on set.'

'Hey, it's the seasick guy,' says the security guard, walking over, a smile on his lips. 'Come back for a little more movie magic, now we're on dry land?'

'Funny,' I say. 'How are we doing today?'

'It's all good, my friend. We're back out on the high seas tomorrow. There's another storm coming. You're invited.'

'I'll let you know.'

The guy laughs, then turns away, the smile still on his face. This has got to be a fairly easy gig for a guard. If you ignore the fact that one of the crew has been murdered, which could be considered something of a security blunder.

'Any chance of having a word with Mr Faraday?' I ask.

He turns back, he laughs again.

'That's above my pay grade, my friend,' he says.

I indicate Faraday and Karlsen standing together by the monitors.

'Would you mind asking Mr Faraday if he'll speak to me. Do it when Mrs Karlsen's with him.'

He looks over, he looks back, he considers it, he says, 'All right,' with some reluctance, and then walks over to them.

'What's your story?' asks the most engaged of the three women.

'P.I. nosing around,' I say.

'About the murder?'

'Partly.'

The security guard is talking to the producers, indicating towards me. They look over. Karlsen says something. Faraday doesn't speak, but he shakes his head and makes a gesture in my direction. Not a very welcoming gesture. He turns away. The security guard starts heading back towards us.

'Not looking good, Mr P.I.,' says the woman.

The security guard starts shaking his head from ten yards

away.

'No can do,' he says.

I nod an acceptance, not a lot other than acceptance being open to me.

I get a whiff of blackberry, then there's a quiet laugh to my left.

'I'll talk to you if you like.'

The director, Curtain. I turn to see him walking back towards us. He looks young for a director. At least, at mid-thirties, young for what I'd assume a director to be. A shock of unruly blonde hair, like Heath Ledger in some movie or other.

'Aren't you doing the scene?' I ask.

'Andrea can handle it. But if you'd rather not, I don't mind…'

35

'Did I sleep with Norah. That's what you're asking?'

We're sitting on a bench, looking out on the ocean. Curtain is drinking Japanese matcha. I mean, these people from the west coast really are going out of their way to tick the boxes. Having said that, I'm drinking as close as you can get in these parts to Tetley, and I'm from Lanarkshire, so he's not the only one ticking a box.

'Yes, that's what I'm asking.'

'She's not dead, is she?'

'Not as far as I know,' I say. 'Nevertheless, it's now six days since anyone's heard from her.'

'Some people like to go off grid.'

'This time last week she was doing a job she loved on a movie she'd really wanted to be a part of. Then, out of nowhere, she vanishes. You don't think that's curious?'

'Maria heard from her, I understand Rebecca or Brian heard from her. What else d'you want to have happened? How many phone calls d'you need the poor girl to make?'

'But that was nearly a week ago. It doesn't explain the week's silence, and it doesn't explain her walking off a movie set.'

'I thought she said she was stressed?'

'That's what she said, but by all account, she wasn't.'

'Interesting. Are we doubting her because she's a young woman?'

'No, we're doubting her because it doesn't make sense.'

He takes a drink from his ethically sourced, carbon-free, reusable mug.

'When did you sleep with her?' I ask.

He looks at me, and then turns back to the ocean. Just to the right of where we are, there's a small stretch of beach. Otherwise, the rocky shoreline stretches away on both sides, here and there a jetty jutting out into the sea.

'Look at it,' he says, his hand sweeping across the ocean,

towards the horizon. 'It's magnificent. There are so many stories to be told, so many mysteries, so many horrors and wonders. Of course, the great nations, the international conglomerates, the leviathans of business, they could not give one fuck about it. They spew their filth into it, they shit in it, they could not care less for it. The ocean, though, the ocean will rise up. One metre, two, five, ten? Who knows, by the time the ice caps have melted. The oceans will rise, life on earth will die, and we will have brought it upon ourselves.'

He takes another drink of tea.

'When did you sleep with her?' I ask.

'And yet, has there ever been a seriously great, and I mean, really,' and he clenches his fist with a thespian flourish, 'really great ocean movie? And don't tell me *Titanic*. That story told itself.'

'*Curse Of The Black Pearl*?'

He looks at me, studies my face for intent, then smiles, shakes his head and looks back out over the ocean.

'Very good, Mr Vikström, very good.'

'When did you sleep with her?'

'None of your business,' he says sharply.

'How many women on set have you slept with?' I ask.

'None of your business.'

'How was Norah?'

He takes another drink of tea, then turns to give me a contemptuous look.

'How d'you mean that? Was she good? Did she use her tongue well?'

'Did she seem stressed?'

He barks out a laugh.

'Is it possible sleeping with the director made her stressed?' I ask.

He laughs again.

'People,' he says after a few moments, 'get so hung up on sex. It's exhausting. It's just sex, come on. We all have sex. Everyone. Every idiot on the planet has sex. Woke assholes who call themselves asexual, as if it separates them in some way from the rest of the humanity? Also having sex. The world is fucked up beyond all imagining, and I know, I know there are people in the world abusing sex. But I'm not one of them. I use my position, I use my authority, I use my,' and he almost sounds abashed as he says it, '*charisma*, but no one, not one of these women think they're getting anything out of me other than a fuck. Full stop, that's it. No favours, no leg up the ladder of success, no big role in my next production. It's for fun, it's to kill an hour, or twenty minutes, or however long we feel needs to be killed, and I am entirely respectful throughout. No one has to do anything they don't want to. I don't strangle anyone, I don't like anal sex, I don't want more than just me to be involved, I don't debase myself or them in any way whatsoever. I've had a vasectomy, I'm not polluting the planet with any offspring, and I'm free to enjoy myself.' A pause, he sounds quite happy with his lot by the time he gets to the end, then he says, 'You should try it.'

A fine speech. I wonder how many of those women really accept there won't be a quid pro quo for having slept with him, or consider him to have been respectful for that matter?

I take my phone from my pocket, and bring up the picture of the guy with the beard.

'You recognise this guy?'

He studies it for a moment, then he smirks, manages to wipe the look from his face, and looks away dismissively..

'Where'd you get this?' he asks.

'It's from a bar in town a week ago today.'

His eyes narrow, he runs a finger along his bottom lip. I get a side-glance, the sense of amusement about him, like he thinks he's toying with me.

'You know how I started out in movies?' he says, though I feel that's a rhetorical question. 'Make-up. I started out in make-up. This is someone who knows he's going to be caught on camera. Who is it?'

'He was seen with Norah Wolfe going to her hotel room the night before she left the set.'

'Interesting,' he says.

'You never saw this guy around the set?'

'Of course not. If he'd been around the set, you wouldn't need to speak to the director to find out.'

He looks at his watch, shakes his head.

'Talking of which, I should get back. They'll be wrapping on fifty-seven, and I want to be there for fifty-eight.'

'The guy in the hotel who recognised him from this, was pretty sure the beard wasn't fake.'

'Is he a professional make-up artist? Because believe it or not, a professional make-up artist will make a fake beard look like a real beard. It's what we do.'

He gets to his feet, still looking out over the ocean, as though he has to tear himself away from it.

'One more,' I say, and he looks back.

I show him the picture of Thomas Riddick.

He studies it, he looks bored.

'Nope,' he says, and I can see his thoughts already moving on.

'You might ask if *Leviathan* is going to be the great movie of the ocean that I say is lacking,' he says, confirming my thought, 'and my answer would be that, of course it won't be. It will be a competent horror. It will have its place. But I want to work on the ocean, I want to know it, so that one day, when that truly great script comes along, I'll be here, I will have earned my stripes. I will be ready to turn that great script into a truly great movie.'

'Tell me about the guy in the picture,' I say.

'I don't know him,' he says, and then he turns and starts walking quickly back towards town. No more than a couple of seconds, and then he stops.

'You should come back over to the island tomorrow. Maybe you'll learn a thing or two.'

He doesn't wait for my reply, and then he's gone.

I watch him for a moment, and then turn back to the ocean.

*

I get a text from Curtain seventeen minutes later.

Boat 2moro at 9am. Your bookd.

I feel a rush of fear down my spine, and immediately look at the weather forecast.

The weather forecast does not help.

36

Back in Salem. Every investigation seems to lead here these days, like it's a thriving metropolis, but it's just another small New England town like all the others. Coincidence is as coincidence does.

I got a call from Gerry Nine Fingers. He's come up with one other sighting of Norah and Roxanne in the town, a week past on Friday.

The bell above the door tinkles as I enter, and there's Gerry behind his counter, looking at another nautical instrument I don't recognise, though on this occasion, not carrying out any repair work. He looks up, he watches me enter.

'You still happy with your compass?' he asks.

'Sure.'

'You got it on display, or you keeping it in your bedside drawer?'

A moment, and then honesty comes from nowhere.

'I gave it to someone.'

He straightens, the rugged, lined face wrinkles a little more.

'You gave it to someone? That's an expensive-ass present my friend? Has Vikström got himself a girlfriend at last?'

'Sure,' I say, deciding blunt, disinterested honesty is the quickest way to bring an end to the conversation. 'You've got something for me?'

'You're not going to let me have any fun over this?'

'We're not in an episode of Seinfeld, so, you know, probably not. What've you got for me?'

'Did she like it? Tell me she liked it at least.'

'She loved it. You've got something for me?'

He smiles, finally accepting that there's no teasing to be done here.

'Hey, good for you,' he says. 'I should tell you the thing. I got another piece of the jigsaw. Your two girls were seen at a couple of boatyards that day. Sounds like they walked along the harbour, you know, did that whole New England shit, know what I'm saying?'

'Anything significant happen at any of these boatyards?'

'Significant? Not sure I can help you with that, but they were seen.'

'You know what time of day this was?'

'Sure. Early on. You know, people come to Salem for all that witch crap, but the out-of-towners, the people that don't know this coast, they always end up drawn to the water. You get out your car, you want to look at the ocean. That's how it works.'

'So, they arrived at the ocean, they had coffee at the Lobster Claw, and then they went along the waterfront.'

'Sounds about right.'

'You know which boatyards?'

'Seriously? Of course I know which boatyards.'

I can't help smiling at that. Then I take out my phone and show him the photo of Thomas Riddick.

'You recognise this guy?'

His eyes narrow a little, then he shakes his head.

'He part of this?'

'He was with the women for some of Friday.'

'He's your six-foot-six-Italian guy, huh? Nah, don't know him. Send it to me, I'll do a little more asking around.'

'You sure?'

'Why not? You think I've got anything else to do up here?'

'You missing the city?'

He laughs.

'Am I missing the city? Not according to Alice. Ha.'

'So what boatyards am I looking at?'

'You need Parker & Frame, and you need The Salem Boatyard.'

'OK, thanks, Gerry.'

I slip the phone back in my pocket, I turn away.

'You want to buy your girlfriend something else? Got lots of nice stuff here.'

'Let's leave it a while, I don't want her to think I'm a psychopath,' I say, and I walk out the store to his laughter.

37

It's getting colder down by the sea, as the afternoon progresses towards evening. The ratio of cloud to pale blue sky has increased, as slowly the bright day gives way to the next weather system moving in from the ocean.

Late Sunday afternoon, and only one of the two boatyards is open. The Salem Boatyard has a few people working on boats, as they get ready for the spring, or perhaps repair damage from this week's storms, and there's a light on in the yard office.

I knock and enter, and am unexpectedly greeted by Petty Officer Second Class Jenkins of the US Coast Guard, sitting behind a large wooden desk. On a chair to the side of her desk, is her daughter, who's sitting with an iPad in her lap, holding both sides, manoeuvring it like she's playing some driving game.

They look at me, and I look between Jenkins and her daughter.

'Didn't expect to find you here,' I say.

'Are you here about the dinosaurs?' asks the girl.

'Mr Vikström,' says Jenkins. 'Are you interested in berthing a boat, or are you working on a Sunday afternoon?'

'Working on a Sunday afternoon,' I say, then I look at the kid and say, 'And yes, I'm here about dinosaurs, but I need to talk to your mum first.'

'Yay!' says the kid, though she hasn't looked up from the iPad.

'I made the mistake of getting her that thing for Christmas,' says Jenkins. 'It's become surgically attached to her fingers.'

'Has not!' cries the kid.

I think of something to say about limiting access, and parental control, but I don't think I'm really the one for that.

'You're not with the coast guard anymore?' I ask.

'I'm still with the coast guard. This is a little volunteer work on a Sunday afternoon. Help out the community.'

'Don't you live in Gloucester?'

'I work in Gloucester, I live in Salem.'

'This is the third time in, what, five cases I've had to speak to you. The two when I didn't talk to you were fairly minor things, one of which was done in a day.'

She leans into the desk, looks at me with a raised eyebrow, her lips slightly pursed.

'Isn't life full of these lovely little coincidences?' she says.

'It's like we're in *Bergerac* or something.'

'I don't know what that is.'

'*Magnum P.I.* then.'

'You're comparing yourself to Tom Selleck. You go right ahead.'

'It's like a TV show where there's a recurring cast. There are obviously new characters every episode, but the same people keep randomly popping up, in a way they wouldn't in real life.'

She sits back, she studies me for a moment. I get the feeling of the kid giving me a quick glance, assessing the silence.

'I'd dispute that,' says Jenkins, 'but I do have some paperwork to complete here – knowing I'm with the coast guard, Ronald likes to leave all that stuff to me, which is kind of him – so let's not waste time discussing the existential curiosities inherent in coincidence. What can I do for you?'

I place my phone on the desk, and bring up the pictures of the two women.

'You know either of these two?' I ask.

Jenkins looks at them, then lifts her eyes.

'Well, I certainly know the murder victim from Rake's Island two days ago. This other girl, I don't know her.'

'Norah Wolfe. She was also working on the movie. She left the set last Monday.'

'Suspicious circumstances?'

'Not sure. It was unexpected certainly. She contacted some people afterwards, insisted she was OK, but it just seems odd, that's all.'

'Odd enough someone hired you.'

'Her mother. Norah was here, in Salem, nine days ago with Roxanne Baudot. I understand they were seen at these two yards. So, they were friends, they had a day out together here, and within a week one of them had been murdered, and the other's missing.'

'That is curious. But I heard the FBI were taking it on. You stepping on their toes?'

'They're taking on the murder case. No one's interested in Norah.'

'Hmm.'

She studies the two pictures, she shakes her head.

'I'm afraid I ain't going to be of much use to you, Mr Vikström. I'm here five hours, every second Sunday. Sometimes a Wednesday afternoon. That's the only part I have to play. So I wasn't here a week past Friday.'

'OK, that's too bad.'

'Sorry I can't be of more help.'

'One more,' I say, and she says, 'go right ahead,' and I show her the Jigsaw Man's image of Thomas Riddick.

Her brow creases, she brings the phone a little closer to herself.

'Where'd you get this?'

'It was drawn by a guy in a café in town. The man in the picture had lunch in there with Norah and Roxanne.'

'Feel like I've seen him somewhere,' she says, and she stares across the office, into infinite nothingness, trying to recapture whatever time it was when she'd seen him in the past. 'You got a name?'

'Thomas Riddick.'

'I feel like...' she begins, then let's the sentence drift off.

Fingers drummed rapidly on the desk, as she closes in on it, then she snaps her fingers, as she finally gets there.

'Damn, of course. Right next door,' and she points to her right. 'Parker & Frame.'

'He was working on a boat?'

'I don't know. He was just a guy. But this area, where our cabin is, we're a little more elevated, we look over onto them. I saw this guy the last two Wednesday afternoons.'

'Doing what?'

'Smoking. That's why I remember him. I've seen him twice, and both times he was just standing there, the back of the yard, looking down over the boats to the water.'

'Phone in hand?'

'No phone. If I'd just seen him once, no way I'd've recognised him or remembered him. Seeing him the second week in a row, that's what did it. I was thinking, maybe that's all this guy does. He smokes. From my perspective, it might as well be. This is who he is to me. The smoker.'

I walk over to the side window in her office, and look over

the fence into the next boatyard. A few boats on cradles, some covered with tarpaulin, some open to the elements, the clang of a halyard in the wind, the familiar detritus of the yard.

'And you don't know which boat he belongs to?'

She smiles at my back.

'I doubt he belongs to any boat. But no, I don't know which is his.'

'This would make sense,' I say. 'Roxanne and Norah came along here looking at boats. Came in here, went into Parker & Frame. They met the guy. Somehow, for some reason, they hit it off, and he ends up spending the rest of the day with them. That place doesn't open until tomorrow morning?'

'That's correct. You'll have to come back, unless you want to go on the hunt for the owners or the yardmaster.'

That's not what I'm thinking.

I turn and look at her, and she sees it in my face straight away.

'I don't think you should do that,' she says.

'Obviously I'm not going to.'

'I think you are. Do not break in.'

I hold my hands apart.

'Put the client first without breaking the law, that's the agency's motto.'

'I know your agency, and no it's not. Don't do anything dumb, Mr Vikström. The dead girl's staying dead, the missing girl is either already dead, or happily living her best life somewhere. Whatever you need to find in there, it can wait.'

'Absolutely.'

She looks dubious.

She knows I'm going to break in, I know she knows, she knows I know she knows, and let's just hope she leaves it at that, and doesn't call it in, so that they have extra security on board after dark.

'Where'd you get this anyway?' she asks, indicating the drawing. 'That is a nice piece of work. Whoever did it is wasted working in a café.'

I feel like I've talked about the Jigsaw Man quite enough, and I lift the phone, and slip it back into my pocket.

'The guy can draw, that's all. I think he might appreciate some discretion.'

'Guess you're talking 'bout the Jigsaw Man. I do not understand what the story is with that guy, but there's something... there's something benevolent about him, that's all. You do mean the Jigsaw Man, right?'

'I do.'

'Weird guy, but, you know, a good kind of weird.'

She looks at the kid. The kid doesn't notice.

'Hey, Luce, say goodbye to Mr Vikström.'

The kid looks up, her brow furrowing.

'I thought you were here about the dinosaurs?'

'I have to go,' I say, 'but I'll tell you something about dinosaurs first.'

She glances back at the screen, thinks about it, dinosaurs win out, she turns it off and lays it down.

'I'm all ears,' she says.

'First time I saw a dinosaur was on an island in the Caribbean.'

'You've seen a dinosaur?' she says, eyes widening a little, though I think she might be old enough to recognise Grade-A bullshit when she hears it.

'An adasaurus.'

She wasn't expecting that. She was thinking I was going to say one of the famous ones. A velociraptor, or a diplodocus.

'Obviously scientists thought they'd died out millions of years ago, but this was on a jungle table top mountain in a remote part of Jamaica.'

'I thought adasaurus was only found in Asia.'

'They called it the lost world,' I say, ignoring the fact check. 'There were all sorts of plant and insect and animal species up there that science had forgotten.'

'Insects *are* animals,' she says, and I think I might have reached the limit of how far I can take this.

'Of course they are,' I say.

'What was the adasaurus doing?'

'Eating tacos.'

She stares warily at me, then her eyes narrow.

'See you next time, kid,' I say, and she gives me a desultory farewell wave, I smile at her mum, she says, 'Thanks for the visit, detective.'

'Thanks for your help.'

'Don't break in next door.'

I smile again, turn away, open the door, and I'm gone.

As I'm closing the door behind me, I hear the kid say, 'Mr Viksum's full of poop, isn't he?'

157

38

Something stops me going to the Jigsaw Man's café while I wait for it to get dark. Feels like there's been a little too much Jigsaw Man, that's all. People knowing him, the mystery of people not even knowing his café exists, the FBI being aware of his existence in an official capacity. It all feels a little odd, I find myself in the middle of something I don't understand, and so I'm just going to avoid it for the moment. The Jigsaw Man, whoever, or whatever he is, would understand.

Sitting in the Lobster Claw as darkness creeps in from the sea, arriving early on the back of grey clouds, and the incoming tempest.

Have a bowl of chowder, some bread, a glass of water. Chowder's not in the class of Al's Diner, but it's passable. The bread has too much sugar in it. The water's OK.

I'm thinking about what Curtain said about the guy with the beard, his smug dismissiveness when I said Malcolm on reception had thought it a real beard.

He's right to be dismissive. I'm among professionals. Wardrobe professionals. Make-up professionals. Acting professionals. Professional constructors of fantastical narratives.

Can I really believe anything I'm told, anything I see, anything at all I've heard, the origin of which lies in the company of fools making the movie? They're literally professional bullshitters, and they'll be much more accomplished than I was when attempting to spin a tall tale to a five-year-old kid.

Perhaps it's time to take some of the certainties in this case, and put them back in the questionable box. Is Norah Wolfe really missing? If she is missing, did she really casually call in the next day, saying she was fine? If she did, was she herself playing a part?

'Everything all right for you?' asks the waiter, wearing a name badge that says *Brad*.

'Thanks, Brad,' I say. 'All good.'

'Hey, I meant to ask about your accent. You're Scottish?'
'I am.'

I don't mind talking to Brad, and Brad does not have a lot else to do.

'Like, what does that even mean?'

There's a question. Seems a little deep for a casual conversation between a waiter and a customer.

'How'd you mean that?'

'I mean, like I follow soccer, and I follow rugby, you know? I love all that stuff, all that like European sport. And you see Scotland. They have soccer and rugby teams, right?'

'We do.'

'You literally beat team USA at rugby last summer. Forty-two to seven.'

'Didn't notice, but that's a relief.'

'But here's what I don't get,' says Brad, and I make a gesture for Brad to continue. 'Scotland doesn't exist. I mean, I know there's this place with like hills and Ewan McGregor and weird food and stuff, but it literally doesn't exist. I've checked. The UN? Nope. The European Union? Nope. The Olympic Committee? Nope. The World Health Organisation? Nope. Like, you know what I mean?'

'I do. Nevertheless, I've been there, I'm pretty sure it exists.'

'Sure, but not as a thing, right? So how come you have rugby and soccer teams?'

Brad and I look at each other. He seems keen to learn. I, on the other hand, living overseas in voluntary exile, feel the pull of the homeland, and a certain sadness about the peculiarity of our place on the earth, and I'm not sure I really want to talk about it with Brad.

'Britain invented those sports and established them as international games. Right from the off, Scotland played England. Now, they don't want to let that go, so I guess they've played politics to keep it that way.'

He smiles.

'And by playing politics, you mean,' and he rubs his fingers together.

'I have no idea,' I say. 'Maybe other countries just want Scotland there so there's someone else to beat.'

'You're like ranked five in rugby, that's pretty good.'

'And yet we never win anything.'

Doesn't take much for the true, pessimistic Scot to emerge.

Brad laughs, and makes a move to indicate the conversation is over. I feel a small flush of relief.

The only thing worse than having to follow the Scottish football team, is the thought that one day it'll get taken away from us because we don't exist as an international entity. Although maybe that would be enough to instigate a successful independence vote.

'Enjoy your chowder,' says Brad, a look about him like he thinks he's made a new friend.

'Thanks, Brad.'

Brad walks off. I take another mouthful of soup, and turn back to the window. The darkness has encroached just a little bit further in the couple of minutes I was distracted.

39

The rain has arrived, and not for the first time in my life, I'm not dressed appropriately for the weather. The positive is that the streets are quiet, the boatyards are deserted, and surreptitious entry to Parker & Frame is more easily gained.

I walk along on the other side of the road on my first pass by, checking the front and sides of the property, looking for security cameras and alarms. Decide on my likely route of entry – climbing over a fence a short distance from the nearest streetlight, and in its own pool of darkness – make another pass along looking for any possible trouble, then, when it comes to it, get to it quickly.

Across the road, hands on the fence with momentum, ease myself up, and then I'm up and over the top, dropping down onto the other side, and finding my way into the darkness of the middle of the yard.

Kneel down, take a moment, assessing where I am. I stood outside Jenkins' office when I left, taking a good look over the boats in this yard. There's a large shed on the side away from the Salem Boatyard. In the yard, there are seven boats on hardstanding, three of which are covered by tarpaulin.

My mission is part *know it when I find it*, and part make a note of everything, names of boats, anything that seems untoward, and then spend time online this evening to see if I can trace anything back to the mysterious Riddick, or any possible connection with the film crew. There has been no talk of them having their own vessel, which makes sense I guess, with all their sea-based work being in rental boats. All part of the substantial budget.

Still, there's connection between this yard, Riddick, Norah and Roxanne, and it's the best place to start looking for it.

Trouble is, I don't want to walk around with a torch. There may not be many people about, but this is still in the middle of town, there are storefronts with apartments above them right across the road, and there are cars and pedestrians passing by, even if not as many as there might have been in more clement weather.

I start with the four uncovered boats. Walk round, decipher their names in the darkness of evening, make a note on my phone, huddled down, the light of the phone at its lowest, and check for anything amiss with any of them.

I come away with four names – *Summer Wind II*, *28-3*, *Belle Epoque*, and *Cressida* – and nothing else. Compared to the boat that takes the crew out to the island, and compared to literally any boat that's going to be able to carry even a rudimentary film crew and its equipment, none of the boats in this yard would be of much use.

Next, to the first boat covered in tarpaulin. Another look around, another check that I've so far managed not to draw attention to myself, and then I duck beneath the tightly drawn tarp. Now enveloped by the sound of the tarp in the wind and the rain, a tent in a storm. I'm standing right beside the boat, the tarp bulging at my back, and I turn on the phone torch.

Let's hope spiders don't linger in the dry spaces beneath the tarpaulin of boats.

And now that thought's in my head.

This tarp could've been in place since early autumn. The height of spider season. They have dock spiders around these parts, don't they? Size of your palm. Maybe one of them's tucked up for the duration beneath the tarp, cosy and warm, and I blunder in, torch in one hand, bare neck waiting to get jumped on.

I shiver and suddenly find myself frozen with fear.

'Jesus, come on.'

Nope, saying *Jesus, come on*, didn't help.

I lower the torch, and press it against my stomach, so I can't see anything.

I have to fight the need to extricate myself from here, to boldly retreat. Like Brave Brave Brave Brave Sir Robin, I'm about to turn my back and flee. High seas are one thing. Heights, totally different ball game, also terrifying. But stuck in a confined space with a spider the size of your palm? *Oh my fucking God.*

'Come on, come on.'

Head down, deciding to do this by feel rather than sight, so that if I do come across a dock spider I hopefully won't know anything about it, I inch my way along the boat, heading towards the bow. I'll put the light on for a second, check the name, then I can get the fuck out of Dodge.

My fingers touch a rough edge. That doesn't make sense. Run my fingers along it, then bow to the inevitable, the fear of spiders briefly forgotten, and turn on the light.

There's a huge rip in the hull, not far from the bow, but above the waterline. I shine the light along the tear in the fibreglass, and it continues all the way to the narrow point of the hull at the bow. Above the gash, the name of the vessel. *Newport 65*.

Not sure that it means anything, but this is what I'm looking for, after all. I take a picture of the boat's name, and then a couple of quick shots of the damage to the hull.

I get the sense of something outside, and I freeze. Phone pulled close to my chest, the torchlight swallowed up in my damp coat. Hold my breath.

Rain on the tarpaulin, the rustling of the fabric in the wind.

What was it I think I heard, with this noise all around me?

God, you really do need to get your head straightened out. So full of demons.

Come on. Forget about the fucking spiders, and stop creating strange, unseen forces out of nowhere.

The tarpaulin is lifted right behind me.

I turn, my back pressed against the boat, and then torchlight travels quickly along the ground, sweeping up my body to my face. I try to shield my eyes, and respond with my inferior phone torch, back at the gap in the tarpaulin.

'Some assholes just don't listen,' says PO2 Jenkins.

'Damn,' I say. 'Scared the shit out of me.'

'You should've known I was coming.'

'Can you lower the... the thing?'

She lowers the torch, and steps closer, lifting the tarpaulin so that it's propped up by the back of her head, creating a little more tent space.

'What're you doing beneath here anyway? What are you looking for?'

And as she speaks, she obviously notices what's behind me, and she lifts her torch again and shines it into the gaping hole in the hull, and I take a step to the side, so she can get a better look.

'Would you look at that?' she says. 'You knew this was here?'

'No. I just knew, thanks to you, that Thomas Riddick had been here, and I wondered what he might've been doing. Basically thought I'd get the names of some boats, check up on them, see if there was anything interesting. Didn't really know what that would be. This, though? This is interesting.'

'Hmm,' she says, running her hand along the rim. Then, 'Here, hold this. I want to get a sample of this,' and she hands me the torch.

I shine it on the edge, then Jenkins takes a small knife from her pocket, scrapes off material from where the contact was made, and slips it into a small see-thru bag that was produced from her pocket at the same time as the penknife.

40

We're back in the café I left no more than thirty-five minutes ago. Brad is still here, slowly wrapping up for the day, food now finished, happy to serve a cup of tea and a chocolate chip cookie. I thought PO2 Jenkins might eschew the cookie as being too frivolous, but she's eating the cookie.

'Where's Luce?' I ask.

'Lucy,' she says, 'only I call her Luce.'

'Where's Lucy?'

'There's a cupboard at home, I lock her in there. That's why I got her the iPad in the first place, to keep her quiet. The neighbours were complaining about the screaming.'

We look at each other across the tea and cookie.

'I can't tell whether you're joking.'

'I get that a lot. I called my mom, she came round.'

'Not that I'm against locking children in cupboards,' I say.

'Good to know. I'm sure you'll make a great father one day.'

'I'm already forty-eight. If I had one now, I'd be over sixty by the time they were a teenager. I don't like the odds.'

'Probably for the best.'

'So, what brought you back?' I ask. 'You just knew I was going to break in there, and you wanted to bust me?'

'I was going to let you go ahead. I mean, I don't really care, you go and do what you're going to do, not my problem if someone had spotted you. And I know, despite everything, that you're not going to go in and steal anything. But you'd given me that guy's name, and I couldn't stop myself looking him up. And he's wanted for some pretty serious shit.'

'He is.'

'And he's been here in Salem, and he spent the day with the murder victim.'

'Exactly.'

'The feds know about that?'

'They do.'

'OK, OK.'

She nods, she takes a bite of cookie, she looks back out at the night, the rain gusting against the window.

We took the time, once we were both there, to look beneath the tarps of the other two boats, and while I also took their names, there was nothing untoward about either of them. I then suggested we break into the warehouse, and she told me we were going to come here and have tea instead.

'Is that the kind of thing you'd've heard about?' I ask.

'The gash in the side of the boat? Depends what it hit. Someone runs into the rocks, then manages to get back to harbour, no need for them to tell us. No different from driving into a tree. If you can drive away, and drive home, no need to notify the cops. However, you drive into someone else? Whole other ball game.'

'What are you thinking here?' I ask.

'I'm thinking this is my job, and I'll handle it,' she says, taking a drink, and popping the last of the cookie into her mouth.

'Is there no possibility you're thinking about the sinking of the *Bel Air* out beyond Grand Bank a few weeks ago?'

She looks across the table, face blank, lifts her tea, takes a drink.

'Because something sunk that boat,' I say, 'and maybe it was another boat running into it.'

'Maybe it was,' she says.

'And that'll be why you took samples from the hull, so that you, or one of your people, can compare it with what's known of the hull of the *Bel Air*.'

'I like that you think I have people.'

'I know you have people.'

She smiles.

'That's exactly what's happening here,' she says. 'Nevertheless, I see this as being of interest to me, not so much to you. You sound like you've been pretty wrapped up in the movie, and maybe you're at the stage where you think it's all connected, everything you learn is intertwined in some mysterious way, but I'm not sure about that. It could be this boat has nothing to do with Riddick. I haven't seen him specifically working on it. The gash in that boat could be perfectly innocent. Sure, it could be his boat. This is the guy who maybe killed those three girls in Washington. Maybe he did some bad shit in that boat. But again, doesn't mean it's related to the film, or either of those women.'

'I feel you're telling me to keep my nose out.'

'I think I am. I'll check with the yard tomorrow to get the story of the boat, and I'll coordinate with the feds on the matter of Thomas Riddick. You? I don't know what you'll do, but it won't be either of those things. We clear?'

'If only you had that kind of control over me,' I say, smiling.

'Don't push it,' she says, and I smile again, and take the last of the cookie.

Brad comes once again into view, and we turn towards him.

'Sorry, guys,' he says. 'We need to close up in five minutes.'

'No problem, Brad,' I say, and Brad says, 'Thanks, guys.'

He disappears out of sight for a moment, carrying cutlery into the kitchen. Jenkins watches the door swing closed, looks at the place where he'd been, then turns back.

'Don't you find it annoying when someone *that* age calls you 'guys'?' she says.

'That's not just me, then?' I say with a laugh, and she says, 'I swear to God one day one of those kids is going to get their *guys* rammed so far up their ass.'

41

I spend some time on the image of the bearded man in the bar with Norah Wolfe, and the images of Thomas Riddick that are available to me. I don't see any similarity, particularly since there was such a height difference, but you never know, and a computer might see something I can't.

I call the agency, and am relieved that it's not Sal who answers. It's a Sunday evening, after all. I get an English voice I don't recognise.

'Mr Vikström,' he says, 'how can I help you?'

'Who's this?'

'Rupert Carrington. I've been with R-K for a few weeks, but we haven't had the chance to talk.'

'Sal never said,' I say.

'Perhaps she didn't expect us to interact, but she has had this weekend off. How can I help you?'

Rupert Carrington it is, then.

'I've got a couple of images, and I wondered if you could run them through Epox-17.'

'Shouldn't be a problem,' says Rupert. 'Send them over now, and I'll get them out to the tech hub.'

Rupert? I mean, if there was anything to make you think this might be genuinely suspicious, that would be it. No one gets called Rupert in real life.

That's just how it is, don't start naming people called Rupert at me.

'Thanks.'

'Not a problem,' says Rupert.

We hang up, I send the images over to the usual address, and can forget about it for now.

The tech hub, I presume, is probably one guy sitting in his basement in Pakistan or Malaysia or Denver or Cape Town, with a bank of computers and a lot of free time.

The answer will come when it comes.

*

'I have a working theory,' I say.

Sitting at the dining table, Natalie and I, a bottle of Pinot Grigio, and take out from the Dragon Boat.

We had a brief chat this morning about the speed of this thing, agreeing we'd leave it a couple of days, only contacting the other if there was some case-related item that needed to be shared. This was an agreement that was made as though neither of us had ever been in a relationship before.

I caved first by making the phone call, nominally by calling just to check up on how she was doing, and she caved by almost immediately saying that she was about to grab the Chinese, would she get extra and bring it round. And here we are.

'Go on.'

'You can't put this in the paper, though,' I say.

'Hmm…'

I make a lips sealed gesture, and she says, 'Come on, you know I wouldn't use anything you don't agree to.'

'What if you decide one day I'm an asshole, and just go ahead and print all sorts?'

'I shall quietly seethe and tell no one but close friends. And family. And people on the Internet.'

She smiles.

'So, here's the theory. The movie people were using the boat *Newport 65* to scout for locations.'

'For locations? It's the sea.'

'There are islands out there. Or they might've wanted to go further out, check the lay of the land, the contour of the coast, what they'd be taking into consideration if they were filming shots that were ostensibly supposed to be on the high seas.'

'Well, OK, I'll give you that.'

'There's an accident. *Newport 65* collides with the *Bel Air*. For whatever reason, the folks on the *Newport* don't manage to save the folks on the *Bel Air*. The accident was their fault. They panic. They nurse their own vessel back to the coast, they manage to get it into dry dock back in Salem. Maybe they pay someone off at the boatyard, but that's a hell of a lot cheaper than paying off the law suit from the families of the people on the *Bel Air*. However that whole thing plays out, there's a damaged boat in that yard, hidden beneath tarpaulin, and it incriminates the movie. It's bad for the movie.

'Then two people from the movie stumble across it by accident. Maybe they heard rumours already. Maybe they go looking for it. But Thomas Riddick's there, he recognises what's happened, and he plays the situation. He befriends the women, he tags along, he spends the day with them. We don't know what he did that night. Maybe, you know, the three of them,' and I make a bit of a gesture, and Natalie rolls her eyes, and says, 'Sure, because women are never done sharing men with their friends, happens all the time,' and I say, 'It does!' and she says, 'Has it ever happened to you?' and that's where my argument falls down, because not only has it never happened to me, I don't know anyone it's happened to.

'Whatever,' I say. 'He plays them. Draws them into his circle, keeps them quiet. He uses Norah, promises her something – something better than she's getting working on this film set – and she leaves. She may have lived long enough to make her phone calls thereafter, but whether she's still alive? After what happened to Roxanne Baudot, I'm not sure she does.'

Natalie has listened throughout, eating chicken chow mein with chopsticks from the carton.

'Not bad,' she says.

'Thank you.'

'But I don't believe it, sorry. Feels a little contrived. A little too hacky.'

'Hacky?'

'Like a pulp fiction novel.'

I take some Korean fried rice, and shrug.

'Maybe it needs work, but it ticks the boxes. Perhaps all the details aren't right, but it feels to me like it's in the right area.'

'Hmm,' she says, sucking up some noodles, licking her lips. I try not to stare.

'What about you?' I ask.

'Do I have a theory?'

'Yep.'

'Nope.'

She sucks up some more noodles.

'You don't have a theory?'

'I don't need a theory. *You* need a theory. I just need to report what's happening.'

'And what's your lead for tomorrow?'

'Sheriff out of ideas, case quickly grinding to a halt,' she says, then she laughs.

'Bugger off,' I say. 'You've got nothing for your day's snooping around?'

'Honestly, you're confusing me with Woodward and Bernstein. I'm just out there, speaking to people, getting quotes. The sheriff's department are being very tight-lipped, but then, it's day three of a murder inquiry. There's no reason they should share, even if they have something to share. Which they might not.'

'You speak to the sheriff?'

She nods to herself, takes a drink of wine.

'I spoke to Deputy Miller.'

A little rush of adrenaline. I've had quite enough of those.

'How'd that go?'

'She didn't really have anything to say. Usual kind of bland sheriff-speak, we're all used to it. But asking around, I don't think she was being intentionally evasive.'

She says all that without looking at me, then she scratches her head, chopsticks held in the air, and says, 'I take it you haven't said anything to her about, you know...'

'I told her this morning we'd had sex.'

She stares, a little of the rabbit in the headlights about her, across the table.

'You did?'

'Yes.'

'Damn. How'd that go?'

I lower my eyes for a moment. Relive the moment. The look on her face, the hurt in her voice.

'It was sad, that was all,' I say. 'She was hurt... It was in her office, she was working, it was brief.'

'Have you spoken to her since?'

'Nope. But apparently you have, so you know, at least she didn't arrest you for some trumped up driving offence.'

We share the look across the table.

'Must've been tough.'

I don't have anything to say to that. It's not like I feel good about it, and it was hardly heroic breaking someone's heart.

'Anyway, it's done,' I say, lurching quickly back to practicality.

The doorbell rings.

We look at each other. I think even Sarah Vaughn, being a little too boisterous from the Bluetooth in the corner – though at least the volume is on low – takes a moment.

'Expecting someone?' she asks.

I don't reply.

There aren't many people who come to this place on a Sunday evening.

'I'll just be a minute,' I say.

I go to the door. I see Elise's outline before I answer, still in uniform.

'Hey,' I say, opening the door.

'Hey.'

A moment, I start to indicate behind me, and Elise says, 'I know, I saw her car.'

Another moment. I'm a little wrong-footed here.

'You going to invite me in?'

'I'm not sure.'

'Sam.'

I stand back, and she walks into the house, gently touching my hand – a peculiarly unexpected, affectionate touch – and then she's through into the kitchen, and I come in behind her, and she pulls up a seat at the end of the table.

I offer her the wine, and she says, 'Better not. I'll be home in fifteen minutes, and Byron might wonder why I smell of alcohol.'

Natalie is looking between the two of us, a little unsure how this is going to play out, but she's not the only one. Then she pushes her chair back, and says, 'I should go, let you two talk it out,' but before she can get to her feet, Elise gestures to her to stay put, and says, 'You're good. Really, I'm not staying,' and Natalie doesn't rise, though she also doesn't pull her chair back in again.

Then Elise's eyes settle on my glass of wine, she reaches out, lifts it, downs it in one, and sets the glass back on the table.

'I'll think of something,' she says, then she taps the table a couple of times, and finally manages to find some words. 'God, you're gorgeous,' she says to Natalie. 'You're not going to fuck with him, are you?'

Natalie laughs a little nervously. Elise has an air of the loose cannon about her, though I know her well enough to know the cannon won't go off. Natalie won't be so sure.

'Sam told you that I know about you?' says Natalie.

'Yes. Very exciting development in my life.'

'I'll never tell anyone, don't worry.'

'Well, I know you mean that, but things happen, and things

have a way of coming out. But I made my bed, and that's for me to worry about. The main thing is,' and she takes a breath, then says, 'Don't fuck with him.'

'I won't.'

'I have powers,' says Elise, then she rolls her eyes. 'Whatever.' Then she reaches out, squeezes my hand, and says, 'Thank you for the honesty at least. I know we'd probably run our course, but you could have played this differently if you'd wanted to.' Another deep breath. 'I'd hoped I'd get you alone, but you know what, this is probably easier. Shorter, certainly. Hey, look, you're still going to do your job, and I'm not going anywhere, so if you need help, you don't have to come in and see Deputy Ed, if it's my case. In fact, probably best for me if you don't suddenly stop coming in, and have folks wondering what happened to you.'

'Thank you.'

She lets go of my hand.

'Dammit. I should go. I have to walk into the house and pretend.'

Natalie and I look at her with awkward sympathy, then Elise gets to her feet, looks at Natalie, says, 'Did I say don't fuck with him?' and she says, 'A couple of times,' and Elise nods, thinks of something else, decides not to say it, gives me a final glance, and then walks quickly from the house before I can get up and see her out.

The front door closes, and then it's the silence of the kitchen. With Sarah Vaughn, and the wind and the rain of the gathering storm.

We stare at each other across the table. It could've been a lot more dramatic than it proved to be, but it was still awkward and sad and full of all the pain we cannot see.

The silence swirls around the room. Eventually I lift my chopsticks and start eating. Natalie follows. Sometime later conversation joins us.

42

Hightower and I are sitting on the edge of a cliff, looking into a deep canyon of thick forest. I get the vague impression we're in China, but I'm not sure why I think that.

I have my legs dangling over the side. There's no railing, no protection. Shuffle forward a few inches, and I'd be plummeting to my death.

'Thought you were scared of heights,' says Hightower.

'I am.'

Hightower nods, then stretches his neck a little, without shifting his centre of gravity too much, to look down the cliff face.

'Interesting location for a coffee break.'

'There's coffee?'

I look around. There doesn't appear to be coffee.

'Curious that you suddenly started panicking about spiders earlier,' says Hightower. 'You've lived in this state for twenty-six years, and you've never seen a dock spider. Then out of nowhere, boom!'

'I was in a dock. A dry dock. Even more likely to see a dock spider. You know they're also called wharf spiders. You literally get them under tarpaulin.'

'Spiders, heights and the ocean. That's a fine collection you have there.'

'Let's not ignore confined spaces and flying.'

'Damn,' says Hightower. 'You're a one-man phobic smorgasbord. Can you come to my office in Vienna?'

I look to my left. Hightower is gone. Sigmund Freud is sitting on a chair, which is positioned perilously close to the edge of the cliff.

'But then I'd need to get on a plane.'

'I don't know what a plane is,' says Freud. 'Wrong generation.'

'You died in nineteen-thirty-nine. They had planes.'

'Let's talk about you. You're lucky you had all that

romantic drama this evening. It saved you from worrying about the boat ride tomorrow.'

My eyes shoot open in the night.

The window is open a little, as it usually is. The air in the bedroom is cold and fresh, smells of the sea. Sounds wild out there, though there's not currently rain hitting the window.

I glance at the clock. Two-thirty-eight.

I think of Elise, and the look on her face as she left.

Time will heal, possibly. Time has a habit of doing that, though only if you let it. I think she will. Me, I'm not so sure about. I tend to let things linger.

Natalie went home after we'd eaten. There was an unsettled atmosphere. That was just the way it was, and there was no getting past it.

'Come to my place tomorrow evening,' she said. 'I'll cook.'

'You don't cook,' I said.

'I'll get something different from the takeout,' she said.

And my first thought at the time was that that would be nice, but I wouldn't be able to look forward to it until after I'd been out to the island.

'You don't have to come if you don't want to,' she said.

I explained my fear. She was squeezing my hand by the end of it.

'You're a one man-phobic smorgasbord,' she said.

'I want *One-man phobic smorgasbord* on my headstone,' I said, and she laughed.

I lie still for a while listening to the night, then I reach over to the bedside table, get my earbuds, start playing *Isn't It A Pity*, and rest my head back on the pillow.

43

Breakfast. Eight-o-seven. I've already called Rebecca Karlsen. The movie people have been on the island since yesterday afternoon. Nevertheless, the sailing at nine is definitely happening. The star of the movie is due to be on the boat. He hadn't been required last night, so had elected to take the rough ride out this morning. 'He loves that shit,' she said.

Why am I so committed to going out there is the question the sports fans are all asking.

The opportunity is there, and not going feels like running away. Feels like avoidance. And there's that other thing at the back of my head. The niggle. That there are answers to be found out there, and by not going, I'll miss them. Perhaps I'm just trying to wish that into existence, but my gut instinct isn't usually too far off.

There's something out on that island, and the only way I learn what it is, is by going out there. I need to face the fear, deal with it, and get over it a lot more quickly once I'm there. No sitting around, looking like a consumptive romantic poet living out his final days in a sea breeze, mainlining laudanum, incapable of logical thought.

Take the last of my toast, finish off the coffee, pour myself another.

My phone pings. Radstone-Kirk. The message is from Sal. Rupert must've gone back to the tennis club.

Morning, coach! Here's the report you asked for. Have a great day!

I type a quick reply, then open the report. It has one line.

Chance that images are of the same person: <1%

Well that sounds pretty definite. The guy in the bar wasn't Thomas Riddick. Maybe it was a guy with an actual beard, as Malcolm Stewart IV thought.

An answer given, but the picture, whatever it is, does not get any clearer.

44

I've done a reasonably good job of not thinking about this too much, but it's too late for not thinking about it now. I'm on the quayside in Manchester, arms folded, jacket pulled tightly around me, beanie and gloves, looking out on the sea.

The sea is not restless. The sea is tempestuous. The sea is pissed off. The sea is all-in, what the fuck do you think you're doing going out on a boat today, motherfucker? The sea has gone full Samuel L Jackson, and is showing no signs of calming the fuck down.

Not that it would matter if it was going to calm down, because the boat's due to leave in nine and a half minutes, and the only thing that can stop it at this stage is the late, or complete non-arrival, of the movie star, Ryan –. I can dream.

'You all right there, buddy?' says the boat's captain, as he walks past. His tone is light, jokey, as though he's going to clap my shoulder and walk on, but he stops in a pretence of genuine concern.

'No.'

'It'll be fine.'

'The regular ferry's off, though, right?' I say.

He looks over his shoulder at the passenger ferry, safely bound by a gazillion miles of heavy rope to the wharf.

'That thing only runs at the weekend this time of year,' he says. 'Anyway, it's a different ball game for those fellas. They got insurance and law suits to think about. Our trip here is on the movie people, and they need it to happen.'

'I know you wouldn't have gone out in this if you hadn't been paid more money.'

He makes a *could be right* gesture, but doesn't seem particularly concerned.

'This is like a scene in a movie when some guy is paid for one last job,' I say, 'and you know it's going to be a disaster. Never take the extra money in exchange for common sense.'

He laughs. He thinks of some glib reply, can't find it, then gives me a reassuring look, says, 'I'd like you on board in five minutes,' and he holds up his hand, fingers extended, and then he's walking on.

I want to think about the case, but when faced with fear like this, I can't think about anything. That's why the ridiculous lighthouse stunt I pulled to save Elise was so much easier than this. I hated that, the heights terrified me, but I had an activity. I had to get on with it. This? I'm just going to be sitting there. Nothing to do, nothing to think about but the waves.

I mean, it's dumb. If I was told I was going to get taken out there and dumped in the sea, I wouldn't care. I can swim. I swim in the Atlantic most days. And yet, a pitching boat, a vessel over which I have no control, and I'm petrified.

I get a heavy clap on the back, and then the movie star comes from behind, smiling.

'Didn't expect to see you here,' says Ryan –. 'You didn't look too happy out there the other day.'

'I wasn't.'

'I don't even know who you are, man. You with marketing?' He snaps his fingers, 'No, wait, you're the Vanity Fair guy, I heard they were coming.'

'Neither,' I say. 'Sam Vikström, private investigator. Looking into the disappearance of Norah Wolfe.'

'Who's that?'

'Assistant storyboarder. Left the set unexpectedly about a week ago.'

'Huh,' he says. 'Don't think I knew her. I always aim, you know, I really aim to get to know everyone. You know, you take them out of the picture, the grips and the storyboarders and the location catering, the whoever, and you don't have a movie, right? Sure, it's my, you know, it's my face up there on the billboard, I'm the USP, the whatever, but come on, without everyone else, no damn movie. That's what I always say.'

Normally I'd engage this guy, but I really don't feel like talking.

'Never seem to get around to it, though,' he says, turning away and looking out over the sea.

His jacket is undone, his hands now thrust in his pockets.

'Two minutes, Ryan,' says a young woman, walking past on the way to the boat, then she holds aloft one of those gigantic Stanley mugs and says, 'I've got the coffee.'

His assistant.

There is nothing that would make me think he wasn't having sex with his assistant. Unless he's gay. Maybe he's gay. I don't know anything about Ryan.

'You really don't like this?' he says, and he sweeps his hand across the seascape before us, then thinks to say, 'Thanks, Kelly!' and Kelly makes another gesture with the mug without turning.

'I hate it,' I say.

He knows this already.

'I love the rush. My people are speaking to the captain, negotiating whether I can drive the boat over there.' Kelly is currently talking to the captain, and I wonder if this is what he means by *my people are speaking to the captain*. 'I want to be the guy, you know. I mean,' and laughs, 'I don't want to sound like too much of a dick, no one likes the guy who's a dick. But I want to be the guy who clings to the side of the airplane. I want to be the guy who climbs up the outside of the Burj Khalifa, the guy who runs along building tops in London, breaks his ankle, then gets up and keeps going. I want to be *that* guy, you know. Tom Cruise? He's got it made. The safety guy says no, the stunt guy, the producer who's breaking out into assholes says no, Tom gets a new safety guy, he gets a new stunt guy, he gets a new producer. I'm not there yet.' He nods to himself, considering his place in the cinematic firmament, then repeats, 'I'm not there yet.'

'All aboard!' shouts one of the small crew from the boat, looking in our direction.

Ryan smiles, beaming with encouragement, slaps my shoulder, and says, 'Up and at 'em, cowboy,' and heads to the boat.

I stand for a moment, looking at the pitch of the boat in the harbour, tied to the wharf.

I knew I should've had vodka for breakfast.

*

The crossing, into the full force of the wind and incoming tide, is worse than either journey three days ago.

I curl into a ball, arms around my head, back pressed against the side of the boat, feeling every movement, every pitch and yaw of the vessel, the spray splashing against the few areas of exposed skin.

Someone tries to speak to me at some point. Someone else is vomiting. I hear Ryan laughing. He says something, loud and attention-seeking, but I don't make it out.

I don't check the time, but the crossing lasts forever. Nevertheless, we do not sink, we get there in the end, and soon enough the boat is being tied up to the small jetty on the island, and once again someone is clapping me on the shoulder, and the captain says, laughing, 'You can come up for air, now.'

45

I assume Elise was all over this island, and perhaps Agent Barnes came out here to do a recce for the Incredible Agent Cameron, or whatever her superhero name is. Far as I know, Elise didn't manage to find anything useful, but there was no reason for her to pass it on if she had done. All I can do is nose around, find out what's happening.

The island is split roughly into two. The ocean side is uncultivated, with shrubs and low trees, a lighthouse at the far end, on a rocky promontory, jutting a little out into the ocean.

On the shoreside, there are ten homes, none of them particularly large by New England standards. There are no other facilities. No shops, no bars, no roads, just a tarmacked path leading from the small jetty to the first couple of homes. Thereafter, the path to the rest of the properties is one of grass and rocks.

In the middle of the island, at the insignificant highest point, a map in bronze atop a standing stone, indicating the surrounding towns on the shore, and then the distance to various other locations in all directions. Two hundred and seventy-one miles to Montreal. Two thousand, four hundred and three miles to Reykjavik. And on to London, Paris, Lisbon, Dakar, Cape Town, Beijing and Sydney.

Of the ten houses, only two are currently occupied, and even those are holiday homes where the owners just happen to be holidaying in late February in a storm. I asked Elise if they'd gained entry to the empty homes, and she said they'd examined them for signs that someone had done that, hadn't found anything externally suspicious, and then had elected not to go so far as to break in. The FBI, when it comes to it, will not be so discerning. Having no need to care about their place in the local community, the FBI would burn down a holiday home if it suited them.

Having attempted to gain use of at least some of the properties, and having been rebuffed, the movie production set up their overnight base in the lee of the small village, living more or less right on top of them. Made sense, from the perspective that the village was obviously situated in the most weather-advantaged location.

I take a few minutes to watch the movie crew in action. They're doing another scene that looks pretty ridiculous while they're about it, but which will no doubt be only partially ridiculous, yet completely consistent with the movie's narrative, once the CGI folks have got their hands on it. So far, I haven't actually seen any filming yet.

I get a cup of green tea and let my head and my heart and my stomach settle. Would be nice to think the storm will have calmed a little by the time I'm returning to land, but no one's talking about that. Nevertheless, this is the last day they're set to film on here, so they are intent on being done by the time evening falls.

Tea finished, recyclable cup placed in the appropriate waste disposal, I turn away from the discussions on set, to take a walk around the island. The wind has not dropped, the sea a tempest on all sides, a spit of rain in the air.

Past the small jetty, our boat tied up and pitching excessively in the swell, and then into this tiny settlement of houses. I guess they're all a similar size to mine. Three of them by the sea, with their own small jetties, four set one house width back, and then another three set a little further behind, against what there is of a rise to the centre of the island.

There's a light on in one of the houses by the shore, and I approach the door and ring the bell, standing back a little, hands in my pockets.

A moment, and then a woman in her forties, wearing a sleeveless summer top, her hair tied up, answers the door, and a wave of heat leaves the house.

'Seriously, I've had enough of you people,' she says. 'No, you cannot use the bathroom. I'm done.'

'I'm not with –,' is as far as I get, before the door is closed.

That was pretty much what I expected.

I ring the bell again. I imagine her in the hallway, deep breath, shoulders tense, contemplating ignoring it, then the door opens again.

'What?'

I have my ID in hand.

'Sam Vikström, P.I.,' I say. 'Wonder if I could have a word.'

'Oh my God, that's almost as bad. I spoke to the sheriff, I spoke to Agent whatever-the-hell-his-name-was. I don't know anything about the girl who got murdered. I never saw her. I never saw *anything*.'

'It's not about that,' I say.

'Oh, well that's terrific, then. Absolutely fine. You selling life insurance, maybe? Or maybe some amazing new medicant that'll get rid of my stretch marks, drop twenty pounds, and make up for all those pelvic floor exercises I never did after childbirth?'

'None of the above.'

'You ever stop and ask yourself why I'm here? Why someone like me might be living on a barren island in the middle of damn winter with only Mr damn Crabapple for company over there? You ever think about that? Well, let me tell you. *I don't want to speak to anyone*!'

She looks like she's about to close the door again, but she gives me a one and a half second window, and I have the picture of Norah Wolfe ready on my phone, and have it placed under her nose before she can make her full retreat.

'You recognise this woman?' I ask.

She gives me a rueful look, and then looks at the picture, sighing at the imposition as she does so.

Hard to read what's going on with her face.

She lifts her eyes, making a small chin gesture in the direction of the phone.

'How come the sheriff and the feds didn't ask me about her?'

'She's missing. There's no crime been committed, far as anyone knows. Her mother just wants to find her.'

'It's tied to this movie, though?'

'She was working on it until a week ago today, then she left.'

'So, nothing to do with the murder?'

'Unknown. The police don't think so, that's why they're not asking.'

'Yeah, I saw her a few days ago.'

'When was that?' I ask casually, as though having spoken to thousands of people who've seen Norah Wolfe in the past week.

She looks away now, pursed lips, actually engaged and giving it some thought.

'Saturday, I guess.'
'Saturday just gone.'
'Yeah.'
'On the island.'
'No, in town. It's Monday today, right?'
'It is.'
'You lose track out here. I do yoga six hours a day.'
'Good detail,' I say. 'So, you saw this woman in Manchester? Somewhere else?'
'Oh, hey,' she says, and she smiles. 'I read this thing, what the Brits say that's different. You know words like pavement and trousers and whatever. I read you guys say somewhere else, rather than someplace else.'
'Yeah we do.'
'Huh.'
A moment. She seems to have forgotten the question.
'You saw Norah Wolfe in Manchester?'
'That's her name?'
'Yes.'
'Norah Wolfe?'
'Yes.'
'Sounds like a thriller writer, right? *Fatal Deception*, by Norah Wolfe, the exciting follow-up to *The Mortuary Murders*.'
She smiles, having amused herself.
'You saw Norah Wolfe in Manchester?'
'Sure. Must've been Saturday. At a café. There was something about her, that's why I noticed. I don't usually notice people, you know. But it was like, what's the word...? What's the word?'
'I don't really know what word you're trying to say.'
'Incognito,' she says, snapping her fingers. 'It was like she was a spy or something, that was why I noticed her. Head down, wearing a head scarf, like she was Taliban.' Yep, like the Taliban. 'But it must've been getting itchy, because she took it off one time, really scratched her hair. Didn't see me looking, but I see things when I want to see them. Then she put the scarf back on, and resumed what she was doing.'
'And what was she doing?'
'Drinking coffee, looking at her phone, same as everyone else.'
'You didn't mention this to either the sheriff or the feds?'
'I didn't mention I saw a woman looking at her phone?'

She laughs.

'Which café?'

'You going to go there and ask questions?'

'Probably.'

'You going to pull some moves?'

'What does that mean?'

'I've seen shows. You going to go over there and grab the guy serving coffee, slam his face onto the counter?'

I make a small hopeless gesture. I glance at the invisible camera, like I'm Guillermo in *What We Do In The Shadows*.

'Of course not.'

'I don't want you causing Harry any trouble.'

'I won't cause Harry any trouble. Where do I find Harry?'

'The Shuttershock.'

'OK, thanks, I know the Shuttershock. Nice place.'

'I know. Don't ruin it with any of your P.I. crap.'

'I'll try to keep my P.I. crap in check.'

'Best chowder on the north-east coast.'

'Al's Diner, Main Street, Glasgow,' I say.

'Really?'

'What time was this?'

'What time was what?'

'You saw Norah Wolfe at the Shuttershock.'

'Hmm. Late morning, maybe. Late morning. Don't know the time exactly. I was back here 'bout lunchtime.'

'Anything else remarkable about her?'

'Such as?'

'Did she meet anyone? Did she talk to anyone on the phone? Was she there so long she was there when you arrived, and still there when you left?'

'That.'

'She was there for the entire duration of your stay, no sign of leaving.'

'It was like she'd moved in.'

'Was it busy?'

She laughs again. At some point she's accepted we're in a conversation, and stepped outside, closing the door behind her. She doesn't look cold, though I don't know how that can be.

'That place is never busy. Maybe a warm Sunday in August. Maybe Labor Day weekend. That's about it.'

'You remember who was serving that day?'

'Harry's always serving. It's Harry's café. That's his life, poor bastard.'

'And you haven't see this woman,' and I have to bring the picture back up on the phone, 'you haven't seen her on the island?'

'I don't think so.'

I look around at the other properties.

'None of these places look properly closed up for the winter,' I say.

'Look at the detective.'

'They're all occupied at various times over the season?'

'Most of them are empty most of the time, but people lie to themselves. They don't shutter up, they don't turn off the electric, they don't turn off the water. I'll be back out in a coupla weeks, I'll be back over the holidays, I'll come for the weekend, yadda, yadda, yadda, and then they vanish after Labor Day and turn up here six months later and hope the sky hasn't fallen. That's who people are.'

I turn, I look over my shoulder in the direction of the film set, but the rise in the middle of the island, while insignificant, is just enough to hide the shoot from view.

'You been over there to watch the movie?'

'Sure, I went over. I'll tell you what, Mr Private Eye, it ain't no spectator sport.'

'Can be a little dull sometimes,' I say, and she nods. 'You see anything exceptional? Any arguments, anything out of the ordinary, anything you might not expect to see?'

'I saw a guy chasing people carrying a ball on the end of a stick,' she says caustically.

'I saw that too.'

'I see what you're doing here,' she says, her tone shifting. 'You reel me in with talk of the Shuttershock, and some woman you might not even be interested in for all I know, but what you're really after is the same thing as the sheriff. What'd you see on the movie set? Well, I'm telling you the same thing I told them. Nothing. I'm getting cold.'

She turns away, back into the house, door closed, and just like that the interview is over.

I don't bother knocking again.

46

I turn away and start walking by the other homes. The other property I know to be occupied does not currently have a light showing. Curtains still closed in a couple of the rooms. Just gone ten-thirty in the morning. Well, if you've come here to shut yourself off from the world, you might not have too much reason to drag your ass out of bed.

I walk past that one, then head away from the shoreline, through the three rows of homes, towards the middle of the island.

From here I can see a little of the equipment on the other side, and every now and again a shout carries in the wind. I turn back and look over the ten homes between me and the sea.

I'm not here, of course, to learn anything about Norah Wolfe. What I just found out there, from yoga woman in white, was entirely unexpected. One of those curious coincidences that come up out of nowhere. Perhaps that's it. That's the thing my intuition was telling me to come here for. After all, it's pretty damned important. Norah Wolfe was alive two days ago. Everyone else might think she's missing, but she knows exactly where she is.

What is she doing? Who is she hiding from? Who is she with?

I'm not going to find answers out here, though. And since I'm here, and it'll be at least two hours until the boat heads back to the mainland, I may as well snoop around. That is, after all, why I came in the first place.

I identify the house to break into straight away. If someone hung around on the island in order to murder Roxanne Baudot, then they would have had to hide somewhere no one is looking to collect stragglers from. And there's one locked-up house that's completely hidden by other houses from the two that are occupied.

Lockmaster pick in hand, I go to the rear entrance of the last house on the right at the back. Casual look around to see if anyone's paying attention, quick check for any sign of a burglar alarm, and then I'm at the door, gloves off, and working on the first of the two locks.

A little longer than I would've liked, then I'm inside, door closed, and standing in a small porch. Shoes off, gloves back on, then open the door and I'm straight into the large kitchen/diner, with a great view over the bay to the mainland. I mean, not so great now, what with the weather being this bleak, but that'll be decent on a sunny day.

I go through this first room, but there's nothing significant leaping off the page. Get a feeling perhaps that there's something amiss, but I can't put my finger on it. One of those insubstantial niggles that refuses to reveal itself. So I stand in the middle of the room, like I'm trying to work out the last clue in the crossword, before giving up, and moving on.

Then through the house, room by room, the place furnished simply to accompany the classic, New England clapperboard style. Floorboards and furniture in rustic white. Whitewashed walls. The art is all of the sea, though it's a little too cute for me. Sailboats and perfect harbours, flags blowing in a gentle breeze. What Edward Hopper would've done had he been commissioned by Hallmark. Two bedrooms, one bathroom, one large closet, the sitting room. The closet filled with all the necessary equipment for fun summer holidays. Paddle boards, an inflatable kayak, a basketball, a stand-alone hoop, a football, a neat pile of laundered swimming costumes.

Back in the sitting room, I stand back from the window and look out over the view. Facing the fact I'm going to have to do in Manchester what I did four days ago in Salem. Manchester is at least a little smaller, with far fewer tourist spots. And, of course, since Wolfe would appear to be laying low, then she's unlikely to have been seen too much in public. I can start with Harry at the Shuttershock, and take it from there.

Nevertheless, I have to accept I haven't made an awful lot of progress, this one, accidental find aside. Five days in, and I have questions and not a lot of answers.

I look around, plonk myself down on a pale sofa, and take out the small notebook that I carry around in my coat pocket, think over the case for a minute or two, then start making a list.

Why did Norah Wolfe leave?
Where is Norah Wolfe staying?
What went on between Wolfe and Baudot?

Where does Thomas Riddick fit into the narrative?
What's the story with the damaged hull of the Newport 65 and is it connected to the Bel Air?

Stop for a moment, think it over, pencil tapping on the edge of the notebook. There seems so much I don't know, but when I narrow it down like this, I'm struggling to think of it.

Then I think to add *Who is Norah Wolfe*? That seems significant as well. I've been asking around, and showing people her picture, but I have no idea who she actually is, beyond her IMDb page.

OK, where do we start? If she's hiding out in Manchester – and wearing a scarf around her head in a café sounds like she might be hiding – she's unlikely to be staying at a hotel. Airbnb seems more likely.

How many Airbnb properties can there be in Manchester? I go to the site and check.

A tonne, it seems.

OK, so we don't know if she's rented a car, but as far as we know she doesn't have one, and so she's liable to have stayed near the centre of town. That narrows it down. Then we can exclude properties that are available for rental right now, assuming she hasn't left in the last two days.

In the centre of Manchester there are currently twenty-seven occupied Airbnb properties. But let's be smart. She's a woman on her own, or at most perhaps, staying with someone else. Thomas Riddick for all we know. She only needs one bedroom. And bleak midwinter or not, places in Manchester ain't a cheap rent.

That narrows it down to four. OK, four is doable.

So, who is Norah Wolfe?

I spent an hour or two on her social media at the start, and found little to identify her beyond the usual whims and interests of her generation, learning little more about her than I knew at the start.

Her dad and stepmother died in a murder suicide, that was the story from Karlsen, and I never bothered checking that out. Something else to be followed up.

That'll do for now.

Damn.

From nowhere the peculiarity that the back of my head identified as soon as I entered the house, finally finds its way to the front of my head, and I get up and walk through to the kitchen.

The coffee machine is plugged in. Everything else is unplugged, everything about the house says that when the owners leave, they make a point of shutting it down, regardless of whether they intend coming back a couple of weeks later. Except the coffee machine is plugged in. Which means they forgot about it as they left, or someone was here and made themselves a cup of coffee.

Far more likely it was that person who forgot to unplug the coffee machine.

I check the bins. No coffee pods. They weren't that dumb. I check the cupboard. A great cache of pods. No one would miss one.

If someone was here, they'll have left something of themselves behind, somewhere in the house.

I start with the bathroom.

The bathroom is perfectly white, and I find what I'm looking for the minute I put myself to the task. There's half-used toilet roll, there's a half-used bottle of liquid soap. Easy enough to use the facilities, and leave no trace. The water hasn't been turned off, why wouldn't you use the bathroom?

Except the person who did that, stood in front of the mirror, they looked at themselves, they had time to kill, they dried their hands on their trousers perhaps, then they ran a still-damp hand through their hair, they decided that, hey, they looked all right that day, and then they stepped out of the bathroom, and they didn't notice they'd left a single hair behind on the floor. Perhaps it hadn't even reached the floor by the time they left the bathroom.

But it's here now.

47

I make a couple of calls, have a careful check of the house to make sure I've not made the same mistake as the previous burglar, check the surrounding area as best I can to make sure I can leave as surreptitiously as I entered, and then I'm outside again, and walking quickly up the small hill behind the village, to where the film crew are in action.

I'm here because Curtain asked me to come, but he'll have forgotten, I think. Either way, he won't care whether or not I'm here, and I've no intention of seeking him out. I'm at the familiar *not sure who I can trust* stage. Really, one should start every investigation with that attitude.

They're filming a scene where Ryan the lead and four others are sitting around a campfire, the fire blowing wildly in the wind. Ryan's having an argument with one of the men, and obviously they're about to start punching each other. As the scene plays out, the three not involved in the argument see something behind, and they have to react to a blank bit of ocean, while Ryan and Man B come to blows, unaware there's a leviathan emerging from the sea.

I'm more interested in the crew, and specifically the ones not directly involved in filming. There are a few people, set back from the action, spread around the periphery of the scene, with one sweep of the island behind the actors kept clear.

I approach a young lad, who's standing with his back to the scene – though really it's with his back to the wind – looking through notes on a clipboard. He glances up at my approach, then ignores me.

'Make-up?' I ask, and he looks up again, doesn't recognise me, which seems to make no difference, he turns, scans the area, then points to a couple of women huddled together with cups of coffee, sitting on camping chairs, watching the action, two large boxes next to them, presumably containing everything they need for this mini-location shoot. An older woman wearing a bright pink puffer jacket, and a younger woman with a fringe so short it contravenes the laws of hairdressing.

I walk vaguely in their direction, watching the action, then, as I get closer, I turn towards them, a couple of steps, phone in hand.

'Hey, how are we doing?' I ask.

'Hey,' says Pink Puffer. Short Fringe smiles curiously.

I hold the phone forward.

'I was wondering if either of you recognised this man?'

They look at the image of the guy with the beard in the bar, and it's obvious straight from the off.

Pink Puffer studies it, face a little blank, then she looks up, smiles again, and says, 'Nope, sorry. Is this to do with Roxanne's murder?'

Short Fringe? She knows. She feels seen. She feels busted. Nevertheless, she's primed for this. She's been told someone might ask. 'Never seen him,' she says.

There's a reason she's in make-up and not part of the cast.

'Thanks very much,' I say.

'You're the private detective?' asks Short Fringe.

'I am. Sam Vikström.'

'You're investigating Roxanne's murder?' repeats Pink Puffer.

'Looking for Norah Wolfe,' I say.

'I thought she left?'

'She did leave, but she's kind of vanished thereafter. I'm just trying to find her for someone.'

'Oh, OK.'

She doesn't really know what to do with that, and she repeats, 'Oh, OK.'

The guilty party is quiet, watching me warily.

I show the photograph again to Pink Puffer, who doesn't really know what's going on here.

'What d'you think?'

'How'd you mean?'

'Does this beard look natural?'

Short Fringe gives her a side-eye, then turns away, teeth working.

'Hmm. I guess. You think this is a disguise?'

'It might be, yes.'

'Hmm,' she says, nodding. 'Yep, that'd be a nice job. Hey, we've got that somewhere, right, babe? That beard, and like, hair combo.' She laughs. 'Even those glasses.'

She looks at her colleague. Short Fringe is staring away across the ocean, attempting to make herself invisible.

'Oh,' says Pink Puffer, and she winces a little.

I look at Short Fringe. She runs her tongue over her teeth behind closed lips.

'Who are you covering for?' I ask.

Her partner is looking at her, brow furrowed. Silence from Short Fringe.

I look at the picture, wondering if this could be Brian Faraday. Nope, nose is too different. Unless that's a fake nose. Doesn't make sense. It's too small. Faraday's nose is prominent.

I show the picture to Pink Puffer again.

'You think this is just a fake beard and wig, or d'you think there might be, you know, other prosthetics going on?'

'I think maybe you should go,' she says, finally coming to the aid of her assistant.

I look at them both, gauging whether there's anything else to be gained from standing here, before deciding quickly there likely isn't.

'Thanks very much,' I say, embracing them with a smile, then I turn away.

I don't hear what they say on my departure. I don't turn back.

A few yards away, I take a moment to look at the filming, currently between takes. Yoga woman isn't wrong. It's not a spectator sport.

I walk back down the other side of the island, to where the tethered boat judders against the jetty. Of the three crew, one of them is on board, while the captain and the other guy seem happy to stand on the jetty, looking at the sea, chatting, drinking from large flasks, which was where I left them, an hour ago.

'You all right?' says the captain. 'You've got a better colour,' he adds, then he laughs.

'Terrific,' I say. 'When are you heading back over?'

'Had word from the boss,' he says, indicating in the direction of the shoot. 'They're wrapping a little earlier than intended, so the first trip back has been deemed surplus to requirements. So we're here for another two, maybe three hours, then we head back, quick turnaround, back out here, second trip, place should be cleared.' He looks at his watch. 'Let's say, we can get you off around two-ish.'

Crap.

I turn away, I look back in the direction of the movie set, then I look over the sea between here and the Manchester inlet.

It looks exactly the same as it did a couple of hours ago when I came over here.

Shit, shit, shit.

Heart in my mouth out of nowhere. You'd think having made the trip, and not died, three times in the past few days, I might be getting used to it. Think on.

'I need to get back now,' I say.

The captain smiles, I think sympathetically.

'Nothing I can do for you, unless you want to speak to Mrs Karlsen and get authorisation.'

I shake my head, and look at the sea. I want to ask him if he thinks the water will be a little less rowdy in a few hours, but I'm not going to. I don't want to be tempted to wait.

'I'll give you a thousand dollars to take me back now,' I say.

His brow furrows, he looks more curious than surprised. Then he indicates the other two.

'A thousand each, or between us?' he asks, laughing.

'Between you. Another couple of hundred if you tell Mrs Karlsen you had to return to the island for other business. It'll be ninety minutes there and back, you'll be here in plenty of time to start loading up. And the first trip is mainly bodies, isn't it, so you don't need to be berthed too far in advance.' A pause, and then I add, 'You have loads of time. Give you something to do.'

'There's that,' he says.

He turns, he looks at the others, eyebrows raised.

One of them shrugs a *why not?*, the other says, 'I'm in.'

The captain looks at me, he says, 'Sure thing, let's do it. You can throw in another hundred for the fuel.'

'Sounds a lot,' I say, my feet starting to drag me to the boat.

'Take it or leave it,' he says, smiling, and I acquiesce with a rueful nod.

'You wanna steer?' he asks.

'Why in God's name would I do that?'

'Take your mind off the fear. Give you an activity.'

I do at least give that two second's worth of thought, then say, 'I think we'd all be terrified if I'm driving. I'm going to do what I did coming over here.'

'Curl up in fear,' he says, smiling. 'You go right ahead.'

48

Back on dry land, I call Sal. Same request as the previous day, running photographs through Epox-17, see if we can get a match on the guy with the beard. This time, all the principal players from the movie. There was something about the look on that girl's face. If she'd been doing that make-up on some junior member of the crew, or some D-lister on the cast, she wouldn't have been as uncomfortable. This, though, this was fear. She'd been busted, and she was worried what that was going to do for her career.

I start with Ryan, the star, and Curtain, the director, and dig up seven other seniors on the creative and business front who've been here on the production throughout. I have no idea why someone would disguise themselves in order to meet Norah Wolfe, but let's start with trying to find out who it could've been.

*

I've come to the Shuttershock. Don't come here so often. It has a different feel than the usual New England café. Darker. As soon as Yoga Woman said she'd seen Norah Wolfe in here, it made sense.

It has the familiar two large windows at the front, but they're north facing, with the hardware store just across the narrow street, so the café doesn't get a huge amount of light. It's also deep set, so that the back of the place is far removed from the front, with only a small side window for natural light. Harry, when setting up the café, obviously decided to embrace the vibe, with natural, dark wood floorboards and furnishing.

Norah Wolfe will come here, and she will sit at the back, and she will keep her head down.

The place is not busy, only four other tables occupied, none of them by Norah Wolfe. Two people behind the counter. Harry, who's in his late fifties, and a young woman, who looks like she's going to be Harry's daughter.

'What can I do you for?' says Harry.

Harry looks exactly like the kind of person who would say *what can I do you for?*

'Cup of regular coffee, hot milk, and…,' and I search the array of pastries beneath the glass panel in the counter, and say, 'The apricot Danish, thanks.'

'Coming right up, Mr Vikström,' he says, and he immediately turns away to the coffee machine.

I look at his daughter, brow creased, and she smiles as I mouth, 'How does he know that?'

'You've been here before?' she asks.

'Once,' I say. 'About three years ago.'

'Daddy remembers everyone, don't you?' she says, and he laughs, as he starts to practise his barista sophistry.

'You remember the date?' I ask, a little dubiously.

'Now that would be silly,' he says, looking over his shoulder, then he can't keep it up, and he laughs. 'Saw your face in the paper last year,' he says. 'That drama when the fella fell offa the lighthouse.'

'Oh, that,' I say.

I didn't like that my name got in the paper, but fortunately it wasn't particularly widely talked about, damned fine drama though it ended up being.

He laughs again, his daughter sees to the pastry.

The grind and the skoosh of the coffee machine, then he says, 'Hot milk, you said?' and I say, 'Please,' and he says, 'Roger Roger,' and his daughter rolls her eyes, and then I'm handing over a ten-dollar bill, and she's giving me the change, and Harry's putting the coffee on the counter.

'Regular coffee, hot milk,' he says.

'Thanks.'

Just as I'm about to retreat, deciding I'll save the inquisition until my feet are a little further under the table, he leans into the counter, after a conspiratorial glance around the café.

'You here working a case?' he asks, his voice low.

Harry's low voice will still be loud enough to hear for anyone who wants to listen.

'Dad!' says the kid. 'Don't be so nosey.'

Well, he's given me an in.

'That's OK,' I say. 'Actually, I'm looking for someone in

town, but I'm just here for a break.'

'Who're you looking for?' he asks, and the kid can't help her own curiosity.

'Really, it doesn't matter, I don't want to trouble you,' I say, lifting the coffee and the Danish.

'S'up to you, son,' he says, 'but we see everyone through here. Your call.'

He laughs, I give in. Lay down the coffee and Danish, take out my phone, open the picture of Norah Wolfe, which I look at for a moment as though reluctant to show it, then lay the phone on the counter and push it towards them.

They look at it, neither expression changes, but they can't hide the recognition in their eyes, then they look at each other, then back to me. As he does so, Harry pushes the phone back across the counter.

'What's the story?' he says.

I look curiously at him, like I'm disbelieving she might have been in the Shuttershock.

'She's been here?' I ask.

'What's the story?'

'Not much of one,' I say. 'She was working on the movie that's been filming up in Glasgow.'

'Oh, *Leviathan*,' says the kid. 'That looks so cool.'

'Doesn't it?' I say. 'Anyway, she abruptly left the set last Monday. No believable reason given, and off she went. She told the producer she was fine, was just feeling a bit stressed by it.' I shrug. 'That's the story, really, except her mother's worried about her. Can't get hold of her, thinks maybe something's happened, asked me to look into it.'

'Her mom,' says Harry, nodding, then he adds, 'You can always rely on moms,' and gives the daughter a smile, like they're in some godawful movie.

'Is it anything to do with the death of that girl over on Rake's?' asks the kid, having played her part in the brief, heart-warming mom affirmation moment.

'Doesn't seem to be any connection. Guess we'll just have to wait and see how it plays out. At the moment, I just need to find Norah, that's all, so I can let her mum know she's all right.'

Harry assesses me for another few seconds, and then accepts I'm on the side of the good guys. At this stage, I'm still not sure whose side I've been taken on by, but at least my intentions would meet Harry's approval.

'She's been here every day this past week. Sometimes twice a day. It's like, I don't know where the girl's staying 'n all, but it's like she doesn't do any cooking, doesn't make herself so much as a cup of coffee, or a Kraft. She comes in here, she has breakfast or lunch. Reckon she'd eat supper here too if we were still serving that time of the evening.' He pauses, then adds, 'Seems kind of lonely to me.'

'I reckon she's waiting for something,' says the kid. 'Or someone. Like in a movie.'

'Has she been in here already today?' I ask.

'You missed her by an hour, maybe more,' says Harry. 'She might be back, she might not. You can sit here and wait, if you like.'

I look outside, think about the direction of the street, and where it leads, and about the location of the four Airbnb's I'm guessing she might be renting.

'Any idea whereabouts she's staying?' I ask, and Harry shakes his head.

'You know which direction she comes from?'

He gives this a moment, but only because he's considering whether he's talking too much about one of his regular customers, then he decides that maybe this isn't giving so much away, and indicates to the right.

'She comes along from Main Street, she heads back along to Main Street,' he says.

'Thank you,' I say, nodding to them both. 'Hopefully, I'll be able to put Norah's mum's mind at ease.'

I smile. Harry, reading something in my tone or my look, seems a little troubled, like he knows he's said too much. It's done now, my friend.

I nod, then take the coffee and Danish to a table by the window.

49

'Hey,' I say.

A pause. I can see Elise making the necessary adjustment to her id on the other end of the phone.

'Hey.'

'You OK?'

'Zippity-ding-dong,' she says. A moment, then she adds, 'No idea where that came from. As fine as I'm going to be. You OK?'

'Yeah. Business call, sorry.'

'That's OK. I won't say we can't use your help on this. Would be nice to get it wrapped before this Agent Cameron arrives. Got a bad feeling about her. What can I do for you?'

'Need you to run a check on someone, if you can. Rebecca Karlsen.'

'You're checking up on the woman who's paying your fee? Very trusting.'

'This is where we are,' I say.

'You got anything on her other than her name?'

'I've got some detail from IMDb, but not a huge amount. Born Los Angeles, March fifth, nineteen-seventy-one. No details of family, or marital status, though she says she's Norah Wolfe's mother. That's all I've got.'

'She *says* she's Norah Wolfe's mother. That's a shift.'

'I have my doubts.'

'I'll run a check, see where it gets us.'

'She also told me that Wolfe's father and stepmother died in a murder suicide three years ago.'

'I'll take a look. Anything else?'

'That's it for the moment,' I say.

'K.'

A pause, which she quickly brings to a close.

'I'll let you know,' she says.

'Thanks.'

I lay the phone down, and look out of the window.

With the abrupt end to the call, the way things are going to be, I feel a moment of crushing romantic despair.

Wasn't it always going to be this way? Weren't we always Springsteen's lovers in *Hungry Heart*? *We fell in love, I knew it had to end...* Didn't really matter whether it was because I met someone else, or Byron found out and made Elise choose, or kicked her out and she couldn't live with herself, or one of us grew tired of the other. Nearly five years of an illicit relationship, with neither of us making any move to change anything, something was bound to happen sometime.

My phone rings. Petty Officer Second Class Jenkins.

'Hey.'

'Thought I'd give you an update, Mr Vikström,' she says, by way of hello.

'You can call me Sam, you know.'

'Let's keep this on a business footing. My daughter still occasionally tells me I should marry the dinosaur man, and I don't want to give her any encouragement.'

'Mr Vikström it is.'

'First off, the *Newport 65* does indeed belong to Thomas Riddick, though under the name Leighton Holmes. Otherwise, however, I'm afraid your theory doesn't stand up. The boat's been berthed there for the past three weeks, and putting pieces together, the yardmaster thinks it was likely damaged during the storm on Thursday evening.'

'The night Roxanne Baudot was murdered.'

'That's correct.'

'You think he was out on Rake's Island?'

'It must be a possibility. We're on it, Mr Vikström, and the sheriff's office has been notified. I'm just doing you the favour of letting you know you can stop conflating the sinking of the *Bel Air* with whatever it is that's going on here.'

'And has Riddick been seen at the boatyard since Thursday?'

'He has not.'

'So, the boat is damaged in the storm, he manages to get it back to the yard, then he disappears.'

'Looks like it.'

A natural pause, I consider telling her I've found Norah Wolfe, but she's not going to care, and so I let it go.

'Thanks for the update,' I say.

'You're welcome.'

She ends the call.

The *Bel Air* thing has been hanging around on the periphery. An unsolved mystery, which could have all manner of mundane answers. But its proximity to this mystery has had me conflating the two, an unnecessary complicating factor. This doesn't completely rule it out, but it feels like it's time to move on.

Pieces are beginning to fall into place, and it's just as helpful when you can discard one.

Take the last of the Danish, finish the coffee, and now it's time to get on with the day. Return the cup and plate to the counter, as there's no one waiting, say, 'Thanks,' to Harry's daughter, as Harry isn't currently in situ, she's says, 'You're welcome,' then throws in a 'Good luck,' and I say, 'Thanks,' again, and then I'm off out into the world to fearlessly continue the investigation.

50

Collar up, beanie on, I take to the streets of Manchester-by-the-Sea, looking for signs of Norah Wolfe. Too early to speak to her, but I need to find out where she is, without her knowing that I've found out where she is.

I speak to people in the vicinity of the properties in my narrowed-down Airbnb list. Could be wasting my time – she could have rented from someone other than Airbnb, she could be staying somewhere else and just happens to come into Manchester every day, because she has business I know nothing about – but sometimes you get a feeling, and you know it's going to pan out.

There will be no absolute negatives here. Just because no one's seen her go in and out of an apartment or a house, doesn't mean she hasn't been. Plenty of people go through life completely unobserved.

'You know this woman?' I ask a guy in a small store.

He looks at me a little warily at first, then looks at the picture of Norah Wolfe.

Almost an hour since I left the Shuttershock. Drew a blank on the first two properties. With the first, in fact, it was almost impossible to find anyone to ask, with it being a quiet, residential street. I doorstepped three houses across the road, and that did not go well. The position of the second property was a little more promising, but no one had anything to give. And so we're on to property number three. A corner apartment, in a converted house, one block away from Main Street. An elegant, well-looked after building, the panel by the front door indicating there are now six apartments inside.

A busy street, a row of shops across the road. The woman in the bookshop was unable, or unwilling, to help.

The guy in the grocery story makes a small gesture to the photograph.

'Sure, I do. That's whatshername, ain't it?' He snaps his fingers. 'The King Kong lady.'

'What?'

'The actress, the one in the movie with King Kong.' Snaps his fingers again. 'Naomi Watts.' He smiles. 'You conducting some kind of, I don't know, market research on audience recognition of, you know, Miss Watts?'

'This isn't Naomi Watts.'

'Oh.'

He looks back at the image, studies it a little more closely, then nods.

'Yeah, good call,' he says. 'Who's this?'

'Her name's Norah Wolfe...'

'Never heard of her. What's she been in?'

'She's not an actress. She's a missing person, and I'm trying to find her. Have reason to believe she's staying in Manchester, and I'm asking around, see if anyone's seen her in town.'

'You a cop?'

'P.I.'

He looks away from the photograph, studying me a bit more closely.

'You're an actual P.I.?'

I'm enjoying his levels of incredulity.

'Yes.'

'You got ID?'

I pull out my ID, hold it open, let him read it.

'Huh,' he says after a few moments. 'Never talked to a P.I. before.'

'So, have you seen her?'

'Well, I think so, but now I'm wondrin', I'm wondrin', is this just the power of suggestion? Because she sure as heck looks like *somebody*, I just can't for the life of me figure out who that is. You come in here asking if I've seen her around town, and presumably you haven't just picked Manchester outta thin air, which means she likely *is* here, somewhere.'

He looks back at the photograph, lips pursed. His concentration face. A few moments, and then we get another finger snap.

'Dammit,' he says. 'I knew I'd seen her someplace.' Then he laughs, looking at me like I should be reading his mind. I ask the question with raised eyebrows, already know what's coming – because I have in fact read his mind – then his smile goes, and he says, 'Hang on a second. How'd I know you're one of the good guys? Maybe *you* don't even know if you're one of the good guys. You think you're helping the girl get found, but in fact, the people who've got you doing this, they're the villains.'

Not many people use the word villain anymore.

'I'm aware of the potential conflict,' I say. 'So, I'll do what I do every time I'm in this position. I find the girl, I tell the girl her mum's looking for her, I give her the option. If the girl says she doesn't want to speak to her mum, then we're good. I'll tell the mum she's fine, she's whatever, and then I bow out.'

'This sounds like it might be a sad story,' says the guy.

'They usually are.'

'That a fact?'

'The P.I.s in the shows, it's all murder and car chases and guns. In real life...'

'And women,' interjects the guy.

'Exactly. Women. In real life, most stories are just a little bit sad, that's all. Husbands cheating on wives, kids running away from home. Had to look for some guy's lost dog a couple of weeks ago.'

No, I didn't.

'Did you find the lil' pupper?'

'Turned out his wife had accidentally run over it in the car, and hadn't been able to bring herself to tell him.'

'Damn. There's a story.'

'Like I say, sad. Have you seen the girl?'

He's nodding now, having decided he's going tell me.

'That's the dumbest thing. She's been here. She's been in here. Been living right across the street, came in here last week. Just the once, but I seen her across the road couple times since then.'

'When was the last time?'

'Don't know.' He looks to the ceiling for answers, can't find them there. 'Nope. Someday, end of last week.'

'OK, thanks very much.'

I slip the phone back into my pocket.

I've looked at the property on Airbnb, and know that it's one at the front of the building. First floor, overlooking this street. If she's sitting up there, keeping an eye out, she may well have seen me come in, but she won't have noticed that I'm standing chatting with the big guy here. Too far into the shop to be seen from the first floor.

'I can't get you to promise anything, and no reason why

you should,' I say, 'but if she comes back in, I'd be grateful if you didn't say anything.'

'Damn, don't you worry, my friend. I tell her you've been asking, I'd end up admitting I told you where she was. She ain't going to like that.'

''preciate it.'

I turn to go, beanie pulled down a little lower over my forehead.

'How'd he take it?' asks the guy, and I turn back.

'How'd you mean?'

'The guy whose wife accidentally killed the dog. How'd he take the news?'

'His wife begged me to not tell him. I thought that was probably best all round. So I told him there'd been a report of a dog meeting the description, living his best life in the woods way up, beyond Concord, like it was heading for Canada or something.'

'He buy that?'

'I don't think so, but he wanted to. Gave him something to cling to when he needed it.'

'Goddam,' he says, shaking his head.

And I leave before I have to embellish that particular piece of unnecessary fiction any further.

51

Two things in quick succession, as the case begins to fall into place.

I get the results of the Epox-17 check back from Sal, and I was right. Eight big fat negatives, and one result more or less bang on the money, >98% accuracy.

So, what was Laurence Curtain doing in a fake beard with Norah Wolfe?

Then Elise calls back.

I'm sitting in another café at the end of the block where Norah Wolfe is staying. The Happy Clam, on Hamilton. I'm just here for the view, though I might also be here for quite a long time. For the moment I have a cup of green tea, and that's it.

'Hey.'

'Well, as I presume you might've been expecting,' says Elise, 'the woman who's asked you to find her daughter, does not appear to have a daughter.'

'OK, thanks. And the murder-suicide?'

'Interesting case. Suspected murder-suicide, but with an asterisk against it. Some possibility that it was just a plain old murder by a third party. Could've gone either way, but ultimately there were no suspects, and the case has gone the way of many a murder in this country.'

'So that was Wolfe's mum and dad, or was it really her stepmum?'

'Pretty sure it was the mom.'

I let out a long breath, looking out onto the street. The circumstantial evidence mounts.

'What are you thinking?' she asks.

'Still in the planning stage.'

'Sure, OK. Well, we have confirmation Agent Cameron reports for duty at nine tomorrow, so if you could have it sorted out by then, that'd be terrific. I hate it when those bums come in here and act like they own the joint.'

The phone vibrates in my hand.

'I'll let you know as soon as I've got something concrete,' I say.

'That'd be great. Me too.'

'Thanks.'

She hangs up. I look at the phone. A text from Natalie.

How's it looking? You OK to come over tonight?

Damn. I hadn't forgotten about that, I just hoped I'd have this all wrapped up, or *something*, so that tonight could happen. But I feel there might be other things to do.

The board is set, the pieces are moving, I type, then I delete it with an eyeroll, and go for:

Sorry, not sure. Might have to work. Will let you know asap.

A moment, then she replies, **OK**.

This is the trouble with the early stages. Now she's not sure I really want to come. She's thinking I'm having second thoughts about Elise, or maybe she thinks I think she herself is not that bothered because she went home early last night. We're in the tricky, misunderstanding period.

I think of replying with some grand gesture, like inviting her to Paris this weekend, or telling her I love her.

I stare blankly at the phone, not writing anything.

I make the final decision not to write anything, then immediately change my mind and type: **If not tonight, am free every night for the rest of the year,** one eye on the front of Norah Wolfe's building the whole time.

I took the precaution of making sure there wasn't a rear exit, as someone who's trying to remain incognito is liable to use a rear exit. There was no rear exit.

Then I type **If you are x**, and she replies, **Will consult my diary x**, and I choose to take that as gentle teasing and reply with the heart, and that should be that for now, and I can stop having this dumb love angst.

Phone pushed to the side, cup of tea in hand, self-doubt and self-loathing in check, I look along the road to the front of the building.

Lift the tea, take another drink. Place the mug back on the table. Push the phone a little further away. Settle in for the long haul, one brain cell on the matter of what I'm going to do if Wolfe hasn't left her apartment by the time this place closes at five p.m.

*

As it is, Norah Wolfe leaves her apartment at just after four p.m. I watch her walk away from me, in the direction of Main Street and the harbour, until she's out of sight, and then I quickly get to my feet and leave the café.

52

This is a nice Airbnb. Small, but perfect for one person to hole up in.

I've no idea how long I've got, but I'm contemplating waiting here. Not sure if that's the best play at the moment. She finds out I'm here, she might just run. But then, I'm not sure what else my client is wanting of me.

Why am I here if not just for my own curiosity? My brief was to find out where Norah Wolfe is staying. Well, I've found her.

In any case, not unexpectedly, there's nothing to see here. This is not Norah Wolfe's apartment, so all she's brought of herself is the bag she would've had at the Market Square hotel.

I go through the bag, and what's been unpacked of her things, in the bedroom. Little of interest. On top of the bedside table, a pair of earbuds, a bracelet, a headband, a copy of *All The Lovers In The Night* by Meiko Kawakami. A few folded-up receipts. A packet of Wrigley's Doublemint.

Receipts are the kind of fool's gold that a detective's life is made of. They can send you off in all sorts of ridiculous directions. Nevertheless, I fold them out and take a look.

One from the grocery store across the road. Cereal, bagels, cheese, beer, coffee pods. A couple of receipts for the Shuttershock, eleven dollars, and seventeen dollars. A receipt from a maritime hardware store. Purchased item unidentified. Seven hundred and seventy-nine dollars.

I hold that in my hand, think about it, and then slip it into my pocket. Right there I'm letting her know that someone's been in her apartment, but I feel like that's not going to be important. She's dumped these here, and they'll likely all end up in the bin.

In any case, maybe I will just stick around and wait for her.

Back through to the sitting room. Still daylight outside and it will be for a while, but the grey is dark and grim, the light levels low, the sun low in the sky and behind thick layers of cloud, and the sitting room is gloomy. Cannot put on a light, however.

Go through all the drawers. Turn on the TV to see the last station that was watched, or any shows she's halfway through streaming, then quickly turn the TV off, having learned nothing. Into the kitchen, through the drawers.

I have more than I thought I'd get coming here anyway. Receipts for seven hundred and seventy-nine dollars don't usually fall out of the sky. Stand in the kitchen for a moment, contemplating staying here while searching through Dick's Maritime Store's website to see what might've cost seven hundred and seventy-nine dollars, or whether I should just remove myself, go to Dick's, or go home to do my research. Still formulating a working plan for bringing this to an end, when there's the sound of a key in the door.

A brief moment of heart in mouth, and then I curse myself.

'Jesus, just speak to the woman,' I mutter, and I return to the sitting room, and sit down, waiting for her to come in.

The door opens, the door closes. Footsteps in the hallway, and then the door to the sitting room opens.

Thomas Riddick stops in the doorway. Something about him that says he shouldn't be here, any more than I should.

'The fuck are you?' I say, aiming to be the first one to act like I'm where I'm supposed to be.

Caught unawares, he doesn't have an immediate answer.

'Looks like I might be in the wrong apartment,' he says, which is pretty weak for a triple murderer. You'd expect him to be ballsier.

'You looking for Norah Wolfe?'

He doesn't answer that. The gormlessness leaves his face, replaced by annoyance, he scowls, then he turns quickly, slams the door shut and runs.

Crap.

And then I'm up quickly and running after him, closing the door on my way out and taking the short flight of stairs three and four at a time.

53

Out onto Hamilton. He's got fifteen yards on me, racing past the antique shop and the woman's fashion store, and then he's turning onto Main Street. The streets are quiet, little traffic, few pedestrians. Get to the corner. Riddick still in sight, distance growing. Long legs, big stride. Past the Lighthouse Bar & Grill and the Pendulum Diner, past Maybole Antiques, and the most high class five & dime you've ever seen. Round the corner at Abercrombie, heading towards State. He crosses the road, times it wrong, gets clipped by a Toyota, sends him flying. A moment, he shakes it off, gets up, but it's too late. He starts to move, and I'm on him, grab his shoulder, bringing him to the ground. I fall on top of him, and he kicks me in the shin, pushes me off. Pain means nothing, the body all adrenaline and intent.

We get up, punches thrown. A miss, a hit. Another hit. No punch heavy enough to be decisive. He aims a kick at my balls, I turn, his foot grazes my thigh. Leaves him open, and I catch him more solidly in the jaw.

Dumb. Should've gone for the balls, throat or stomach. He takes the momentum from the blow, and returns it, fist at my throat. Doesn't quite catch it right, but it gives him a second's advantage, and he turns and runs. Catch my breath, contemplate giving it up, and then take off after him again.

Round the corner onto State, and then there she is, Norah Wolfe, twenty yards away, walking towards us. She looks curiously at Riddick as he approaches, and I call out, a mindless, 'Hey!' and she backs off a little at his approach, and then he's right by her, and running full pelt towards the harbour.

I make the decision as I get towards her, and choose to let him go. Thomas Riddick isn't my problem.

I stop beside Norah Wolfe, hands on my knees, panting. I'm reasonably fit, but like a footballer who's spent six months training in the gym, I'm not match-fit.

'What the fuck is going on?' she says. She looks curious, amused almost, but only in her lack of understanding.

'I was looking for you. Caught that guy coming out your apartment. Guess he shouldn't have been there, and when he saw me he ran.'

I straighten up, hand at my throat. Swallow. Pretty damned happy he didn't catch me properly, hurts bad enough as it is.

Take another few breaths. She's looking at me, still not sure what's going on.

'I don't even know who he is,' I say. 'He ran from me, so I ran after him. Detective's instinct. Then he hit me when I caught up with him.' I laugh at that, like it was such a dumb thing to have happened. 'You know him?'

She looks a little confused.

'I don't understand. Why were you even at my apartment? You're the cops?'

'P.I. I've been looking for you. Managed to track you down to that place.'

'What? Who hired you?'

'I don't know.'

Breath recovered. Now we're just standing in the street, as darkness falls, and I'm not sure either of us really knows what's playing out here. I look in the direction that Riddick ran, but there's no sign of him.

'How can you not know who hired you?'

'I work for an agency. Radstone-Kirk.' Reach into my pocket, produce my ID, which she looks at with continued bemusement. 'Clients often don't want to reveal themselves.'

We stand and look at each other, then she finally says, 'Great. What now?'

'I report back that I've found you and where you are.'

'What if I don't want to be found? I can just leave now, and whenever whoever's looking for me shows up, bingo, I'm gone. You'll come looking for me again?'

I take a breath, look up and down the street.

'Look,' I say, 'I'm always a little cautious with this. I'm supposed to find you, not make any contact, report back, then the client knows where you are and acts accordingly. But… I'm always wary when someone's looking for a young woman. Any woman, in fact. Sometimes it feels off, that's all.' I shrug. 'Made the call, especially after that other women from the movie crew was murdered, that I'd maybe interfere this time. Make sure you were OK to be found. Which, to be honest, I'm not entirely sure you will be.'

She lets out a long sigh, and then looks down the street in the direction Riddick took off.

'Damn,' she says.

'You knew that guy?'

'Look, we should talk,' she says. 'Come back to the apartment.' She laughs. 'You were coming there anyway, right?'

'Sure.'

'Don't have much food, but I've got coffee and a bottle of Jack.'

She smiles, and then we're walking back towards her apartment, taking it in turns to look over our shoulders.

54

Blinds closed, lights on low, she's walking around the apartment, checking it out. Looking in drawers, looking in her bag, making sure everything's where she left it, checking the items on her bedside table.

She comes back into the sitting room. I'm in a single armchair, sitting back, watching her. She gets a glass, pours herself a stiff shot of whisky, holding the bottle aloft.

'I'm good, thanks,' I say.

'You don't like Jack?'

'Nope.'

'Isn't Scotland like the home of whisky?'

'America's the home of mass shootings and corporate asset-stripping. You ever done either of those?'

'Fair,' she says, taking her first drink. 'It's this or coffee.'

'I'm good, thanks. You were telling me if you knew who that guy was,' I say.

She studies me, eyes narrowing a little, then she looks around, deciding where to sit, but it's not like there are many options, and she sits on the sofa, on the other side of the TV.

'Not taking your jacket off?' I ask.

'You wanting me to get undressed? Is that what this is about? You pretend to be concerned, then when it comes to it, all you're after is some twenty-three-year-old tits?'

'Really?'

'You're a P.I., right? Your life is women and alcohol and car chases, pulling a gun at the slightest sign of trouble.'

'You've been watching too many movies.'

She smiles, she crosses her legs, though she's wearing jeans, which rules out the full *Basic Instinct* manoeuvre.

'You carrying?' she asks.

Hmm. There's been a shift in the atmosphere. She doesn't trust me, and it's hard to read how she's playing this.

I pat my pockets.

'Left my PPK at home,' I say. 'I was on a stakeout. Didn't

think there would be any action.'

'Let's hope you don't need it then.'

'Are you going to tell me the story?' I ask.

'Which one?'

'You were working on the movie, everyone seemed to think you were happy, and then you upped and left. What happened?'

She takes a drink, lowers the glass. She swirls the liquor around. This girl is twenty-three going on forty. I don't have this much self-confidence, and I don't suppose I ever will.

'I was stressed. Just needed to get away for a while, that's all.'

'Why didn't you go home? You left the set, why stick around?'

'Maria's totally got this. But I felt a bit guilty, and there was part of me that was just like, I don't want to completely disappear in case there's some sudden emergency.' A pause, then she laughs. 'Though I have no idea what a storyboarding emergency would actually look like.'

'Where'd the stress come from?'

'You know the budget on this movie?'

'Read it was north of fifty million.'

'Closer to a hundred. They're going for a theatre release, so once you've racked up the marketing spend, the ad buy, all of that shit, you're north of two hundred million. That's a lot of money, even now, and when the people involved, the director, the producers, when they know they're in line for a cinema release, they know they can't fuck up.'

'Thought this was being done for GuLu+?'

'Sure, but Curtain's their new whatever. They've got him pegged as Del Toro multiplied by Michael Bay. They're all in on him, and this goes well, the sky's going to be the limit for that guy. So the producers are stressed, he's stressed, and that stress flows down through every level of the production.'

'I spoke to Laurence Curtain yesterday.'

She lifts her drink, takes a sip. I wondered if it would be a prop, something to hide behind, or something she could throw at me perhaps, but she's genuinely drinking it.

'Must have been lovely for you.'

'He certainly didn't seem stressed.'

She rolls her eyes, a small head shake.

'Who'd have thought Laurence Curtain could be such a

walking cliché? The man's near enough a psychopath, you know? He is whoever he needs to be, in any given situation. You should see him with the press. Jesus, they love him. You come snooping around, he's probably a little wary, you know. Doesn't want to be found out.' She makes a face, imagining the scandal. 'And so he'll have been perfectly pleasant.'

'What is there to find?'

We have the same routine every time I ask a question she doesn't want to answer. The pause, the slightly narrowed eyes, the pursed lips, then the lifting of the glass, and this time she takes more of a drink, then kind of chews it.

'So, how'd it play out with the guy you chased?' she asks. 'If you saw him at this apartment, you must've been inside the building already? How'd you get in?'

'There was a guy coming out as I arrived. He thought about it, then either decided I looked OK, or more likely, just thought he didn't feel like getting into an argument.'

'Then you came up here, and what? The guy was at the door, he was leaving the apartment?'

'He was leaving. Something about him. The look of the guilty.'

'I expect you've got a good instinct for that, in your line of work.'

'So I asked him if he'd been seeing you. Guess he read something in my eyes, that's when he ran. When I saw you in the street, I was pretty relieved. I'd wondered if something had happened to you. So I was chasing after him thinking, shit, I need to get back there.'

'Huh.'

She nods. Lifts the glass again. With every drink it seems the atmosphere chills a little further.

'You're not really a storyboarder, are you?' I say.

'No? What d'you think I am?'

'I'm curious,' I say, deciding I may as well play my part in getting to the point.

'Good attribute for a detective.'

'Since you spent a week past on Friday with the guy who just punched me in the face, I'm wondering why he ran right by you in the street. He didn't stop to say hello, didn't stop to make sure you'd be all right.'

Her face hardens at me electing to be the one who shifts the narrative of the conversation.

'I'm also curious,' she says. 'Was he really leaving this apartment, or were you the one who'd been through it? Because someone's been through it. Maybe it was him, or maybe it was you.' A pause, another drink, and then, 'I think it might've been you.'

'You first,' I say. 'Why'd he run right past you?'

'*Me first…*' She shakes her head, looking more than a little disappointed in me. 'Like we're in the schoolyard.'

She reaches a little uncomfortably inside her jacket and produces a gun. A Walther PPK. The exact same gun that I use, on the rare occasion I use it.

I get a slight thrill of fear at its introduction, though peanuts compared to choppy seas and wharf spiders. Which is dumb, of course, because chances are neither of those things will kill you. A Walther PPK on the other hand…

55

'You know what they say about guns in movies,' I say.

'What would that be?'

'Once you put the gun in a movie, you're going to have to use it. Why else is it there?'

'What makes you think I won't use it?'

'Nice line of work, by the way. Being a storyboarder not exciting enough for you?'

'We've all got our talents,' she says, smiling.

'You talented, or are you just cold-blooded?'

I get raised eyebrows at that, then a wry look, and, 'Maybe we'll find out.'

'Who's the guy?'

'Who's the guy?' she repeats.

She takes another drink. So she looks like she's right-handed, but she's disadvantaging herself by having the gun in her left hand. She'll still be able to fire it, of course, she can still put a bullet in my head, but there's a handicap there. It's just not as comfortable. Regardless of the closeness of the range, she ain't intending to use that thing just yet.

'Interesting question. Thing is,' she says, 'I think you already know.'

'How so?'

'You found me here. Sure, I obviously haven't locked myself in my bedroom, I've been around and about, but still. That's a nice bit of work. I think you might know what you're doing. And if you found me, and you know I was in Salem a week past Friday, then I think you're more than capable of finding out who that man is.'

'Let's say I have…' She laughs. 'My question remains valid. You spent the day with him in Salem, therefore you know each other. Why'd he run past you?'

'Sure, perfectly valid question. I don't know why he ran past me. You like that answer?'

'Really?'

'Really. I don't know. He knows me, he knows my name, he knows what I do, and off he went, high-tailing it down the street. He must've been pretty scared of *you*.'

Another drink. I'm just sitting here, she gets all the activities. Drawing the gun, taking the booze. Wouldn't mind a drink myself to hang on to.

'So, here's where I think you begin to lose control of the narrative,' I say, and she smiles. 'You're too cocky.'

'Oh, really. OK, OK, this should be good.'

'I was out on the island earlier today. I was wondering where someone might have hidden out while waiting to illicitly meet Roxanne, because they had unfinished business with Roxanne. Picked the house on the far right of the small settlement. And just like Indiana Jones in *Last Crusade*, I chose wisely.'

She smiles at the Indiana Jones reference.

'You are such a dweeb,' she says.

'You left one of your hairs in the bathroom. You were on the island, and you were in that house, hiding.'

She doesn't say anything to that.

'You've got that, you know, distinctive green whatever that is.'

'Dye,' she says, her voice with a tone of contempt it hasn't had before. 'It's called hair dye.'

'And here, in Manchester, you don't think anyone's going to find you, or that anyone will come snooping around, so you stay here with no precautions. You wander around town with little more than a scarf draped around your head. You happily sit in the same damn café *every day*. You're careless. And you leave receipts lying around, so that the casual observer of your life can find out you paid Dick's Maritime Store nearly eight hundred dollars, and one has to wonder what that was for.'

'One does,' she says coldly.

'I would wager it was to pay for some means by which you got out to Rake's Island, where you waited for Roxanne, then back off again after you'd killed her.'

Well, that gets all the cards on the table, doesn't it?

She sits back, she looks coldly across the room, and now we come to it. She slams back the rest of the drink, lays the glass on the floor, and then transfers the gun to her right hand.

'The last time a woman pointed a gun at me, I was saved by a capuchin monkey called Joey,' I say.

219

I get the full coldness of the stare – this girl is one hundred percent getting played by Sydney Sweeney when this gets made into a movie – then the slight, contemptuous head shake.

'I have no idea what to do with that,' she says. 'Who even are you?'

'I showed you my ID.'

'You don't seem real, somehow.'

'And yet I worked out you killed Roxanne.'

Her lips purse again, she neither confirms nor denies.

'All right, detective, why would I do that?'

My phone pings. I ask the question with a raised eyebrow, and she makes a small movement of the gun.

'I'm not done with you,' she says, 'so the first bullet isn't necessarily going in your forehead, but you take the phone out your pocket, your hand and your phone are getting a bullet put through them.'

The phone pings again.

I ignore it.

'You were seen with a bearded guy at the Seaside Shack, then back at the Market Square.'

'The beard was a little criminal, fair enough,' she says.

'Nice disguise.'

'Oh, yeah? Who'd you think was in disguise?'

I hold her in the moment, leave another beat, and another, then say, 'Laurence Curtain.'

She stretches her neck. Leans across herself to lift the whisky tumbler with her left hand, drains the dregs.

'This starts with Curtain,' I say. 'I thought it was Faraday, but it's not him. He's just a guy. Sure, he likes young women, but he doesn't mistreat young women. He's also likely expendable. Lots of people can make money. Indefinable artistic talent, however? Much rarer commodity. A studio isn't going to want to let that slip through their fingers when they've got hold of it. Question is, why does Laurence Curtain put on a disguise when he's hitting on women from the crew? Do they really not know it's him?'

She laughs. She gets to her feet, still keeping her distance, eyes still on me, gun still on me.

'Hey, I like this scene in the movie, the part where it all comes out,' she says. 'It's cute.'

A pause, while she gives herself a substantial refill, then she adds, her voice becoming theatrically colder, 'You're still going to die, though.'

'Did you know you were having sex with Laurence Curtain?' I ask, and she laughs again, as she sits down.

Thought about making a move there, when she was pouring the drink, but it's too early. And the longer this goes, the more she drinks, the better my chances.

'*Everyone* knows they're having sex with Laurence.'

She slurps the drink, grimaces a little, then sets it back. Again, the glass is in her right hand. She watches me, wondering how far to take this. While I consider that I'm playing for time, she's likely doing the same thing. Contemplating her options. A gun shot ringing out in a small town, probably isn't her best case scenario at this stage.

'Three, four movies ago, I don't know when it started. He was hitting on some girl. You know the score. She said no. He didn't like that. He pulled some moves, he threatened her career, he did what he could, but that girl still said no. Laurence, though, he's born and bred in the classics. He decides to pull some Shakespeare level shit. He goes in disguise to woo his prey. God knows how he pulled it off, but it worked. Word gets around. The girl's part in it is forgotten, but everyone thinks Laurence is pretty funny. Laurence is one cool motherfucker. It became Laurence's thing. A couple times during every shoot, he'll pull that shit. Fake whatever, go on the prowl.'

'And everyone knows who he is?'

'Been a long time since someone didn't see him coming, I expect.'

'What about Roxanne?'

The cold look again, the slurp at the glass.

'He just told her to come to his room one night, and she did, like an obedient little puppy.'

'And he abused her.'

Another drink.

'She went back.'

This is where I need to lift a drink, and look as cool and calculating as Norah Wolfe does. Maybe when this drama, such as it is, gets made into a movie, my character will drink that same stuff she's drinking.

'But after a week or so, Roxanne decided that Curtain had gone too far,' I say. 'Did Roxanne start making threats? Did Roxanne imply she might start telling people about who Laurence Curtain was, and what he liked to do to young women?

Maybe Roxanne asked for something in return, but the studio didn't want to give her anything in return. And there went Roxanne. Same as happened to Nella Lombardi last year.'

'Very good. I'd clap if my hands weren't full.'

'Like I say, though, you're getting cocky.'

She laughs, makes a small go-ahead gesture with the gun, takes another drink.

'A year ago you felt the need to make sure all trace of Laurence's debauchery was covered, and Lombardi's body was debased, along with her two friends. Now, though, who knows how many murders later, he doesn't feel the need for that. Or perhaps, you don't see the need for it. Like I said, you're getting cocky.'

'How many murders later,' she says, with a smile. 'Funny.'

'How many murders?'

'None, Sherlock, none, but don't let me stop your flight of fancy there.'

'And how about your mum and dad?'

Oh, she doesn't like that. Face sets like concrete, the temperature in the room drops fifteen degrees.

Silence as she ponders her options. The bullet in the head will likely remain her favourite, but there's the issue of the noise, and of removing the corpse.

'Why'd you leave the set?' I ask.

Part curiosity, part just spinning this out, while she gets drunker, and I hopefully think of some way out of this.

A contemptuous sigh, but this time I don't think the contempt is aimed at me.

'Mr Faraday,' she says, and she smiles. 'Mr Faraday did not like Laurence hitting on me, nor me accepting his advances. I mean, Laurence doesn't know what's being done in his name to cover his tracks, does he? Laurence is a fool. He goes through life with eyes closed, misunderstanding all he sees. But Mr Faraday was unhappy. He told me to get off the set.' She rolls her eyes, then adds, 'Jesus,' and takes another drink.

I'm not sure how much sense this made before I got here, but it's starting to make sense now.

I was wondering why I'd been brought in at all, but at last it begins to unravel. Rebecca Karlsen suspects this is going on, or knows and doesn't like what's going on. She wants to go to the police, but if she does that, there goes her career in Hollywood. No one likes a whistleblower. So, she anonymously gets a P.I. involved. Lets me dig around and get to the bottom of it. It all comes out in the wash, she's still there, producer on the movie, and Faraday is screwed.

Not sure about Curtain, but perhaps she has someone waiting in the wings to take over. She has it all planned out, and I'm just a small part of it.

'How much are they paying you?' I ask, which is something I don't care about *at all*. It's a non-question, but it won't seem like a non-question to a professional fixer. To the professional, it's always about money.

'It's a big business world, Mr Vikström. There's money everywhere. GuLu+ may not yet be Netflix or Prime, but they're owned by the Erebus Corporation, and Erebus are a leviathan. Leviathans always win. So GuLu+ have a gazillion dollars behind them, and they're coming for Netflix and they're coming for Prime. They're coming for them all. They need people like Laurence, and they just have to accept the quid pro quo. There's collateral damage with Laurence, and it needs to be managed.'

'So, who's Riddick?' I ask.

'Tall, isn't he?' she says, smiling, then lifting the glass to her lips.

'Who is he?'

'By the way, I know what you're thinking, and I'm afraid you're wrong. I'm not going to have a problem with shooting you here, and leaving your body. Because you've helpfully informed me that our fleet-footed friend was seen at my apartment. Therefore, when you turn up dead, the blame can easily fall on him.'

'After he was here, I was seen chasing him down the street.'

'Which came first, though? People are unreliable. And even if they're sure about that, hardly out of the question that he came back for you. And if you don't think the GuLu+ people will come up with a reliable witness or two to back up their story, while I move on to wherever Laurence next sets up base, you're much stupider than you've seemed up until now.'

Damn, that's a good point.

We sit in silence for a few moments. Horrible feeling this thing might have run its course. Begin to feel a little of the nervousness that one really ought to feel when looking down the barrel of a gun, particularly in a country where people are more than happy to discharge them.

'Maybe we could have sex now,' I say, and at least that makes her laugh.

'Funny, grandad,' she says. 'You ain't James Bond, you ain't just jumping into bed with the gorgeous assassin.'

'You're going to have to shoot me then,' I say.

Because obviously sex and death are the only options.

She tilts her head back a little, and I wonder what it is that's actually staying her hand, and for the first time think that, aye, maybe I am just about to get a bullet in the head.

There's a key in the front door.

'The fuck now?' escapes her lips.

She leaps up, the drink splashes from the glass, the gun still trained on me, her eyes darting between me and the door.

'Don't you fucking move,' she says.

Then, 'Do not fucking move.'

56

Her moment of twitchiness passes, and now she just looks pissed off at the interruption.

'Who'd you tell you were coming here?' she snaps. As she says it, she takes another gulp of whisky then lays the glass on the floor.

Sports fans, I didn't tell anyone. Whoever this is, it's unlikely they'll be coming in on the side of the good guys.

'Fuck it,' she says, in response to my silence.

I have to take advantage of the distraction. Eyes fly around the room. What can I get behind, what can I grab and throw? I just need a second.

Whoever's there, they're hesitating, assessing in the silence what might be going on in here.

'What's the plan?' I say, loudly enough that whoever's in the hallway will hear, and she scowls.

'Zip it,' she says, through gritted teeth.

The gun's on me, and I can see the consideration, the idea of firing and getting it over with running through her head.

The door starts to move, a footstep, and then suddenly Thomas Riddick is standing in the doorway. I have no idea whose side this guy's on, or whether he's some lone wolf, playing his own game, but I'm at least hopeful he'll have a gun on him.

'Thank fuck you're here,' says Wolfe. 'You're going to have to find something to tie this guy up. He's the one who killed Roxanne. There's also something about murders in Washington, I don't know what's going on with that yet.'

Riddick doesn't move.

'Come on!' she says, and she gestures with the gun in his direction.

He still doesn't move.

She stares at him coldly, and he looks back with a similarly harsh stare.

'No?' she says. 'Not buying it?'

'Looks like the game's up,' says Riddick. 'I know you killed Roxanne. The fact you've got the gun on this guy suggests he knows what's going on.'

'So, why don't I just kill you both and be done with it? Call in the wolfs, job done.'

She gives him a slight shoulder raise.

'I'm over here, he's over there. Someone's going to get the jump on you.'

'Are they though? You've met me. I don't get paid a hundred thousand k a week for nothing.'

'Wait, a hundred thousand dollars?' I say, deciding it's time to toss in a little more conversation, waste a little more time. 'Who even are you?'

'Thought you had it all worked out, genius boy?'

'You can't call me that, by the way. Doesn't work. I'm old enough to be your father.'

'You literally just asked if we could have sex.'

Put like that, it doesn't sound great, does it? Even though I wasn't actually looking to have sex.

'And who are you?' I say to the guy.

'P.I. investigating the actions of Brian Faraday in covering up the crimes and sexual deviance of Laurence Curtain. Miss Wolfe here was suspected of two murders in LA; then I followed her to Washington, and it was there three women were killed in a cabin in the woods. Miss Wolfe rendered me unconscious before that happened.'

'And then the company did a nice PR job of pinning the blame on you.'

'Exactly.'

'So, how come the three of you spent the day together in Salem?'

They look at each other. Something of the estranged lovers about them when they look like that, but that's not it.

'It was an accidental cat and mouse,' he says. 'They were spending the day together. I presume she was checking out Roxanne, making sure she wasn't going to do anything foolish with regards to Laurence Curtain. I was staying on a boat down at that yard. I got talking to Roxanne, not realising she was with Miss Wolfe. Then she appears. I know who she is, she knows who I am, Roxanne is oblivious on both counts. I stuck with them, to see how it would play out.'

'Like the most boring game of chess you ever saw,' says

Wolfe, then she laughs harshly. 'And that's a high fucking bar, by the way.'

'If you know about her,' I say, 'and you know about Curtain, why haven't you just gone to the cops?'

'He's the new biggest thing in Hollywood. He has a gazillion dollars behind him. There is no just going to the cops. There is no just making an allegation. You need to have proof, and you need to know victims are going to talk. So far, that hasn't happened.'

'Might help if they didn't keep dying,' says Wolfe, then she smiles.

'How'd *Newport 65* get damaged?' I ask.

'I heard you'd been snooping around,' he says. 'I tried to get out to the island last Thursday. Was barely beyond the harbour when I was driven into the rocks. Took nearly an hour to get back, even though it was only a couple hundred yards.'

'So, who's employing you?'

'Yawn yawn yawnity yawn,' says Wolfe. 'Seriously, Tom, or whatever your name actually is, you're going to have to get over there, right now. Sit down beside your chum, P.I.s together. Go on, squeeze in, boys.'

'No,' he says.

'So, who's employing you?' I ask again.

'Really, no one gives a fuck!' shouts Wolfe, suddenly losing her cool, then she lets out a long breath. Gritted teeth, coming down from the anger. 'Get *the fuck* over there.'

Damn it. She's not so sure of herself that she thinks she can take us both out, and we're only five, maybe six yards apart. Firing the first shot gives the other guy little more than half a second maybe, but she's worried that's all it'll take for her to lose control.

She might have the cold-bloodedness required of her job, she might have the callousness necessary to be able to leave someone dead, but from her current inaction, I'm going to say she doesn't have the skill.

Use it before you lose the opportunity.

'Trouble is,' I say to Riddick, 'you don't have the faintest idea what's going on.'

He looks curiously at me. She rolls her eyes, scowls, looks at him.

I move.

Push myself back, over the seat. A sudden explosion of

noise. The gun discharged, the thud of a bullet into the wall. The crash of Riddick diving to the ground. Gunfire, two quick shots in Riddick's direction.

Need a weapon. Nothing to hand.

My phone.

Dive out from behind the chair. The gun goes off. Phone in my right hand. Throw on the move. The angry cry of, 'Fuck!' as it hits in her in the face, and then I'm up and running towards her. Dive at her legs, the gun goes off, loud in my ear. The bullet flies waywardly, another thud into the wall. She crashes back, out of control. Her head bangs on the floor. I fall on top of her. Her hand hits the ground, the gun flies.

Her knee comes up, catches me in the groin. But this is the height of battle. Pain is for later. This is a scrap to the death, except I can't be the middle-aged guy killing the young woman.

Her mouth on my neck, and she bites. Jab her in the eye, harsh and deep and she backs off with a yowl, and then there's an, 'Everyone calm the fuck down!' shout from our right, and there's Riddick, on his knees, blood pooled around him, though the wound is not immediately apparent, the anguish of the injury on his face, the gun in his hand.

'Call it in,' he says to me, as I push myself off her. 'And you,' he says to Wolfe, 'I don't give a fuck what you do, after what you've put me through. You move, I'm putting a bullet *in your face.*' A beat, and then he says, for added cinematic drama, 'Your choice, sweetlips.'

On my knees, away from the girl, instantly feeling the pain of the roll over the chair, the awkward fall, the whack in the testicles, the bite in the neck. Lift my phone. There's a large crack down the middle of the glass, but it still works.

I get to my feet, look at Riddick.

'You all right?'

'Ankle,' he says. 'I'll be fine, though I might miss spring training.'

A baseball gag, and a previously concealed sense of humour. Nice.

'Hey,' I say to Elise.

'What's up?' she asks, recognising something in my voice.

'Four-seventeen, Hamilton Street, Manchester. Apartment three. Norah Wolfe killed Roxanne. We've got her here. We'll need medical.'

'You're all right?'

'It's not for me.'

'Who's we?' and then, 'Doesn't matter, on my way.'

I lower the phone, I look at Riddick.

'Sure you're all right?' I ask, though the question is needless. Riddick is obviously locked in.

'Yeah. If I think I'm going to faint from bleeding out, I'll put a bullet in her head before I fall,' and she scowls and laughs humourlessly, and this action-packed mini-drama is over, thank God.

57

'You did a good job,' says Elise.

CSI are in the apartment. Riddick is on his way to ER to get patched up. Anderson, the Manchester deputy, has taken the murder suspect off for overnight incarceration, while the initial moves play out.

'Thank you.'

'She's not going to talk,' says Elise. 'You know the type.'

'Yep,' I say. The pain of the brief hostilities came and it went. Wolfe didn't get to bite too fully into my neck, and there's a small patch over the wound. 'If she talks now, she'll lose the protection of the company. They'll be waiting to see what she does, and if she plays ball and keeps schtum, then they'll lawyer up and get behind her.' A pause, think of the alternative option. 'Or else they throw her under the bus, finding a way to keep her quiet in the process. If I was her, I might be worried when I get bailed.'

'She looked a little too confident in her own position.'

'Hmm.'

'Won't be our problem, anyway,' she says.

'Agent Cameron still coming in the morning?'

'Yes, she is. This development has neither hurried her, nor slowed her down. She'll be here exactly when she said she would be.'

'Like a wizard.'

She looks at me, shakes her head.

'Don't,' she says.

'Don't what?'

'Don't find a stupid *Lord of the Rings* quote for *everything*. It always makes me laugh, and... I don't want you to make me laugh,' she throws in, her voice a bit lower. 'What's the score with Rebecca Karlsen?'

'Just had a quick call. She was cagy, and not at all surprised. I told her what I knew, including that Norah's not her daughter, and she responded to none of it. I suspect she knows about Laurence, and she knows Norah's a fixer, not a storyboarder. Agent Cameron's going to need to find out who it was who ordered Norah to kill Roxanne.'

'You don't think that was Karlsen?'

'I think that was her partner, Brian Faraday. Bringing me on board, was Karlsen's way of trying to stitch him up. That might take Agent Cameron a bit of work to get to the bottom of.'

'You were a power play?'

I smile at that.

'Quite possibly. Norah goes down, and she'll end up taking someone down with her. I've no idea whether Karlsen will want Curtain to go, but I'm sure she'll want Faraday dealt with. However it plays out, it'll be to her benefit.'

There's always the possibility that she genuinely felt bad for these girls being abused by Curtain, but if that was the case, she'd actually have done something to help Roxanne before she was murdered.

'There'll be a lot of people looking over their shoulders,' says Elise. 'They'll have known about it, and they'll have kept their mouths shut, because it was better for their career, or because they wanted to protect the asset. This is how the world works.'

I nod, I look around the room, I watch the CSI guys at work.

'Agent Cameron is going to want a statement from you in the morning,' she says.

'I'll be easy to find.'

'OK.' A moment, then, 'OK, I need to get back to the office, start writing this up.'

We stand there, in our new state of awkwardness, that will be a long time getting over.

'Thanks,' she says. 'Should've been me solving this damn crime.'

'Team effort,' I say.

The look extends into a few seconds, and then finally she turns, and walks quickly from the room.

58

There are forces at play, as there often are. I'm not entirely sure who those forces are, in this instance, but when Thomas Riddick was set up for the murder of those three girls in the cabin in the woods, it wasn't just a bunch of studio executives who managed to pull that off. They have someone, somewhere in law enforcement on their side.

There are leviathans everywhere. Always have been, and they're not going anywhere. Not until humanity is brought to its knees and laid waste.

The studio will be fine, of course. They're not ditching this movie, even if Curtain has to fall on his sword in the coming days. They'll bring in someone else, or they'll hand the reins over to Andrea, the first AD. I suspect, they'll rope in as big a name as possible, and Laurence Curtain, and his part in it, will be whitewashed.

Entirely possible, however, that he's been blissfully unaware of what's been done in his name by Brian Faraday. In which case, if he escapes arrest and ruination, no doubt he'll be back once the scandal has run its course, and the public have moved on. Which shouldn't take more than a couple of months.

But this isn't my story. Barely any of it is. It's Thomas Riddick's. He's the one whose life has been screwed over for the past year and a half. He's the one who's stayed on the case, not that he had much choice if he wanted to clear his name. He's the one who rented a boat, so that he could try to keep an eye on the island where they were filming. And who tried to get out there on the evening Roxanne Baudot was murdered, but was run into the rocks within a short distance of leaving the yard.

I still don't know who hired him in the first place, but I wouldn't be surprised to find it was Rebecca Karlsen. Good of her not to fill me in on anything that had gone before.

*

We talk this through, Natalie and I, over Sarah Jarosz on the Bluetooth, and Chinese takeout out of cartons. Rain against the windows, wind whistling around the building.

'This is going to keep me busy for a long time,' she says. 'Particularly with the unexpected vampire aspect.'

She's been making the most of the bite on my neck, currently hidden behind a small bandage.

'You need to get an interview with Riddick,' I say.

She smiles.

'You already interviewed him?'

'Nine tomorrow morning.'

'Damn. Nice work.'

'Thank you. He said he'd tried to tell a lot of people at a lot of outlets, and none of them wanted to know. In the hour before I spoke to him, he'd had about fifty calls from all the same people. Told them all to,' and she jerks her thumb, and demurely doesn't say *get to fuck* like the rest of us would've done.

'Guy's going to have a story to tell,' I say.

'Yes, he is. Nevertheless, I don't think you should undermine your own part in this. You too have a story to tell.'

'My part was to be Nick Carraway in a sea of Gatsbys. When the movie gets made, Riddick gets played by Brad Pitt, and I get played by that guy who was in some movie, whose name no one can remember.'

She smiles softly, elbow on the table, her chin resting in her hand.

'I always had a thing for the guy who was in some movie, whose name no one can remember,' she says.

'You don't need to say that. You had me at *you a cop*?'

'What does that mean?'

'That's the first thing you ever said to me. You asked if I was a cop.'

'Was it?'

'Sure. On the Fischer compass case.'

'And you remember I said that?'

'Of course. You were really irritating.'

She shares my smile.

*

I lie in bed, listening to the storm. Wide awake, though possibly just with the unfamiliarity of sleeping somewhere new.

An uncomfortable feeling sits in the middle of my chest. Not sure where it's come from. Had a perfect evening, and I'm not at all daunted by stumbling unthinkingly into romance. It'll play out like it'll play out. Things happen. Or not.

Maybe it's guilt. Maybe it's sadness at what I've chosen to lose. Though, I'm not sure the choice ultimately was mine, regardless of how difficult Elise might find this.

I hear a sound in the night. Something moving across the floor. Like a heavy rug being pulled. I stare at the ceiling, trying to work out what it could be. I think of Hightower, then remember I'm at the wrong house.

It comes again, a little louder.

I sit up, but the sound is coming from Natalie's side of the bed.

In the half-light, I see a movement beneath the duvet, as though something is reaching up from the floor.

I swallow, fear growing in my chest, and then I whip the duvet quickly away.

Natalie is asleep, naked. She stirs, but does not wake.

A giant tentacle is slithering up onto the bed, and then another, and they begin to creep easily up Natalie's legs, one on each side. She snuffles, and then she turns, rolling onto her back.

And then the arms of the squid appear, heaving the body of the giant beast up onto the bed. I want to kick it off, I want to react, but having sat up, I can't move.

For some reason I can't explain, it's not my part to move. I'm Nick Carraway in a sea of Gatsbys.

Natalie's legs part a little, as the squid's body moves up between her legs. Its tentacles reach up, and start to caress her breasts. She moans softly. I recognise the sound. Then the squid's mouth reaches the top of her thighs, a moment, and then it latches onto her pussy. Natalie gasps loudly, her back arching.

I shoot awake in the night, breathing hard, the feeling of haunting evil heavy on my chest.

I turn to her, Natalie, still asleep, facing me, one hand between her head and the pillow, the other pulling the duvet close into her neck.

The window is open, the curtains are open. The night is dark, the rain spatters the glass, the wind whistles quietly through the gap.

I look at her face, pale in the night, long enough for the ill-feelings to leave. She rubs her nose, and I think she's going to wake up, then she settles down again, still fast asleep.

I lay my head back on the pillow and stare at the shadows cast across the ceiling by the lights of the night outside.

Somewhere there's a dog barking.

The night is old.

Printed in Great Britain
by Amazon